IF *Love* WAS ENOUGH

ERIN CB

Copyright © 2024 Erin CB.

All rights reserved.

No part of this publication may be reproduced, distributed or transmitted in any form or by any means, including photocopying, recording or other electronic or mechanical methods, without the prior written permission of the publisher, except in the case of brief quotations, reviews and other noncommercial uses permitted by copyright law.
Library of Congress Control Number: 2024921922

For Jimmy

"No, no, no!" Hannah whined. She pounded her fists against the steering wheel, watching the drawbridge lower across the highway. She glanced out toward the water on her right to find the cause of the delay, spotting a sailboat with a tall mast approaching the harbor.

Hannah grabbed her cell phone from the cup holder to text her boss: *I'm going to be late. I got stuck at the bridge again. Sorry.*

Her phone buzzed almost immediately with a response: *Thanks for letting me know, but this is the third time this week. Get here as quickly as you can.*

Hannah dropped the phone back into the cup holder, shifted her car into park, and let her gaze drift to take in the view of Highgate City across the bay. She noticed how small the skyscrapers seemed from this side of the water. Hannah often daydreamed about what was happening in the city, spinning tales about people she would never meet; it was a game she liked to play when she was bored or needed a distraction.

Her mind slowly drifted to someone she had once known better than anyone, who had once lived there among the hustle and bustle. He was someone she had loved with every square inch of her heart, and his name was Jimmy Taylor. He had dashed through her thoughts occasionally in the years since then, sometimes because of a song or an old photograph that popped up somewhere. Every time, it led Hannah to search his name online, even though she would never dare reach out because of the distance that had grown between them.

She again plucked her phone from the cup holder and typed his name into the Google search bar: *Jimmy Taylor, Riverside Springs.* Hannah looked up from her phone while the results loaded, a small smile creeping across her lips as she remembered that there had once been a time when she could imagine her first name joined to his last name.

Time seemed to stop then as Hannah's eyes drifted down to the first search result, an obituary announcing that Jimmy had died about three months prior. She felt her heart sink in one sudden rush while the coffee in her stomach churned. Hannah rolled down the windows, feeling like all the air had been sucked out of the car. She gulped in oxygen, imagining all four sides closing in around her. Hannah pulled her long brown hair into a ponytail to let the cool air touch her neck as tears slid down her cheeks.

She was surprised by her own reaction; Hannah and Jimmy had been strangers for the better part of a decade, and it didn't feel right somehow to cry for him. A voice inside spoke to Hannah quietly, reminding her of everything Jimmy had meant. *You and Jimmy are two sides of the same coin,* it said, *just two pages ripped from the same book. Time and space couldn't ever change that.*

Noticing the drawbridge was back down and the safety barriers were nearly fully up, Hannah collected herself as best she could. She wiped the tears from her face, smearing most of her makeup in the process. She exhaled deeply, hoping she might get stuck at the railroad crossing near the office so she would have a few minutes to fix the facade she had painted on earlier that morning. It was imperative to keep it in place, to hide the pain trying to poke its way through to the surface.

How am I ever going to get through this day? Hannah thought as she shifted the car back into drive.

Hannah remained distracted for most of the work day, periodically searching Jimmy's name at her desk to read the obituary again and again; at least it looked like she was working intently on the client progress notes that she was behind on. She barely recognized him in the obituary photo that, no doubt, his mother had chosen. It was one in which he wore a suit and tie with his hair cleanly cut, one where he looked downright uncomfortable. Hannah smiled slightly, recalling his 80s punk style: hair spiked out in every direction and a ripped denim vest he had decorated himself with patches and safety pins. The Jimmy she remembered was always trying to make a statement.

Hannah searched for more information about Jimmy, clicking on a blog article by an old college friend named Brad. In it, he detailed a trip to Riverside Springs to visit Jimmy and explore the vibrant underground music scene there. Jimmy had always loved music; he had sung and played nearly every instrument in who-knows-how-many bands through the years. He wrote songs about all kinds of things like politics, everyday life, and even random things like a conversation he overheard in a parking lot somewhere.

As she read the article, Hannah could almost picture herself in those dive bars, smelling stale cigarette smoke and Bud Light. She could imagine sitting on a wobbly bar stool, watching Jimmy jump around, giving everything he had to the music he created with his fingertips. He was so free on a stage with a guitar in his hands, always having the time of his life. Hannah could still make out a glint of sadness in his eyes through the haze of this memory, with a pounding drumbeat that she could almost feel reverberating in her ears. It had been there in all the years leading to Riverside Springs and, apparently, beyond.

When it was finally time for her lunch break, Hannah walked to the train station near the office and sat on a bench on the platform. It was her favorite routine, sitting in a crowded place and watching people pass by her as if she were invisible. That was all she wanted today: to blend into the background and disappear into her pain. Hannah's phone was back in her hand with the Google search results for "Jimmy Taylor" pulled up again. She clicked on each link, putting the pieces of her past back together. She listened to recordings of songs he had performed with one of his more recent bands and stared at photos that friends and family had shared on the obituary web page. Even if it sounded like a recording made inside a tin can, hearing his voice again transported Hannah back to those days when they were strangers and then suddenly lovers.

It felt like a lifetime ago, yet somehow so close that she could almost relive it all again; Hannah could still feel how her heart lit up when Jimmy smiled at her or how his husky voice spoke her name. A cavernous pit began to open up in her stomach, remembering all the good times with him while her heartbreak lingered underneath.

Hannah recalled her college days when it all started between her and Jimmy. She had been a lanky eighteen-year-old when she began her first year at Safe Harbor University in September of 2005. The school was also known as S.H.U., but locals preferred pronouncing it like "shoe." Her hair was long back then, too, without any hint of gray. Hannah's green eyes were accented with a splash of golden yellow around the pupil, and that year, they were on full display since she was finally allowed to wear contacts. Trying to escape the tomboy image she held onto all her life, Hannah dressed differently, trading oversized hooded sweatshirts, baggy band t-shirts, and chunky Vans for more fitted tops and girly ballet flats.

Hannah was a walking ball of anxiety in those days, but she was also so full of hope—hope that she could start over and be someone she always wanted to be. Someone more outgoing and confident. Someone that other people genuinely wanted to be friends with. Someone that boys were happy to be seen with in public. Someone who just felt free.

Hannah sat on the bench, still lost inside her thoughts, watching commuter trains come and go every fifteen minutes. She watched the people getting on and off, wondering where they might be going to or coming from. Hannah wondered if any of them had a "what if"? When they talk about falling in love, people often talk about finding "the one," but what about the other one? The "what if?" In hindsight, it was easy to question that if one thing had been different in her story, even the tiniest thing, would everything else have been different, too? She eyed the strangers walking all around her, wondering what one thing they would change in their own stories. What would life look like had that fight never happened, or had the timing been just a little more right? Hannah rubbed her eyes, trying to hold the tears in with her fingertips, as she considered her greatest "what if?"

Hannah's mind returned to the present moment as Jimmy's voice and the accompanying music faded in her earbuds. She thought about her husband, Jake. He knew her too well, and this heartache was too big to hide from him. Jake would instinctively know that her puffy eyes and quiet mood were more than just "a long day at work." How would she explain the utter devastation she felt over the death of a man she used to love?

Of course, Jake had heard about Jimmy; they had shared stories about past lovers early on in their relationship, but Hannah had kept many of her memories to herself. She never talked about how deeply she and Jimmy had been connected or how it nearly ruined her. Jake didn't know that Hannah still thought about Jimmy, wondering at times what would have been had she not run all those years ago. Hannah deliberated on how much she should tell Jake, knowing it was inevitable that she would have to come clean about all of it.

Hannah took the long way home that evening, excusing her lateness on traffic. Jake was in the kitchen plating their dinners when she finally walked in the door. He had gotten home long before her and had changed from his work clothes into basketball shorts and a T-shirt from his favorite video game. His thick black hair was still styled into place with the hair gel he had used that morning, while his musky cologne still lingered on his skin. Hannah's body tensed as Jake hugged her, feeling guilty about the day she spent reminiscing about Jimmy.

"What's wrong?" he asked.

She didn't move from the place in his chest where her head fit just right, letting the tears flow faster than her words. Having felt Hannah shuddering against him, Jake pulled away from her. The look on his face turned to one of alarm when he saw the wetness on her cheeks. As he reached up to wipe it away, he asked, "Hannah, what's going on?"

With a shaking voice, Hannah told him, "An old friend of mine from college died."

Jake was so much taller than Hannah that when he pulled her back into a hug, he rested his chin on her head, encasing her in him. Her tears quickly turned to sobs. "I'm so sorry, honey. Who was it?"

"Jimmy," Hannah choked out.

Jake paused. It was a name he hadn't heard Hannah mention very often; she had always been guarded about that relationship. He had always been curious why she refused to open up, knowing that the story would likely be painful. But he wondered who would it be more painful for—Hannah or Jake? "Like, SHU Jimmy? Riverside Springs Jimmy?" he asked.

She nodded her head slowly against his chest. "Yeah."

"Damn. What happened?"

Hannah took a step backward, looking up at him. "I'm not sure, really, but I have this sinking feeling," she replied, not wanting to accept what her heart already knew.

"What's that?"

Hannah's voice caught in her throat. "I think he did it to himself."

Jake looked at her, confused, knowing Hannah hadn't spoken to Jimmy in years. "Wait—how did you even hear about it?"

"I looked him up this morning," Hannah said. "Sometimes, I just—I don't know. He came to mind for some reason, and I was curious. So I looked him up, and his obituary was the first search result."

Jake knew how nostalgic Hannah could sometimes be, pining away for the simpler times before bills, mortgages, and careers. He knew that her heart had always been a deep well from which anything and anyone she had ever loved could never escape. He knew how deeply she missed being young and carefree, how she missed the friends and the life she used to have. He sometimes worried that Hannah would never really be happy with the life they'd built together, but she always insisted that she was.

Jake scrapped his dinner plans, thinking this night called for Hannah's favorite pizza and a bottle of wine. He poured her a little more wine than usual, knowing the alcohol would permit Hannah to reminisce about her college days more freely. He took in every word, trying to remember all the characters and laughing at some of the inside jokes he didn't quite understand. Hannah cried and laughed while retelling her stories, amazing Jake with the many things he still didn't know about Hannah, the many layers of her life.

Hannah hesitantly talked about Jimmy, fearful of revealing too much. She and Jake had met about a year and a half after she had returned home from Riverside Springs as a completely battered and broken version of herself. Jake had done so much to help her put the pieces of herself back together in the years that followed, always so patient and kind.

"I want to tell you more about Jimmy, but I don't want to upset you," Hannah confessed. "I love you so much, and—"

"Honey," Jake interrupted, "you can talk to me about this. I want you to. He was a part of your life, but it's one that I know hardly anything about, and he was obviously special to you if you're this torn up about it. Besides, I know there were other guys before me. I know you *loved* other guys before me."

Hannah smiled and wondered, *How did I get so lucky?*

She slowly opened up to Jake about how, even after all the years apart, she still held a place in her heart for Jimmy. She admitted she held on to regret that they had just let each other go, both with wounds too deep to heal together.

"The world just looks so different now that I know he's gone," Hannah cried.

"I'm so sorry," Jake said simply, hugging her tight.

He tucked Hannah into bed early that night and sat with her for a while, his hand rubbing her back to help her relax. Hannah had pretended to fall asleep so she could be alone in the dark with her thoughts, letting the waves of grief crash over her. Eventually, she drifted into a fitful sleep, thinking that if she could go back in time and change how things had turned out, maybe she could save Jimmy from himself. But what else would have changed as a result? What would that have meant for her relationship with Jake? Would they have ever even crossed paths?

When Hannah awoke the following day, Saturday, she felt a pounding in her head that she hadn't experienced since her twenties.

I definitely had too much wine last night, she thought.

She lay in bed for a while, staring at the ceiling, feeling like she could almost hear the ghosts of her past calling out to her from the attic. To call it an attic was generous. Hannah and Jake's small seaside cottage boasted a rickety fold-down ladder that led to a small crawlspace that ran the length of their home. Jake had installed sheets of plywood to make the space usable to hide away the things that were sometimes better left out of sight.

She wandered to the kitchen to find Jake sitting at the table with coffee and a plate of scrambled eggs. Hannah stood quietly in the doorway for a moment, just watching him. Jake was wearing only a pair of basketball shorts, his thick black hair messy from sleep.

Hannah took a few steps into the room and greeted him in good morning. Jake handed her a cup of coffee made just how she'd always liked it, light in color from a healthy pour of milk and sickly sweet with sugar, something that Jake could never stomach; he preferred his coffee black.

Jake noticed Hannah's surprised look. "I heard you rustling around in there, so I thought I'd get this ready for you—figured you might need it after last night," he said with a chuckle.

"Thanks, I definitely do," she told him. "I think I'm going to go up into the attic today. There's some stuff I wanted to go through."

"Okay. Do you need any help?"

"No, it's just something I want to do. Alone, actually. Do you mind if I take this coffee up there and get started?" Hannah asked, feeling an urgent tug in her chest like an invisible string pulling at her.

Jake smiled. "Sure."

"Thanks," replied Hannah, giving him a quick kiss before leaving.

The attic entrance groaned loudly as she pulled the tattered cord hanging from the ceiling, unfolded the old wooden ladder, and climbed into the warm, dusty space. Hannah headed for the back corner where she kept boxes from her youth, untouched since they had moved in five years ago. During high school and college, Hannah had meticulously crafted time capsules of memories in photos, journals, and scrapbooks. It was like she always knew there would come a day when those moments would be the salve she would need to heal some profound wound.

Hannah frowned, wishing she had kept up the habit of documenting her life in such a way; it just hadn't seemed necessary anymore with the advent of social media and cloud drives that were accessible from anywhere. Even then, there had been lulls in her recordkeeping when life felt too hectic or stressful. She would always find her way back to her journals and pictures, though, even if not consistently. Hannah found it funny how she tended to move so far away from things, like writing and art, that could push her through tough times or heal her broken spirit. Jimmy had done the same, just in different ways.

Hannah used to carry a maroon digital camera everywhere she went as if it were an extra appendage. She took pictures of the cool things, the weird stuff, and all the small, beautiful bits she noticed back when she kept her eyes open to such things. She loved taking pictures of her friends the most, hoping to freeze them in those happy moments, having thought they could stay that way forever.

Hannah dug through boxes of artifacts like old journals, full-to-bursting scrapbooks, old copies of *The Inkwell,* and unorganized shoe boxes of photographs. She tossed aside journals until she finally found one labeled "SHU 2005" on the front. Its black and white marbled cover was wrinkled and worn, warped by time and humidity. This book was the beginning of everything, the place where she needed to start. This was where she could find proof of Jimmy's life—the proof that he had once belonged to this world and to her.

Hannah sat in her 1991 bright red Chevy Cavalier outside the University Diner, desperately trying to talk herself into walking inside. She peered at herself in the rearview mirror.

"You can do this. You can do this!" she whispered to herself.

There was an introductory meeting for a student-run publication that some kids were trying to get off the ground. Hannah saw a flier in the Student Center seeking out students interested in joining as writers, editors, and artists. It piqued her interest then, but she had become absolutely panicked sitting there in the parking lot. Hannah had always been shy and reserved, especially around new people in new situations. She had promised herself over the summer that she would make an effort to branch out and work through the distressing feelings that had plagued her for as long as she could remember. Hannah had never felt entirely comfortable in her own skin, nor did she ever feel like she really fit in anywhere. The familiar, menacing voice in her head chimed into her positive affirmation speech, reminding Hannah that no matter how hard she tried, she would probably always be the same scared little girl she always had been.

Hannah sighed and asked herself, "Why am I even bothering?"

She flipped open her cell phone and texted her long-distance boyfriend Manny: *I can't do it.*

He quickly texted back: *Baby, you can. Just go. You'll be ok.*

Hannah rolled her eyes. She appreciated Manny's easy-breezy attitude sometimes, but it mostly felt like he was just brushing her off. He never could quite understand the chokehold Hannah's anxieties had on her.

She took one last deep breath before exiting the car. It was mid-September in the northeast, and the sun was still warm and comforting on her face that afternoon. Once inside, Hannah peered around for what might look like a meeting taking place. Her eyes scanned the booths, decorated in dark green floral patterns; it reminded Hannah of an old couch at her grandmother's house. She turned to her left and was met by about a hundred identical images of her own face blinking back at her through an entire wall of mirrors. Taking a couple more steps inside, Hannah noticed a large U-shaped corner booth in the back of the dining room where a group of students huddled together in conversation. With her head down, Hannah walked over to them.

A stocky guy with curly hair dyed a bright blue sat in a forest green chair at the end of the booth. When he turned around to meet her, Hannah noticed his eyes were so dark that they were nearly black.

"Hey! Are you here for the newspaper meeting?" he asked in a warm and welcoming voice, a stark contrast from his appearance.

"Oh, uh, ye-yeah. I am," Hannah said, tumbling nervously over her words.

"Cool. I'm Chris," he said, sticking out a hand for her to shake. She grasped his hand, aware then that her palms were slick with sweat. He let go, unbothered, and motioned to the person sitting to his left. "This is Joe. We're the ones who posted the fliers!"

"Hi," Joe said curtly, adjusting his silver metal-framed glasses and running a hand through his red hair that looked like it had been freshly trimmed earlier that day. He, too, reached out and shook Hannah's hand. In contrast to Chris, Joe looked miniature in the big booth. Hannah wasn't sure how to take his brusque attitude, but she tried her best not to feel offended; she figured that Joe was the much more serious one of the two.

"I'm Hannah. It's nice to meet you both," she said sheepishly.

Chris went around the table, introducing the others who had come to the meet-and-greet, explaining that a group of other students had already come and gone. Those sitting on Chris's right side made space for her to sit in the booth. Chris and Joe talked about their vision for the newspaper: to print real news stories, but also to have fun and be a little weird. Joe then asked for everyone to pass forward their writing samples that they had been instructed to bring.

"Oh, I've only really ever done short stories and poems, so that's all I brought," she told them, avoiding eye contact with both of them. "I was a finalist in a couple of state-level competitions, if that counts for anything," Hannah mentioned with a shrug.

"That's okay. We'll still take a look at it," Chris said as he took the papers from Hannah, scanned them quickly, and passed them to Joe to review.

"Yeah, we'll figure out a spot for you," Joe stated.

Hannah's face flushed as that voice in her head spoke up again, telling her how stupid she was for bringing those writing samples. Chris and Joe reviewed materials from the others, commenting positively on most of them. With her shoulders slumped, Hannah stared off at a faded poster hanging on the wall above Joe's head, which depicted maple syrup being poured over a stack of pancakes.

I wish they had something nice to say about my stuff, she thought. Hannah knew that it hadn't been enough to get her in, and she just wanted to bolt from the lumpy plastic booth she had been swallowed up in.

"Here," Chris said, pushing a pen and paper toward her. "Write down your contact info so we can let you know when the next meeting is."

Hannah scribbled down her name, email, and cell phone number but doubted they would reach out to her after that day. It had been her first genuine attempt at branching out, and Hannah felt like she had already blown it.

She called Manny on the drive home to tell him how the meeting went, admitting she felt utterly dumb for bringing her short stories and poems when everyone else had brought actual newspaper articles they had written for other publications.

"They must be all laughing at me now," she told him.
In his usual way, Manny told her, "Just stop worrying about it so much."

I t was three weeks before Hannah received any communication from either Joe or Chris. She figured that they were just being nice at the diner when they told her they could find a place for her. She had fully prepared herself for them to pass on her as a contributor, so it was a surprise when an email came through from Chris:

> To: Hannah O'Malley
> From: Christopher Rivera
> Subject: Newspaper Meeting
> Date: October 3, 2005
>
> The next meeting will be on Thursday at 1:00 in the Student Center, Room 202. See you there!
>
> Chris and Joe

Her first instinct was to smile, but then her stomach flipped as the worry set in over what she had gotten herself into. She imagined there would probably be some kind of icebreaker, which opened up a rabbit hole of anxiety; Hannah found herself already rehearsing answers to questions nobody had even asked yet.

Hannah sent a text message to Manny to tell him the news.

He replied: *That's great, baby!*

She smiled, and tried to forget the rest for a while.

That Thursday morning, Hannah could barely concentrate on her two prerequisite classes, history and algebra. When she was done at noon, Hannah tried to eat lunch at the small cafe on the third floor of the Student Center, but her backflipping stomach had put a stop to that. She threw the food tray into the garbage and walked downstairs to the second floor, sitting in the hallway outside of Room 202. She peered at her phone for the time; it was only 12:30 P.M. She buried her nose in a book, trying to get ahead of some homework for the next half hour.

A friendly voice boomed out of the silence at the end of the hallway. "Hey! Hannah, right?" Chris was walking toward her, waving.

"Yeah, hi! You're Chris?" she asked. "Sorry, I'm terrible with names."

That had been a lie, one she had told acquaintances before to somehow make her seem less offbeat. Hannah worried that people felt weirded out, rather than special, that she remembered them after only a brief encounter. The truth was, she remembered the name of everyone she'd ever met. Hannah had never wanted anyone to feel as invisible as she did.

"Yep! Don't worry—I'm not offended. No biggie," he laughed. "What are you reading?"

Hannah held up the book to show Chris the front cover. "It's just my textbook for a Child Development class I'm taking," she replied.

"Let me guess!" Chris closed one eye, tapping his puckered lips with the tips of his fingers, before pointing at her. "Education major?" he guessed.

"Wow, you're pretty good!" Hannah nodded, feigning amusement.

"It's a hidden talent of mine. I'm a Computer Science major," Chris told her. Hannah noticed the T-shirt he was wearing, which bore a techy pun written in 8-bit font across the chest.

Yeah, that fits, she thought.

While they were chatting, a few other students appeared in the hallway. "Well, I guess we should go in," said Chris, ushering the group into the empty classroom. He instructed them to rearrange the desks into a large circle.

Joe popped in, breathless, as they were maneuvering the last couple of desks into place. He mentioned something to Chris about how his one professor made it a habit to keep them past time, annoyed he'd had to run across campus to get there in time. "Anyway," Joe began, "I think we're just missing one person, but we'll get started."

Joe announced everyone's duties for the newspaper, and it was Hannah's job to sell ad space to help bring in funds for printing. She felt like the last person who should be selling ads, but she accepted the assignment with a smile. She didn't dare ask for a something different; it just wasn't like her to make a fuss.

Nearly halfway through the meeting, the classroom door whipped open with a bang as it hit the wall, and a new face appeared. "Hey! Sorry I'm so late—I got the time mixed up with something else!" The voice was loud and gravelly, contrasting the small frame that swaggered through the doorway, skateboard in hand and arms open wide as if to say, "What can ya do?" His hair was dirty blonde and wildly spiked, standing straight up and down, like he had stuck a fork into a light socket that morning.

Joe told him to grab the last open seat across the circle from Hannah. Crazy Hair Guy, as Hannah dubbed him, gave Joe a nod and a crooked smile. She noticed a sizable scar on his top lip, revealing a chip in his front tooth.

Crazy Hair Guy walked past Hannah to sit at the empty desk when her nose was filled with a mix of cigarettes and something strong and herbal. She couldn't quite place it, but she felt oddly soothed by it. She looked him up and down, fascinated by the character who had just taken charge of the room without even trying. Crazy Hair Guy wore a denim vest that had evidently been a whole jacket in a past life, with frayed edges where the sleeves should have been. Safety pins and band patches covered the front and back. She scanned them: Misfits, Dead Kennedys, Black Flag. Others were more politically motivated, like a picture of a fist raised in protest and one that read: "No blood for oil!" Under the vest was a wrinkled, black button-down shirt. He wore jeans with a chain attached to a wallet in his back pocket. On his feet were a tattered pair of black Airwalk sneakers.

Hannah looked up to notice that Crazy Hair Guy was watching her take him in, and she felt her face flush instantly. She felt something shift inside her as he held her gaze. It was something Hannah couldn't quite name, but it felt something like a long hug from an old friend; his eyes seemed to hold her in ways no human hands ever had before. She looked away quickly, her embarrassment spreading from her cheeks down her neck, still feeling his eyes on her. Hannah imagined herself melting into a puddle under her desk.

She shifted her gaze back to Chris, who announced they would go around the room to introduce themselves since everyone was accounted for. Luckily, Hannah didn't need to dig through her memory banks to recall her favorite band or hobby, only the basics: her name, hometown, major, and what year she was in. Two girls sitting to her right went first, Katie and then Whitney. They were both in their first year, too, and both majored in nursing.

When it was Hannah's turn, the red flush refreshed itself across her cheeks. She made it a point to avoid eye contact with anyone, especially Crazy Hair Guy, so she focused on a knotted cord from the blinds that hung in one of the windows across the room. "Hi, I'm Hannah. I'm a commuter, and I live in Harborvale. It's my first year here, and I'm an Education major." She gave herself an internal pat on the back, proud she had gotten through it without a misstep.

The conversation continued around the circle until it was Crazy Hair Guy's turn. "What's up? I'm Jimmy. I'm a double major in Communications and Marketing, and it's technically my first year here, but I did two years at Cedar Cove Community College. Let's see, um, like everyone else at this place, I'm a commuter. I live over in Stonebridge." Hannah dared to look at him at the mention of Stonebridge, which was two towns over from Harborvale. She made accidental eye contact with him again. Jimmy smiled at her from the corner of his mouth and waved at her. "Howdy, neighbor," he added.

Before they were all dismissed, Chris and Joe announced that the group would meet again on Monday to brainstorm article ideas and outline a plan for the first issue. Hannah grabbed her backpack and headed straight for the door, anxious to leave. Her path was blocked by the two girls who had been sitting to her right. Whitney was tall, like a model, with rich brown eyes and wavy dark auburn hair that fell nearly to her waist. Katie was much shorter than Hannah, with pale blue eyes and pale skin with acne scars covering her cheeks. Her hair was cut into a short bob, and was so blonde that it was nearly white.

Katie told her that they were going to grab some lunch and asked Hannah if she would like to join them. The invitation caught Hannah by surprise, but before she could answer, Whitney stopped another girl from the circle, Jenny. They invited her to tag along, too. Hannah stared at Jenny's smooth, milky skin and brown almond-shaped eyes. She was instantly envious of how perfectly in-place Jenny's long black hair hung in a ponytail high up on her head. Jenny immediately agreed to lunch, leaving Hannah feeling like she couldn't decline.

The cafeteria was full of school pride: navy blue, white, and gray stripes were painted along the cement walls, encircling the room in school colors. A massive flag of the school mascot, a sea lion with big tusks, hung on the wall beside the food line. A banner of dark blue with "Safe Harbor University" printed in white hung from the ceiling at the main entrance. Hannah had never been one for school spirit, finding the overt display of pride a bit much.

The wait for a soggy sandwich or hot mystery meat dish was relatively short despite still being early afternoon. She looked over the depressing lunch options, choosing a bowl of penne vodka. Hannah paid and found the other girls sitting at a large, blue table along the far wall. She anxiously looked at the time on her phone—

1:15 P.M. She reminded herself that she needed to be at work at 3:00 P.M. but had to go home first to change.

Whitney, Katie, and Jenny were chatting about the meeting when Hannah plopped down into the open seat next to Jenny. Katie immediately turned to her and asked, "So what did you think?"

"About what?" Hannah asked.

Katie laughed. "About the meeting, silly!"

Hannah wasn't sure what to say, thinking the meeting had been nothing special. Feeling the pressure to come off the right way and not wanting to scare away potential new friends, Hannah answered casually, "Oh, it was okay, I guess."

"What about your assignment?" asked Whitney. She was going to be one of the writers, along with Katie. Jenny would be in charge of graphic design since she knew her way around design software from when she helped run her high school newspaper.

"I mean," Hannah paused, "I'm not *excited* about it, but I'll figure it out. Hopefully."

"I can help you design ads if you need," Jenny offered with a friendly smile.

"Cool, I'll definitely be asking you for some help," Hannah told her.

The conversation naturally turned to more casual topics, such as their favorite types of music and books, where they worked, and their hobbies. Hannah gathered that Katie and Whitney knew each other already since they were in the same program, and Whitney knew Jenny from a prerequisite art class they were both enrolled in. Hannah couldn't help but feel like an outsider, seeing as how the three of them already had some history together.

During the meeting, Hannah remembered Katie saying she was from Union Bay and asked if she knew Manny or Amanda, Hannah's best friend from high school. She didn't, though, probably because they both had gone to a private Catholic high school, whereas Katie was a public school kid.

"Are any of you dating anyone?" Hannah asked, before shoveling another forkful of her meal into her mouth.

"Single as can be," Whitney announced loudly, as Katie and Jenny echoed the same. Whitney went off on a tangent about the lame boys from her high school and how she was just too mature for any of the guys she had met at SHU. Hannah wondered if Whitney was just really confident or a little conceited, deciding it was too thin of a line between them to figure out.

Katie interrupted Whitney's speech to disclose, "Well, I think Joe is really cute!"

Whitney folded her arms across her chest, leaning back in her seat. "Ugh, he's so uptight," she said, rolling her eyes. There was a long silence as a certain tension hung over them.

"Ooooohhh! Is there a love connection already?" Jenny teased Katie, bringing a lightness back to the conversation.

Katie giggled. "Oh, please!"

"Well, he's not really my type. I don't really go for the ones with the dangly bits," Jenny said as she winked at Hannah.

"What about you, Hannah? Did anyone catch your eye?" Whitney prodded, seeming to get over her bad mood pretty quickly. Hannah's face flushed lightly, and she wondered if they had noticed her staring at Jimmy.

Katie elbowed Whitney. "She already said she had a boyfriend!"

"So? She can't look?" asked Whitney.

Hannah shrugged, feeling flustered by the question. "Um, I don't know! I hadn't thought about it, I guess!" She looked down at her lunch, letting her hair conceal the terrible poker face that showed itself when she was lying. If Hannah were to be completely honest, Jimmy had caught her eye but it felt so wrong to admit since she had been dating Manny for nearly a year by then.

Hannah glanced up at the clock on the wall in front of her. It was 2:30 P.M. "Shit!" she exclaimed, standing up suddenly. Whitney, Katie, and Jenny looked up at her with startled expressions. "Sorry, I have to go. I'm gonna to be late for work!" Hannah told them.

"Wait! Write down your number so we can do this again," Katie said, ripping a paper from her spiral notebook and passing a pen to Hannah. She scribbled her number down, shoving the paper and pen back to Katie, doubtful she would actually call.

"Okay, I gotta run! Bye!" Hannah shouted over her shoulder. She jogged through the cafeteria and out the back door of the Student Center. The parking lot she frequently used was only a couple-minute walk down a steep sidewalk, but she kept jogging, in hopes of saving a few precious seconds.

Hannah threw her backpack on the passenger seat, floored it in reverse out of the parking spot, and maneuvered through the maze of cars. Once she hit the street outside the main gates, she started practicing the story she would tell her boss when she unfailingly walked in late.

On Monday, Hannah walked across the SHU campus from the shuttle bus stop toward the Student Center for the next newspaper meeting. She was lost in her own world, watching squirrels chase one another across the perfectly manicured lawns marked with signs every few feet that read, *Keep Off Grass.*

Jimmy had spotted Hannah walking ahead of him on the sidewalk and yelled, "Yo! Harborvale!"

Hannah had heard someone shout, but hadn't noticed what they said or where it had even come from. She was near the main door of the Student Center when she heard the voice again, louder and more clear.

"Harborvale!"

She turned around to see Jimmy jogging toward her. A backpack swung loosely on his shoulders, but he took care not to spill the coffee he held in one hand while the other held a skateboard.

"Hey, Harborvale," he said with a grin, slowing down as he approached her.

"Hi?" Hannah replied, confused as to why he was talking to her—if he even was. Hannah quickly looked around her but didn't see anyone else he would have been addressing.

Jimmy stared directly into her eyes. "What's up?" he asked.

Hannah shifted her weight, uncomfortable with the eye contact. "Um, nothing—just going to the meeting," she said, pointing her thumb at the building over her shoulder.

"Ditto," said Jimmy. "Hey—have we met before? I mean, before the meeting the other day."

Hannah considered his face, knowing she would have remembered him. "No, I don't think so, why?"

Jimmy shrugged. "I don't know. You just seemed familiar."

"Oh, I get that a lot," Hannah told him with an awkward smile. "I guess I just have that kind of face."

"No, it wasn't just that…" Jimmy responded, his voice trailing off. He cleared his throat suddenly and reached around her to open the door to the Student Center. Hannah's breath caught in her throat as he leaned forward toward her, so close that their bodies were mere inches apart. She looked more closely at the scar on his upper lip, before her eyes traveled up his face where she noticed the hazel hue of his eyes. "Ladies first," Jimmy said, motioning the large Dunkin' Donuts cup toward the open door.

"Oh, thanks," Hannah said. She pivoted her body around his, carefully avoiding contact, and walked through the door. "My name is Hannah, by the way. So you can stop calling me 'Harborvale.'"

Jimmy chuckled. "I know your name, Harborvale."

"So why don't you use it?" she asked.

Jimmy shrugged again. "It's just more fun this way," he replied.

"Right, real funny," Hannah said sarcastically, rolling her eyes at him.

"Fine. If that's what you want, I'll call you Hannah from now on," Jimmy conceded.

Hannah bent her head in a slight bow, feeling victorious. "Thank you."

Jimmy raised his eyebrows, his mouth opening wide with excitement. "Oh! I know! How about 'Hannah Banana'?"

"Oh god, no!" Hannah gasped, playfully pushing him in the shoulder. As soon as her hand made contact with Jimmy, she quickly retracted it, mortified.

Jimmy threw his head back and squinted as a deep laugh rumbled from his belly. His hand rubbed the spot on his arm where Hannah had shoved him. "Ow! C'mon! What's wrong with that? I'm still calling you by your name!"

"You could've come up with something more original," she teased. "I've been called that since, like, the first grade!"

"I can always shorten it. How about just 'Banana'?" Jimmy snickered.

"That's even worse," Hannah whined.

Jimmy opened the door to Room 202, letting Hannah walk in ahead of him. "Well, you better get used to it, Banana. I happen to like it," he told her.

Hannah tutted her disapproval as Jimmy sat on the far side of the circle of desks, exactly where he had sat at the first meeting. Hannah chose the same spot in the circle across from him. She beamed as she replayed their exchange over in her mind, deliberating if he had really been flirting with her or not. She secretly hoped he had been, even if she shouldn't.

Later that night at work, Hannah briskly walked out to her car for her thirty-minute break. If she didn't move fast enough, her manager would undoubtedly pull her into some new project, and she could forget all about that break. Under the electric glow of the thrift store sign, she dialed Manny's number. Hannah hadn't had a chance to talk with him about the first two official newspaper meetings she'd attended, or her impromptu lunch date.

Manny picked up on the last ring. "Hello?" His voice was deep and groggy as if he had been sleeping or, maybe just annoyed that she had called.

"Hey, it's me," Hannah replied.

"Oh, hey, Hannah." She noted that Manny had called her by her name. He never did that.

Hannah thought she heard hushed voices in the background. "Did I wake you up or something?"

"No, I'm fine. I'm just a little busy," Manny said as if he was suddenly in a rush.

Hannah started feeling uncomfortable with his short responses but tried to look past the feeling. "Oh, what are you up to?" she asked.

"Uh, well, Kyle came up from school, and we've been pre-gaming before we head out to this Halloween party soon," Manny told her.

Hannah couldn't stop a groan of loathing from escaping her lips. Kyle was Manny's best friend from high school, though Hannah thought "best friend" was a loose term; it had always been obvious to Hannah that Kyle talked down to Manny just because he had been on a scholarship.

"Who else is there? I thought I heard a few people," Hannah prodded.

"Just some other people from my floor. We're all going to the party together," Manny replied. Hannah could still hear the other voices in the background, and was able to make out some laughter. She couldn't help but worry that they were laughing at her somehow.

"Cool. Well, I was on my break and thought I would call you. I had two newspaper meetings…" Hannah said, tracing her finger in circles on the steering wheel.

"Oh, right. How was that?" Manny asked. Hannah could tell from his tone that he didn't care to hear the answer.

"It was interesting," Hannah began. "A couple of girls asked me to go for lunch after the first meeting, so that was nice."

"Cool," said Manny flatly. There was a long silence, and the awkwardness of their conversation caused Hannah to squirm in her seat. "Hold on a sec," he said.

"Okay," Hannah said quietly. She could hear Manny rustling around and whispering indistinguishably to someone else in the room. A heavy door opened and closed, and she could hear Manny's footsteps on the linoleum floor of the empty dorm hallway.

"You still there?" he asked.

"Yep."

Manny hesitated. "Listen—I, um. I don't know if I can do this."

Hannah looked confused as she picked at the peeling Chevrolet emblem on the car horn. "Do what?" she asked.

"This. Us." Manny said simply. "It's just so hard, being so far apart."

Hannah felt her heart stop, then start again in a fury. "What?"

"I'm sorry, Hannah. I like you—more than that. It's just—it's just too hard," Manny said again.

"So, what? You want a free pass, or something? To hook up with one of those girls in your room tonight?" she spat.

Manny raised his voice suddenly. "No! What? No. Look—I've been tossing this over for a few days and talked to Kyle about it. That's why he's here. The party and everything was his idea."

"So this was all Kyle's idea, then? For you to break up with me?" Hannah's voice grew louder. "And how, with him going to school in another state, did he just-so-happened to know about a party on your campus tonight? *And* Halloween is still, like, two weeks away!"

Manny sighed. "No. Kyle came here, and we talked to some people on my floor who are hanging out with us now. They were the ones who mentioned the party, and Kyle thought it would be a good way to get my mind off of things."

"Whatever," Hannah muttered. She sat silently, trying to decide if Manny was playing some weird prank on her. If he was, she knew it was probably Kyle's idea—he had never really liked Hannah, anyway.

"I'm sorry, Hannah." Manny's tone became more serious then, and she realized there was no joke to be had.

Sure, real sorry, Hannah thought. *If he were so sorry, he wouldn't be going out with a bunch of drunk bimbos.*

Hannah didn't know what to say to Manny, so she hung up and threw her phone to the floorboards. Hannah rested her forehead on the cool steering wheel. She felt like she should dissolve into tears, but they weren't coming. Instead, she just felt numb.

The thought of being alone covered her like a familiar, heavy blanket. Hannah had been relentlessly bullied in middle school and struggled to find her place in high school. She felt constantly lonely in those days, which weren't very far in her past. She would rather forget those years, but it was hard to ignore the scars they left. In high school, she was friendly enough with all kinds of people—the popular kids, stoners, goths, theater kids, nerds—but they were merely acquaintances. She had friends, sure, but they had always flitted in and out of her life. Hannah didn't feel like anyone really knew her, which, she could freely admit, was partly her fault. She had a tough time opening up to other people since so much of what she had shared in the past was spread around school like wildfire. Hannah curated narratives that she wanted people to know about her—mostly true, but with some bits of fiction sprinkled here and there.

She had one best friend through middle and high school: Amanda. They remained close through Amanda's abrupt move during the second half of their senior year because of her dad's job. That's how Hannah and Manny met—he had been going to the same school that Amanda had been switched to. Hannah had been visiting Amanda one weekend toward the end of the school year when they had crossed paths with Manny at a house party. Fireworks were being set off somewhere nearby that night for some unknown reason. Their separate groups of friends had seemingly disappeared, leaving Hannah and Manny alone on the lawn of a random house. They sat in the grass, too drunk to stand still, reveling in the explosion of color overhead. Manny kissed Hannah that night under the stars and bursting fireworks. It was all so breathtaking, but that only lasted so long in the real world, outside of the romance novels Hannah guiltily enjoyed reading.

Hannah thought about calling Amanda then, thinking that the news of being broken up with would finally motivate Amanda to want to talk to her. If Hannah were honest, though, she didn't feel like she had a best friend anymore. Since Hannah and Manny had started dating, Amanda got busy finding a new life at a college far away: new friends, activities, and a lot of partying. Whenever Hannah called, Amanda would say she couldn't talk because she was in the middle of another theater project or studying in the library. She barely texted back, either.

Hannah glanced at the clock on the dashboard to notice that she only had one minute left of her break. She picked up her phone and put into the front pocket of her apron, her body feeling heavy under the weight of her sudden loneliness. She took a deep breath, putting on her sweetest and most artificial smile, before trudging back into the store to finish her shift.

Hannah was in the Student Center getting a coffee between her classes when she ran into Katie, dressed down that day in SHU sweatpants and a matching sweatshirt.

"Katie! Hi!" Hannah called to her.

Katie waved. "Hey, dude!"

They found they had the same schedule on Tuesdays, and had some time to kill before their next classes. Katie and Hannah found an open table and sat down with their drinks. Katie mainly talked, which was okay with Hannah; she had never been much of a conversationalist, but more of a listener.

"So, tell me about your boyfriend!" Katie said. "I asked a couple of people from home if they knew him, but none of them did. What was his name? Matty?"

"No, Manny," Hannah corrected, enunciating the 'n' sound. "But he's not my boyfriend anymore. We broke up, like, two weeks ago."

"Oh. I'm sorry, dude," Katie said, wide-eyed and flustered. "I mean, are you okay?"

"Yeah, no, I'm fine. Totally fine. It's dumb—he felt like the distance was too much or something. I don't really know. I think I'm more angry than sad. But also, like, kind of 'whatever' about it?"

"That's so dumb! I mean, he knew you guys would be long-distance. If it was such a problem, then why commit?" Katie rolled her eyes. "Honestly, sometimes I think Jenny has the right idea, being a lesbian and all."

"True!" Hannah agreed with a chuckle. "But, yeah, I'm fine. I just want to move on, frankly." She shrugged like she could hoist the lingering disappointment off her shoulders if only she tried hard enough.

After a pause in the conversation, Katie took out her planner and flipped through its empty pages. "Hey, do you know when the next newspaper meeting is?"

"Um, I think it's next week?" Hannah replied, pulling out her own planner to double-check. "Yeah, a week from today. Same time, same room."

Katie wrote it down on the empty square marked November 8th. "Are you going?"

Hannah nodded as she sipped her coffee before saying, "I was planning on it, yeah."

With even just a mention of the newspaper, Hannah's mind went back to Jimmy. Her curiosity begged to know more about him; he had this bizarre pull over her, and she found herself thinking about him any time her mind became too quiet. Hannah eyed Katie, curious as to what she knew about him.

With some hesitation, Hannah asked, "Hey, what's that guy's name? The one with the hair?" She motioned her hands randomly around her head as if she were messing up her slick ponytail.

Katie laughed at Hannah's miming. "You mean, Jimmy?"

"Jimmy! Yeah! That's the one. I just keep calling him 'Crazy Hair Guy'!" Hannah laughed awkwardly. "I couldn't remember his real name."

"I think everyone seems pretty cool. Should be pretty fun to work together," Katie said.

"Yeah. You seemed to know a couple of people before the first meeting, like Whitney. Who else did you know?" Hannah asked. She would have to be careful with how she approached the topic of Jimmy, not wanting to expose her little crush.

"Well, Fernando. He's in my program, too. Brad, kind of—we have Algebra together," Katie rattled off as she marked each name with a flick of her finger.

"What about Jimmy?" Hannah blurted out. Her face flushed, knowing she was leading the conversation in an obvious way.

"Not really. He's friends with Brad, I know. He must have a class near our Algebra class because he is always with Brad beforehand, but I haven't really talked to him. He seems nice enough, but he kind of smells like… I don't know what," Katie chuckled.

Hannah laughed, too, trying to hide the way she swooned inside thinking about the smoky earthiness that wafted off of him. "Yeah, like a dirty hippie or something!" Hannah stuck out her tongue in mock disgust.

Whitney approached their table. She was dressed in a floral sweater, her skin as dewy and tanned as ever, a holdover from the summer. "What's up, ladies? My Bio class got out early today—it's a damn miracle!" she told them.

Hannah offered Whitney the extra chair at their table, which she immediately threw her bags down on and walked off to order herself a green tea.

Katie eyed Hannah suspiciously. "Why are you asking about him, anyway?"

Hannah fidgeted with the coffee cup between her hands, stumbling over her words, "I wasn't really. I was just making conversation."

"What did I miss?" Whitney asked as she sat down at the table with her tea. She could sense some drama was brewing and wanted in on it.

"I don't know," Katie muttered as she continued to study Hannah, pointing a finger in her direction. "This one over here is being a little weird."

Hannah's tone turned defensive, giving her away. "I am not! How am I being weird?"

"You tell me," Katie said, turning to Whitney. "Hannah was asking me about some people from the newspaper, and she keeps mentioning Jimmy."

Whitney's eyes went wide over the rim of the paper cup. "But I thought you had a boyfriend! Miss I-can't-look," she jested.

Katie cleared her throat. "Hannah and Manny broke up a few days ago, but she's over it. He couldn't handle the long distance anymore. Which is bullshit, but whatever."

"I was just saying that I didn't remember Jimmy's name, and Katie seemed to talk to everyone, so—I don't know! I was just making conversation!" Hannah shrieked.

"Uh-huh. Right," said Whitney.

"It's not a big deal! I'm sorry I asked," Hannah said, desperately wanting to change the subject, even though she could sense she was backed into a corner with no escape. Remembering the promise she made to herself about being more outgoing, Hannah knew she wouldn't be able to keep everything so close to her vest. She let out a long sigh and looked up at the ceiling. "Okay, fine," she started again. "I guess I'm kind of into him! There's just something—"

"I knew it!" Katie shouted before Hannah could finish. The girl at the table beside them, who had been diligently reading, turned to glare at them.

"Oh, lighten up. This isn't the library," Whitney sneered at her. The girl collected her belongings in a huff and left.

"Yeah, okay, I get it," Hannah said, throwing her hands up in defeat. "He's weird, I know!"

"Hannah, you can't say you like him and then call him weird!" Katie laughed, shaking her head in disbelief. "I mean, maybe he does need a little cleaning up, but he seems really nice!"

Hannah let out a loud groan and collapsed, resting her forehead on the metal table top.

"Oh my gosh! You're *so* dramatic!" Whitney muttered. "But you're not wrong—he is pretty weird. You could do better."

"That's not helpful, Whit." Katie thought for a moment. "Isn't he in a band or something? That's pretty cool, right?"

"How should I know? Does he look like someone I'd hang out with?" Whitney retorted. "If he is in a band, though, it just kind of makes him even dorkier."

Katie shot Whitney a look, gesturing to Hannah, who was still hiding her face. "Dude," she whispered.

Whitney smiled, suppressing more laughter. "Sorry, you're right. I'm not being nice, I guess."

Katie stood up from her place at the table and announced, "Well, I have to run off to class, dudes." She nudged Hannah in the shoulder. "That means you do, too!"

Hannah groaned and glanced at the clock on the wall. Whitney sipped on her tea, watching Hannah with her eyebrows raised. Hannah could tell by the look on her face that Whitney wanted to hassle her some more; Whitney thought her over-reactions were hilarious. She and Katie said goodbye to Whitney and walked down the stairs to the main floor of the Student Center.

"My next class is Algebra with Brad. Maybe Jimmy will be with him," Katie teased. She winked at Hannah as she turned to walk in the opposite direction.

"Why do I not trust you?" Hannah shouted to the back of her. Katie turned around to wave and tauntingly stuck her tongue out at Hannah. "Please don't do anything stupid!" she called out, as she watched Katie disappear around the corner.

Katie called Hannah later that night to tell her she hadn't seen Jimmy that afternoon, only Brad. "I got some information from him," she said to Hannah.

"What? No, you didn't," Hannah sighed.

"Relax, it was fine. I didn't tell him I was asking for *you*, only a friend," Katie assured her.

Hannah sat on the edge of her bed, her eyes growing wide. "You didn't think that would be a little obvious?" she questioned, waiting for Katie to realize that her plan had not been a good one.

"It could be *anyone*, Hannah! Whitney, maybe!" Katie suggested.

Hannah rested her face in the palm of her hand. "Oh, please! He wouldn't believe that for a second!"

Katie countered again, "Then Jenny!"

"Pfft. Do you hear yourself? *Everyone* knows Jenny is gay, Katie!"

"Fine, maybe you're right," Katie conceded. "But do you want to hear what I found out or not?"

Hannah laid back on her bed and sighed. "Fine."

"So Brad and Jimmy have been friends for, like, six years or something. They met when Jimmy's family moved to New Jersey during their freshman year of high school. He's a friendly guy and just, literally, talks to everyone. He skateboards, which we knew already, and he *is* in a band! They're called Cat Hair, which is weird, but whatever." Katie paused. "Let's see… he likes to read—just like you! Oh, and he's pretty into politics."

"That doesn't sound so bad, I guess, right?" Hannah asked.

"No, but there is bad news," Katie admitted.

"What is it? Is he moving back to wherever he came from or something?"

Katie laughed. "No, but he does have a girlfriend."

"Oh. Well, whatever," she mumbled apathetically, even though her heart was slowly sinking.

"Sorry," Katie murmured.

"Don't be. It's fine," Hannah said, busying herself with a loose thread on the blanket underneath her. "It's just a dumb crush. I'll wake up tomorrow cured, I'm sure of it."

After they hung up, Hannah continued to lie on her bed, staring at the pattern in the popcorn ceiling above her. With her anxiety on high alert, she feared Brad would tell Jimmy about his conversation with Katie; Hannah just knew Jimmy would realize that she was the friend in question. Hannah tried to talk herself out of feeling disappointed that Jimmy was in a relationship with someone. She tried to discredit her new crush on her recent breakup with Manny, convincing herself she was only looking for someone to replace him.

Not like it matters, anyway, she told herself. *He already has a girlfriend.*

Somehow, Hannah knew that when she awoke the following day, she wouldn't be over it.

Hannah arrived at the next meeting at one o'clock. She was perfectly on time, or so she thought. When she opened the door, all the other staff members had already gathered in a circle. Hannah checked the clock on the wall to be sure she hadn't misread the time, but she hadn't.

"Ooh, you're late, Banana," Jimmy announced, silencing the chatter in the room. He was sitting with his arms folded across his chest, a playfully smug smile on his face.

"Oh, sorry. I thought it started at one," Hannah said bashfully.

Katie and Whitney giggled from the left side of the circle, turning the room's attention to them. Hannah walked over to the only open seat next to Whitney, which the girls had been saving for her.

Whitney leaned in toward Hannah, hardly trying to stifle her laughter. "Banana?"

Hannah glared at her. "Don't call me that," she said quietly to avoid being overheard by the room.

Whitney smirked and whispered back, "Why not, *Banana*?"

"Because it's not my name, Whit. I don't like it," Hannah snapped.

"You didn't say that to *him*," she huffed, nodding in Jimmy's direction.

Hannah's gaze followed Whitney's to where he sat, obliviously doodling in his notebook. His body sagged in on itself with a certain sadness. Hannah frowned, feeling disappointed that the moment between them was over; she found herself beginning to enjoy his little taunts.

"I already did," Hannah said as she turned back to Whitney. "He just does what we wants."

"Or maybe you really do like it," Whitney suggested. "Or *him*." Side conversations had sprung up throughout the classroom, creating a chaotically noisy mixture of voices. Katie, who had been listening to their exchange, elbowed Whitney so she would stop badgering Hannah. Joe clapped his hands loudly, trying to get the attention of the room. When silence was finally restored, Joe explained, "Chris and I initially had a name for the newspaper but, after a lot of thinking, we've decided it just doesn't fit our mission. So, we're bringing it to all of you. This is a group effort after all, so we want the name to be something that reflects us all."

The group shouted ideas at Chris, who wrote them on the class whiteboard in his severely slanted script. Jimmy sat quietly at his desk, still sketching, not even noticing what was happening in the room around him. Hannah thought he would have been the loudest voice in the room, shouting out the craziest name ideas.

The running list consisted of:

- The SHU
- Safe Harbor News
- Safe Harbor Happenings
- The GumSHU
- Safe Harbor Chronicles
- The Inkwell

Eventually, the group whittled the list down to the top three choices:

- Safe Harbor News
- The GumSHU
- The Inkwell

Joe handed everyone scraps of paper to write their votes on, then walked around the circle with a plain paper bag to collect all of them. After Chris had finished counting, he announced, "It's official! *The Inkwell!*" He looked at Hannah, giving her a thumbs-up for the winning suggestion. She couldn't help but smile big, feeling happy that the group had picked her idea. It almost felt like they had picked her, not just her idea.

Joe changed the conversation back to the business of running a newspaper, which was sleep-inducing for the whole room. "We need to raise some funds to help with the publishing costs. Hannah, this is where you come in," he explained.

Hannah smiled and nodded as the mention of her name snapped her back to the present conversation.

"We need some businesses in the area that students frequent, or might frequent if they knew about them," Joe continued.

The group compiled a list of about six places, which Hannah diligently wrote down in her notebook. Joe then took Hannah aside to discuss how to approach those businesses about *The Inkwell* and review ad sizing and pricing information. She took thorough notes as they spoke, outlining all of the information she would need to try to make it a success; Hannah felt a lot of pressure to get it right since the funds for printing were dependent solely on ad sales. Chris, meanwhile, talked with the writers and artists on staff.

By the end of the meeting, Hannah was overwhelmed with all of the information she and Joe discussed. Her mind spun, too, at the idea of walking into businesses to pitch a sale to a stranger. She figured her sales skills were terrible; Hannah barely knew how to talk to her friends, let alone a business owner who had built a career selling stuff.

As everyone packed up their belongings to leave, Hannah took her time with nowhere in particular to be that afternoon. She busied herself with putting her notebook and pen into their respective pockets in her backpack, then checked her phone for messages before finally standing up to leave. When she did, Hannah found herself nearly nose-to-nose with Jimmy, who had been standing next to her, patiently waiting for her to notice him. She stumbled backward a step, tripping on the leg of her desk.

"Jesus!" Hannah shouted in surprise.

Jimmy reached for her, grabbing Hannah by the shoulder to help steady her. "Sorry, I didn't want to startle you," he told her.

"Well, that obviously didn't really work," Hannah sarcastically said before she noticed the frown on his face. "Sorry. I just hate being startled like that."

"Don't be. I'm sorry," Jimmy said again, looking at the floor. "Listen—I was just thinking—I know this cool comic book shop off Route 11. You should hit them up for an ad."

"Yeah, cool, that's a good idea. What's the name of it?" she asked, sliding her backpack off her shoulder to dig out her notebook and a pen again.

"The Comic Closet," Jimmy shared. He paused as Hannah unzipped her backpack. "Actually—I thought if you're not busy, I could take you over there now. I know the manager pretty well."

Hannah went rigid, panicked that he was asking her to hang out. Just the two of them. She grabbed her phone from her jacket pocket to check the time as if she had somewhere to be, trying to buy herself a quick second to think it over. Surprising herself, she spontaneously blurted out, "Yeah, that works! As long as you don't mind. I don't want to impose or anything."

"Not at all. I asked *you*, Banana," Jimmy said, nudging his index finger into her shoulder. "Really. It's not a problem," he added with a smile. Hannah noticed that only his mouth was smiling while his eyes seemed downturned and sad, unlike how they usually were. She knew what it was like to feel so low on the inside, trying your best to cover it with a disguise of false happiness; like recognized like.

Hannah could feel her heart fluttering with anticipation at the thought of spending time alone with Jimmy, but that mean voice in her head quickly squashed that feeling. *He's only doing you a favor,* it said. *Remember—he's just really friendly and nice, so don't take it so seriously.*

Hannah met Katie's eye just then, who gave her a not-so-discreet thumbs-up.

Brad, Jimmy's friend and resident comic artist for *The Inkwell*, interrupted their conversation. "Yo! Did you say you were going to The Comic Closet?"

Jimmy turned to Brad, giving him the same fake smile. "Yeah, I'm gonna take Hannah to talk with John about buying an ad."

Brad's face lit up. "Bro! I'm going to tag along! I've been wanting to see if they have the newest release of this manga I've been reading. I've been waiting forever for it!"

Hannah tried to hide the disappointment from her face, turning to look out the window. Jimmy looked from her to Brad, suggesting, "Why don't you and I just go tonight, man? Hannah and I will probably be there a while talking business, ya know? It'll be boring."

"No, it's okay. I can keep myself busy," said Brad. "Let's go!"

Jimmy looked at Hannah once more, frowning slightly. "I guess we should head out then."

Hannah picked up on the hint of melancholy in his voice, eager to know if it was because of the hiccup in his plans or if something else was bothering him. She concluded that it probably had nothing to do with her.

The three of them walked down the steep hill behind the Student Center to the parking lot, the same one Hannah always parked in. "I'm over on the far side," Jimmy said, pointing off into the distance. Brad had Jimmy's ear, going on about the manga series he had mentioned back inside. They hadn't even left campus yet, and she already felt like their third wheel.

Brad and Jimmy walked fast, creating a considerable distance between them and Hannah; she found herself almost jogging to keep up with them. Brad was over six feet tall with a wide stride, so she could understand how he moved so fast. Jimmy, though, stood about six inches shorter than him. She mused that Jimmy must get his speed from the large coffees he was always drinking.

Jimmy turned around, pointing to an old gray Oldsmobile with peeling paint and rust stains. "I'm right here," he said.

Brad was already at the passenger side before Hannah reached the car, so she accepted her place in the backseat. Jimmy unlocked the door, opening it for her with a weak half-smile in apology for Brad. Hannah slipped into the car, which was comfortably warm compared to the cold afternoon air. Looking around, she noticed a large rip in the seat and how the car reeked of cigarette smoke.

As they pulled out of the crowded lot, Brad was still talking but had switched to another topic by then. It was hard to hear him over the screaming punk music that flowed from the car's speakers, but Hannah had stopped listening to him anyway. Jimmy reached down to turn the volume knob a couple more clicks to the right, drowning out Brad even more. Steering with his knees, he opened a blue pack of American Spirit cigarettes and placed one between his lips. Before flicking the lighter, Jimmy peered at Hannah in the rearview mirror, briefly turning the music back down.

"Banana, do you mind if I smoke?" he asked.

Hannah met his eyes in the mirror, but before she could respond, Brad said, "Nah, bro. Go ahead."

Jimmy looked over at him with a confused look on his face, "Since when do you answer to 'Banana?'"

Brad looked back at him, equally puzzled. "Huh?"

"Nothing, man," Jimmy said with a chuckle.

He looked back into the rearview mirror, where Hannah was still watching him. He rolled his eyes, which caused her to chuckle. Jimmy gave her a questioning look and held up the cigarette. "Do you mind?" he mouthed.

Hannah shook her head and mouthed back, "No."

He smiled more genuinely that time, holding eye contact with her a second longer than necessary; something stirred in her, and she wondered if he felt it, too.

Brad hadn't even noticed their exchange, so lost in a conversation with himself. Jimmy lit the cigarette and turned the music back up to drown him out again. Hannah leaned her elbow on the armrest for the remainder of the ride, watching the world go by.

The drive took about fifteen minutes as they wound through various back roads. Once they parked, Hannah looked around and realized she knew the area but not that building. It was so unassuming that Hannah knew she would have never found this place had she come alone. Jimmy and Brad started walking toward the rundown building, wrapped in beige siding, which looked more like a house than a store. A simple neon sign was lit up in the front window reading, "The Comic Closet."

Hannah stood in the doorway to the store, surprised at how much bigger it was than it had appeared from the outside. It was a long, narrow room with floor-to-ceiling shelves along all four walls and groups of smaller double-sided shelving units running down the middle of it.

Jimmy tapped her arm and spoke softly, "John's here. I'm going to talk to him real quick. I'll be right back." She nodded in response as he walked over to the glass display case at the front of the store, with a register at the far-left end. A heavy-set man with a ponytail and a sizable bald spot at the back of his head was perched on a stool behind the register, watching them.

Brad had already disappeared to the back of the store where the manga was kept. Hannah stood on the spot momentarily, unsure what to do with herself; comic books weren't really her thing. Feeling out of place, she walked up to the nearest shelf and flipped through the merchandise, pretending to be interested.

Brad appeared at her side again before she knew it. "Bro! They have it!" he said with a goofy grin, holding up the manga to show her. Hannah likened him to a Golden Retriever who had just found the best stick in the park.

Trying to match his enthusiasm, Hannah declared, "That's great!" After a few seconds, she asked more seriously, "Hey—is Jimmy okay? He seems a little off today."

Brad's smile faded. "Oh, yeah. It's just Kelly."

Hannah busied herself again by thumbing through comic books on the shelf. "Kelly?" she asked.

"Yeah, his girlfriend. Well, I guess, his *ex*-girlfriend. He told me they broke up the other day after another fight," Brad said, trying to sound indifferent.

"Oh!" Hannah exclaimed loudly before clearing her throat and lowering her voice. "Well, that sucks, I guess."

Brad shrugged, turning to shuffle through the comic books on the shelves in front of them, too. "Eh, she sucks. They're not good for each other."

"What do you mean?" Hannah asked.

"They're always breaking up, getting back together, and breaking up again. It's been that way since high school. It's crazy," Brad said.

"Oh, wow. Jimmy's been dating her that long?" Hannah probed, hoping she didn't sound too nosy.

Neither of them noticed Jimmy approaching from behind one of the center aisle bins, having stopped in his tracks when he got close enough to hear their conversation about him and Kelly.

"Yeah. Since, like, sophomore year," Brad replied, eyeing Hannah curiously. "You know, I had an interesting conversation with Katie the other day—"

Jimmy reappeared abruptly, talking only to Hannah, "Let's go talk to John, yeah?"

"Sure," Hannah said, thankful for the disruption.

I knew this would happen! I wonder if Brad said anything to Jimmy about it, she thought. *Ugh, don't be stupid, Hannah. Of course, he would have.*

She selfishly had to admit that she was happy to hear about Jimmy's breakup, but she did feel terrible that it made him so obviously sad. Hannah felt the sudden urge to hug him, thinking it somehow might be enough to heal his heart. Maybe hers, too.

Hannah and Jimmy walked to the cash register, where Jimmy introduced her to John. She talked with John about the newspaper's available ad space, but she kept stumbling over her words, having to backtrack through the conversation awkwardly. Jimmy quickly picked up on her nervousness and scanned the notes she had laid out on the counter. He jumped into her sales pitch to help steer the conversation back on course while still allowing her to own it. Hannah watched in amazement at the ease with which Jimmy explained everything, even though he had only briefly looked at the details.

John wound up buying a medium-sized ad that day. As they left the store, Jimmy high-fived Hannah and told her, "Nice work in there."

"Pfft. Yeah, right—"

"Don't be so hard on yourself," he said reassuringly.

Later that night, Hannah was online doing homework for her Child Development class when she got a chat room invite from Katie, Whitney, and Jenny, who wanted to know all about her afternoon. They couldn't believe what an airhead Brad was, inviting himself along like that. Hannah confessed that she had really fallen for Jimmy, watching him just ooze charisma at the sales counter. She instantly regretted putting that into writing, making it permanent and hard to refute if it got into the wrong hands; verbal conversations were much easier to deny in her experience.

Hannah frowned, feeling deflated by her lack of trust in her friends. She couldn't help but think about the time in middle school when her friend stole her diary from her backpack. Her friend had taken it home to read from front to back and then told everyone about it the next day at school. She showed it to some of their other friends, divulging what Hannah thought about all of them. The friend told anyone who would listen about the boys Hannah thought were cute and the fighting going on at home between her parents.

Hannah did her best to disregard the negative memories, allowing herself to feel happy to have people with whom she could share some of the good stuff with. She had also seen Amanda online that night but didn't bother sending her a message. They were practically strangers by then, and Hannah knew Amanda wouldn't make the time to hear about what was happening in her life, anyway.

Continued

Hannah only now realized that Jimmy was the first person to see her for who she was without any shame or guilt. Not even her parents really knew who she was deep down. They didn't understand the paradox of her soft yet hard nature, her love for the arts, or that she lived so deeply in her thoughts that she hated being inundated with constant small talk. It didn't click for them how she could get so emotional, often crying over a movie or a book.

Hannah reflected on all the fights she had with her parents in those days, arguing over how she chose to spend her time and who she wanted to date. She remembered the day that Jimmy met her parents for the first time. Neither of them saw in him what Hannah saw, blinded only by his scruffy appearance. Her mom had often made fun of his hair, calling him "Pinhead" behind his back when he wore it particularly spiked out. They thought Jimmy was too wild, calling him a nuisance for skateboarding in public places around town. Her dad disliked that Jimmy took up so much of Hannah's time, keeping her out of the house late and causing her to skip dinners with them. At least they were fair in that they held a lot of judgment against Manny, too, thinking he just wasn't good enough for Hannah. Whatever that meant.

Hannah learned so much from Jimmy about being self-assured and outgoing; he had been a great teacher without ever meaning to be. As she recalled that day at The Comic Closet, Hannah reveled in Jimmy's natural charm. He had swooped in like some superhero and saved her from the anxiety that clung to her back for years. She often envisioned herself putting on Jimmy's confidence like a cape, drawing strength from him to dampen her insecurities. Hannah continued to use that visualization in her adult life when things felt too overwhelming, allowing the peace she once felt with him to wash over her again.

Hannah looked back on those days, on her budding relationship with Jimmy, and pictured herself being swept out to sea by his current. Like a tsunami wave—gentle, almost, when you saw it coming from a distance like it could carry you safely back to shore. In reality, though, it was so incredibly destructive and powerful enough to destroy whole villages.

Hannah found herself spending a Friday night pricing new merchandise for the men's department that had come in during the morning shift, and she was annoyed all the work had been left for her on the night shift. Even though Christmas was only three weeks away, she had been customer-less for most of the night, so she couldn't be too mad. Her manager was holed up in the back office finalizing some paperwork, so she was pretty much alone in the store. She clicked the pricing gun in time with some catchy Christmas song playing on the Muzak system overhead; the same song had already played five times in the three hours she'd been there. Without wanting to, Hannah shook her hips and bopped her head to the rhythm. The pricing gun turned into her microphone, and she sang along while hanging new shirts on the racks.

As the song ended, Hannah whipped around in surprise at the sound of someone clapping. Jimmy was standing a few feet away at the end of the aisle, leaning against a display unit, having witnessed her entire performance.

"That was impressive, Banana," Jimmy said with a crooked smile. He flashed her a thumbs-up as he walked up the aisle toward her.

Hannah stood frozen on the spot, her eyes and mouth open in horror. She couldn't believe that she had unknowingly embarrassed herself in front of Jimmy like that. Hannah blinked hard, hoping that when she reopened her eyes, she would find herself in bed in the midst of a bad dream. Instead, when she opened them, Jimmy was still approaching her.

"What are you doing here?" she managed to squeak out.

Jimmy chuckled, motioning his hand toward the racks of clothing around them. "Um, shopping? This is a store, after all, right?"

"Right," Hannah said with a slow nod. "I just didn't know anyone was here—didn't hear the door chime."

"I'm not surprised. You were pretty devoted to your craft," he teased. Jimmy thumbed through the shirts on the rack next to her.

Hannah watched how his jaw muscles tensed and how his Adam's apple bobbed with each hard swallow. Her embarrassment seemed to melt away somehow. Jimmy had this effect on her that softened something hidden deep inside.

"Shut up! I'm so embarrassed," Hannah replied.

Their eyes met for a fleeting moment before Hannah quickly looked away, busying herself with the pricing gun again. No matter how calm he made her feel, Jimmy just as quickly made her entirely too nervous.

"You shouldn't be," Jimmy told her in earnest. He cleared his throat and changed the subject, "I didn't know you worked here."

"Only for, like, the last year," Hannah quipped.

"Really?" Jimmy asked. "I feel like I come in here all the time. How have I never seen you?"

"I don't know." Hannah shrugged. "I feel like I practically live here."

Jimmy only nodded in response as silence fell between them. Hannah desperately tried to think of something, anything, to say to prevent the moment from ending. Before she could think of something clever to say, Jimmy asked, "So, what are you doing tonight?"

Hannah chuckled and motioned to the boxes of clothing stacked in front of her, mimicking Jimmy's sarcasm. "Stocking shelves? This is a store, after all."

"Oh, duh," Jimmy murmured. "So, like, *big* plans then."

"Huge," Hannah laughed. "I'm just booked solid with fun for the next few hours."

"Hopefully you get a break at some point?" Jimmy inquired.

Hannah took out her cell phone from the front pocket of her apron to check the time. "Soon. I can't wait to just step outside for a little bit; it feels claustrophobic in here sometimes."

"It's not real cold tonight, so it should be good out there for you." Jimmy hesitated, then cleared his throat again. "I should probably go. I've got some big plans myself," he told her.

"Oh, what are you up to tonight?" she asked, trying her best to sound upbeat even though she was sure her face was giving away her disappointment.

"Oh, uh, the usual stuff," he stuttered. "Well—see ya 'round, Banana." Jimmy began to walk away from her quickly but stopped suddenly at the end of the aisle. He turned around to face her again, admitting, "I lied. I've actually never shopped here before." The edges of his lips turned up in a smile for only a brief second before he abruptly turned to leave.

Hannah just stood there, wanting to run after him or at least say something. No matter how hard she tried, her body didn't respond. *What did he mean by that?* she wondered. *Did he come here to see me? No, he wouldn't have. Would he? How would he have known where to find me if he did?*

Hannah pushed the thoughts from her mind, the voice inside telling her that she was reading too much into his words. There was no way someone like Jimmy would ever fall for a girl like her. She continued pricing and hanging shirts, unable to stop replaying his last words in her mind.

Twenty minutes later, Hannah poked her head into the back office to let her manager know she was going on break. She usually would have sat out back behind the store, but it was too creepy in the dark. Hannah exited through the front door, heading to her car to sit and listen to the radio for a while. She checked her phone for messages as she stepped onto the sidewalk, snorting at a text she had received from Katie. Hannah momentarily looked up from her phone to find Jimmy sitting on the trunk of his car in the parking lot, his face lit by the neon sign above them.

Jimmy grinned. "What's up, Banana?"

"What are you still doing here?" Hannah asked, feeling completely stunned that he was really sitting there in front of her.

"Ya know, you keep asking me that," he joked, careful not to answer the question.

"Sorry, I just mean—you said you had plans," Hannah stuttered.

Jimmy chuckled. "Eh, yeah, I don't have plans. I walked out here and just thought I might sit for a minute."

"It's been a lot longer than a minute," Hannah jested.

"Yeah, I guess it has," Jimmy said. "Do you want to sit?" He slid over to make room for her.

"Um, sure." Hannah wanted to pinch herself as she walked toward the car. She lifted herself backward onto the trunk, her feet resting on the bumper.

Jimmy laid back on the rear window, his hands under his head like a cushion. She could see the Rancid T-shirt he wore under a navy blue canvas jacket with a red armband around the left sleeve. It had ridden up, exposing the portion of his stomach below his belly button and a pair of green plaid boxer shorts. Hannah looked away, embarrassed she had let her eyes linger like that.

"I love looking up at the stars," he told her. "I just wish I lived further from the city, though, so they'd be more visible."

Hannah looked up at the night sky, following his gaze. "I don't know that I ever really just sat and looked at the stars," she admitted.

"Oh, you're missing out, Banana," Jimmy told her. He pointed to a cluster of stars. "See those three bright ones there that look like they're in a row?"

Hannah slowly laid back for a better view, feeling Jimmy's eyes on her. She followed the path of his finger, noticing fresh scrapes on his knuckles. "What happened?" she asked, touching his hand lightly with her index finger.

Jimmy turned his hand over to see what she was pointing to. "Oh, that. I fell skateboarding earlier. It's nothing," he said and again pointed toward the sky. "Anyway, do you see the ones I'm talking about?"

"I think so."

"That's Orion's Belt, probably the easiest one to find. They all have stories about them, ya know. Folklore, I guess."

Hannah marveled at the night sky, wondering what stories the stars could tell. "I had no idea," she told him.

Jimmy excitedly lectured Hannah about the stories of Orion's Belt that existed across cultures, each somewhat similar to the last. Hannah particularly liked the Egyptian version of the story, which said the belt was the resting place for the Egyptian god of the dead.

"Some people say that you become a star when you die," he told her wistfully. "I don't know what I believe about that. What happens when we die, I mean, but I hope that's true. I'd love to be a star one day."

Hannah thought that was the most beautiful thing she had heard and hoped it was true, too. Jimmy cleared his throat and continued to point out other constellations and stars, spouting off different mythologies. Hannah watched him as he talked, taking in the enthusiasm he poured into each word.

Jimmy eventually turned to face her, realizing she had been watching him the whole time. Hannah swore she saw his cheeks redden in the dark. They both turned to look back at the night sky, afraid to acknowledge the growing thing between them. "I don't know," Jimmy continued. "There's just something about looking up there at something so big, and being this tiny little speck that's literally light-years away. It puts so many things into perspective." Hannah heard a twinge of emotion in his voice. "Hannah?" he asked.

She looked over at him. "Hm?"

"Do you ever feel this pressure to—I don't know—just be perfect? To get it all right?"

"Get what right?" she asked.

"Everything. Life."

Surprised by the serious turn the conversation had taken, Hannah momentarily contemplated his question. "Yeah, of course. I think we all do."

"You think so?"

"Yeah. I just think some people are better at hiding it than others. I don't think anyone really gets it right—not the first time, anyway," she replied. "And what is perfection, anyway? Or normal, for matter?"

"Sometimes I just feel like the weight of the world is on my shoulders because of it," he confessed.

Hannah exhaled loudly. "Pfft. I know how that feels. Some days, I think it's a miracle that I walk upright." She and Jimmy both laughed at that.

He propped himself up on his elbow, studying her face. "Ya know, your eyes kind of look like sunflowers," he said dreamily. She wasn't sure if it was just her imagination or wishful thinking, but his face seemed to slowly creep closer to her own. Hannah squirmed as the possibilities of what might happen next played out in her mind, but then Jimmy pulled back suddenly with a sharp inhale. He looked back at the store. "Your break is probably over soon, right?"

"Oh, yeah. Maybe," she said. Hannah pulled her phone from the front pocket of her apron to check the time. "Just kidding! I'm actually late!" She sat up and jumped down from the car. Jimmy hopped down in front of her. "Thanks for the impromptu astronomy lesson," she said.

Jimmy grinned big. "Sure thing."

She turned to walk back inside but felt a hand on her arm.

"Hannah?"

She turned to face him, surprised by how close he was standing to her.

"Thank you," Jimmy said earnestly.

Hannah looked away and laughed, feeling uneasy in their closeness. "For what?"

Jimmy shrugged. "Just thanks." He turned and got into his car, slowly pulling out of the parking lot. She saw his eyes in the rearview mirror, watching her as he left.

Hannah walked back into the store to finish her shift that night, but her mind was still out there somewhere, floating among the stars. Jimmy had surprised her by showing a more sullen and serious side of himself, and it felt good that he had come to her seeking… what, exactly?

With the end of the first semester only a week away, Hannah noticed how unusually quiet the SHU campus had become, with students too busy to be anything but serious. Hannah had spent the morning alone at the cafe of the Student Center studying for her Sociology final, feeling pretty confident that she'd get an 'A.' She was surprised that she didn't run into any of her friends from the newspaper, but she was thankful to be able to review her notes uninterrupted one last time.

Hannah packed her textbook and notebook into her backpack before throwing away the coffee cup she slowly sipped from all morning until her drink had gone ice cold. She descended the stairs to the first floor, making a detour to the bathroom before leaving the Student Center to make the trek across campus to the Humanities Building.

When Hannah left the bathroom stall, she noticed a female campus police officer talking to some girls nearby. She was tall and thin, with blonde hair pulled into a severe bun at the base of her head. Hannah didn't think much of it, still reviewing the material to herself as she washed her hands. The officer approached Hannah as she turned off the faucet and asked, "What stall did you come out of?"

She eyed the badge on the officer's uniform: *Officer White.* Hannah directed her attention over her shoulder toward the stalls as she shook the water from her hands. "I'm sorry?"

Officer White repeated more slowly, "What stall did you just come out of?"

Hannah was put off by her demeaning tone. She looked back at the stalls, unable to remember which one she had gone into; she had been too busy reciting gender inequality statistics to notice. "Oh, I'm not sure, to be honest. Either that one or that one," Hannah said as she pointed to the two doors in front of her.

Officer White pulled a paper from her pocket. "Well, this note was found in the stall on the left just a moment ago." She stared at Hannah, searching for the guilt in her eyes.

Hannah looked from the officer to the bathroom stall. "I didn't see anything in the stall I was in, so I must've been in the other one," she stated simply.

"Come outside with me," Officer White said matter-of-factly as she grabbed Hannah by the arm and tugged.

Hannah blinked hard, taken aback by Officer White's attitude and force. "Oh, uh, okay." She trailed behind the officer into the busy hallway, where another campus police officer was waiting. *Officer Black,* Hannah read on his badge and smirked. *Oh, that's funny. What are the odds of that? Officer Black and Officer White.*

Officer White looked at Hannah disbelievingly and asked, "Is there something funny about this?"

"No! No, sorry. I'm sorry," Hannah stuttered. "What's all of this about, anyway?"

Officer Black shifted his body weight between his feet and hooked his thumbs through the belt loops of his pants. She noted his tall and stocky stature, and how the change in his posture made him look more menacing. With a deep voice, he explained, "We received reports of two bomb threats in this building this morning. One note was left at the front desk there." He pointed over his shoulder. "The other was found in a bathroom stall here," he said as he pointed to the door of the women's bathroom.

"I don't know anything about those notes," Hannah said as she looked between the two of them, their expressions stern. "I didn't leave those notes, if that's what you're thinking!"

Officer White put a hand on the strap of Hannah's backpack, causing Hannah to duck away from her. "You have a notebook in there? Something with your writing on it? We'll need to see something to compare to the notes."

"Yeah, sure. I've got a ton in here," Hannah told them, hoping to resolve the dispute quickly. She dropped the backpack from her shoulder to the ground and bent over to unzip it.

Officer White stopped her, saying, "I'll do that." She bent down, snatching the backpack away from Hannah, unzippering it briskly. She pulled out the first notebook she found, opened it to a random page, and huddled together with Officer Black. They compared the two notes with Hannah's notebook, whispering and nodding to one another.

Can she be any ruder? Hannah thought to herself, shooting a furtive glare at Officer White.

Hannah fixed her expression to a more neutral one as Officer Black addressed her again. "They look pretty similar." He held out one of the notes and her notebook so Hannah could see for herself.

She glanced from the note to her notebook and then back again. "I'm sorry, but I don't see the similarities at all," she told them. "That's so… round and bubbly. My handwriting isn't like that; it's all slanted and tight."

She looked at the note again:

I've planted a bomb in the SC. It will detonate at noon.

Hannah's eyes then shifted toward her notebook:

Theories of Self-Development:
Freud – phases of maturation, failure to engage/disengage
from one phase emotional/psychological consequences
Erikson – personality never finishes developing
Piaget – socialization, self develops as we interact with
the world as it exists to us
Harlow – social relationships, esp. isolation and maternal
deprivation

Disregarding her insight, Officer Black sighed and said, "We're going to need you to come down to the station with us."

"But—I have a final at noon!" Hannah told them. "I can't miss it!" Her eyes pleaded with him to let her go on about her day, to believe her, to see what she could so clearly see: those notes were not Hannah's doing.

Officer Black looked Hannah over suspiciously. "This one note here mentions noon—what a coincidence. Look, the faster we get down there, the faster we can figure this all out," he said promisingly.

"It wasn't me!" Hannah said, her voice rising. She noted the sass in her tone, making a mental note to calm down.

"Come on," Officer White said as she took Hannah by the arm again and guided her out the front door of the Student Center. Hannah looked at the faces of students who had lost all interest in their studies, instead focusing on the scene unfolding. She could feel them all passing judgment on her.

Officer White directed Hannah to sit in the back of the white and blue patrol car parked outside. A small crowd had filtered out of the building behind them, whispering and watching as Officer Black drove slowly away. Hannah stared out the window, her eyes widening when she noticed Jimmy in the crowd. He stared back at her, his mouth open in shock. He raised his hands to her in question, but all Hannah could do was shake her head and look down at her lap; she felt so ashamed of herself for something she didn't even do.

Hannah flung open the front door of the campus police station, rushing to make it to her sociology final on time. She had begged Officer Black and Officer White to let her leave so she could take her exam. They finally agreed to let her go, but under the condition that Hannah leave her belongings with them. The officers wanted to examine her backpack and compare the handwriting samples thoroughly. Hannah agreed to their terms, unsure of what else to do to prove her innocence.

A voice called to Hannah from behind the open door, "Banana! Hey!"

Hannah turned around, startled to find Jimmy leaning against the brick building. He was smoking a cigarette while fiddling with something on the underside of his skateboard. She felt almost angry to see him then; Hannah was so embarrassed, and he was the last person she wanted to see her like this.

"What are you doing here?" she asked him.

Jimmy pushed himself off the wall and walked toward her. "Are you okay? What happened?"

Hannah narrowed her glare at him. "You first. What are you doing here?"

"I'm starting to feel like you don't want me around. First at the store, now here," he joked, but Hannah's expression didn't change. Jimmy shrugged, putting his hands up in defense in front of him. "I don't know, okay? I just saw you in the back of the cop car, which was really fucking weird. I came to see what happened and if you were alright."

"They thought I wrote some bomb threats and planted them in the Student Center."

Jimmy blinked fast several times in disbelief. "Wait. A *bomb* threat? *You*? You've got to be kidding."

"Pfft. I wish I was kidding," she told him. The overwhelm of the last thirty minutes was finally catching up to her. Hannah's head spun with all the scenarios of what might happen when she returned to collect her things.

Jimmy frowned at the sight of tears building up in her eyes. "Are you okay?" he asked again.

Hannah shook her head. "Not really. They really think I did it, but I didn't! Jimmy, I *swear* I didn't!"

Jimmy took a long stride toward her, hugging her tightly. It all happened so fast that Hannah didn't have a chance to comprehend what was happening as Jimmy wrapped his arms around her. Hannah's arms just hung limp at her sides. "I believe you, Banana. I know this isn't who you are."

Hearing his immediate belief in her was enough to crack open the dam of sobs she had been holding back.

"It's okay," Jimmy continued while Hannah shook against him. He rubbed a hand on her back, which did help to comfort her. For a moment, Hannah forgot it was Jimmy holding her. She forgot all about her feelings for him and the awkward, romantic tension between them. "Hey, where's your backpack?" he asked suddenly.

Hannah sniffled and pulled away, trying to compose her fevered mind. "They kept it all to go through while I take my exam. I have to come back when I'm done."

"They can't do that, Hannah!" Jimmy shouted. "They have no right! That's bullshit!"

Hannah looked at Jimmy, shocked by his sudden anger. "Well, I had no idea you were some secret lawyer."

Jimmy scoffed at Hannah's sarcasm, "I'm not stupid—I do know some things, ya know."

"I'm not stupid either," Hannah retorted.

"That's not what I meant," Jimmy moaned.

"It's fine. I gave them permission. I mean, it's not like I have anything to hide, so... ." Hannah looked to the ground as silence fell between them. "Hey, do you know what time it is? I don't have my phone to check."

Jimmy pulled his cell phone from the front pocket of his jacket, the same one he wore when he showed up to Hannah's job last week. Hannah briefly zoned out, lost in the memory of Jimmy leaning back on the trunk of his car in the darkness. "It's, uhh, 11:45."

Hannah's eyes went wide. "Shit! I have fifteen minutes to get to my exam, and it's on the other side of campus!" She turned from Jimmy and started to walk away quickly.

"Hey!" he called out to her.

Hannah stopped and turned back around.

"Can you ride? Do you want to take this?" he asked as he held up his skateboard.

Hannah unexpectedly roared with laughter. "I don't know. Which do you think is the better excuse for failing my final? A broken neck or being arrested for making terroristic threats?"

Jimmy smiled, happy to see her lighten up a little. "Hmm, that's a tough choice! I mean, I'd offer you a lift, but I can only fit myself on this thing."

Hannah let another small laugh escape her lips. "Thanks, though," she said sincerely. "For being here."

Jimmy gave her a slight nod in response as she turned away from him again and began to jog across campus. By some miracle, Hannah made it to the Humanities Building in just five minutes. She hesitantly approached a group of students in the downstairs lobby, asking for some change to use the payphone. With her hands shaking, Hannah deposited the quarter and dialed her mom's work number.

"Greenline Distributors, how can I help you?"

Hannah breathed a sigh of relief that her mother was the person on the other end. "Mom, it's Hannah."

"Hi," her mom said in surprise. "What's going on?"

Hannah whispered into the phone, not wanting to be overheard by the students pushing past her. "Something bad happened. There were these bomb threats made at school, and somehow, the cops think it was me."

"Oh, Jesus, Hannah! Why would they think that? What did you do? Do I need to get a lawyer or something?"

Hannah was shocked that her mom actually thought she might have been involved. "What? No! I don't know!"

"What did they charge you with?"

"Nothing yet, but they said something about terroristic threats. They let me go to my exam, so I guess that's good? It's in a few minutes, and then I have to go back for my things."

Her mom sighed. "Your things? What do you mean?"

"They kept my backpack and stuff to go through. I don't have anything with me right now. I'm using the payphone to call you. I had to ask some people for change."

"Well, call me back when you figure out what they're doing. I have to go, Hannah. I'm trying to work," her mom snapped.

There was a dial tone in Hannah's ear; her mom had hung up on her. Hannah felt like crying all over again, having only wanted her mother's support and love, not the cold bitterness she received instead. She hung the receiver back onto its cradle and looked at the clock on the wall: 11:55 A.M. Hannah headed for the stairs and climbed the three flights to the third floor, walking into the sociology classroom just in time. Hannah asked to speak to her professor in the hall before beginning the exam, wanting to tell him what had happened to her that morning. She hoped he might take pity on her when grading her test.

Hannah spent the entire hour on her exam and was one of the last students left in the classroom by the time she had finished. Although she had felt prepared for the test, she could not remember anything when she sat at her desk with the test materials in front of her. All that swam around in her mind were images of herself wearing an orange jumpsuit, handcuffed, and pacing the tight space of a jail cell.

As Hannah returned to the campus police station, she noticed Jimmy riding his skateboard on the sidewalk outside. "What are you still doing here?" she called out to him.

Jimmy stepped off his skateboard, letting it roll onto the grass, and walked over to her. "I figured I would wait for you to come back when you were done with your exam. I wasn't exactly sure where your class was, but I knew you had to come back here eventually. Plus, I figured it would annoy the shit out of them if I rode around right outside their front door."

Hannah squinted her eyes at him wearily. "But why? Why did you come back?" she asked.

"I don't know, Hannah. Can't a guy just want to make sure you're okay?" His voice had the same annoyed edge to it that it had earlier. Jimmy looked down at his feet, trying to play it off. "So—how did your final go, anyway?"

"Unironically, I think I completely bombed it," she told him, her voice reflecting the resignation she felt. "Seriously, though, I just couldn't concentrate. I won't be surprised when I find out I failed, but that might not matter anymore, anyway."

"I'm sure you did fine," Jimmy reassured her.

Hannah cleared her throat. "Didn't you have a class today? You didn't have to wait here for me… ."

"I had a final at noon, too, but I didn't need the whole hour, so I just came back here to wait."

Hannah nodded. "Well, I don't know what will happen when I go back in there. You don't have to keep hanging around here."

"I can come in with you if you want. For support? I mean, I do moonlight as an attorney, after all," Jimmy jested, trying to get Hannah's mind off whatever might await her inside.

Hannah snorted. "Oh, right. How could I forget? It's fine, though. You don't have to," she said and waved him off.

"It's really okay, I don't mind," he insisted.

"Yeah, no—it's fine. I'm all right."

Jimmy's lips moved into a tight smile. "Alright then. The Hannah Banana has spoken. I'll leave you to it, I guess."

"Thanks. I'll see you around, Jimmy," she said quietly, walking around him and into the front door. Hannah noticed the dejected look on his face and how his shoulders sagged, but she knew by then that she could only rely on herself. She couldn't expect Jimmy to save her, not when her own mother wasn't even bothering to. Hannah knew she was on her own and would need to ride into battle unaccompanied.

The secretary behind the front desk directed Hannah into the same interrogation room she had been in before. She sat in a hard metal chair and waited. A couple of minutes later, Officer White came in carrying Hannah's backpack, simply handing it to her without an explanation or apology. "You're free to go."

"Um, thanks," Hannah replied, reaching for the backpack. Officer White stepped aside so Hannah could walk past her and out the door.

As she left the building, Hannah hoped to see Jimmy still riding his skateboard on the sidewalk. She pouted at the sight of the empty walkway, disappointed. Hannah slid her backpack off her shoulder and onto the ground, digging around for her cell phone, which she found at the bottom of a mess of papers; the officers seemed to have just dumped all of her things clumsily back into the bag without a care. She flipped the phone open to see a bunch of missed text messages from her friends, surprised at how quickly word had spread about the incident.

Hannah opened a string of messages from Katie, the last one saying: *I just ran into Jimmy, and he told me what happened. I can't believe that, dude! Text me when you get this. We're meeting at Chris's after the noon exam slot. Meet us there if you can.*

Hannah texted her back: *I'm okay. I just left the police station. They let me go. I'll head over to Chris's now.*

Hannah then called her mom as she walked to her car, letting her know nothing more would happen from the situation. She told her mom, "I'm going to go to my friend's house for a little bit, though, so I won't be home before I have to go to work."

"See you tonight then," her mother responded dismissively, hanging up on Hannah for the second time that day.

Chris lived in a small bungalow a block from the bayside beach on a crowded, narrow side street between the SHU campus and the coastline. Hannah circled the block about four times before settling for an open spot a block away. As Chris had instructed on the phone a few minutes earlier, Hannah walked around to the back of the house and opened the creaky storm door. She had two options: go right through another door into the home's kitchen or down a set of steep steps.

Hannah bounded down the stairs to find Jenny, Katie, Chris, and Brad watching some horrendous black-and-white horror movie. Chris had the whole bottom floor of the house to himself, which consisted of a small kitchen, a bathroom, a bedroom, and a lounge area equipped with an old couch with no legs and a projector for movies.

Katie jumped up from her seat on the couch and ran over to Hannah, embracing her tightly. "Oh my god, dude! Are you okay?"

Hannah huffed and nodded. "I'm fine, really."

"What happened?" Katie asked.

"Yeah, what happened exactly?" Chris chimed in. "We heard the story from Katie, who heard from Jimmy that you were *arrested*?"

"Well, I guess it was more like 'taken into custody,'" Hannah said, making air quotes with her fingers.

"I'm not sure what the difference is, but *why*?" Katie asked.

Hannah told them the whole story from beginning to end, pausing occasionally to laugh at their faces with awed expressions plastered on them.

"Whoa," Chris said as she finished the story. "You are the *last* person I would peg for a domestic terrorist!"

"I can't believe that! Those rent-a-cops are such idiots!" Jenny shrieked.

The sound of heavy feet plodding down the steps echoed into the room as Jimmy appeared in the doorway. His eyes immediately found Hannah. Smiling at her, Jimmy joked, "They let the jailbird out after all, huh?"

"Ha-ha," Hannah replied sarcastically, shoving Jimmy playfully.

Committing to the bit, he continued to rag on her. "Hey, did someone pat her down for explosives?"

"No, we figured you'd want to do that," Jenny countered, winking at him.

Jimmy's voice caught in his throat with a slight cough. "We should make sure to check the backpack, too. Those cops aren't too bright, man. They probably missed something."

"They aren't even real cops!" Brad added.

"Yeah, yeah. We get it," Hannah said with a roll of her eyes.

Jimmy threw his head back and cackled. "Oh, come on! It's pretty funny. This whole thing is so crazy!"

"I mean, it is *now*, but it wasn't before!" Hannah squealed.

"I know. I'm sorry," Jimmy said as he hugged Hannah again. She tensed up at his touch but then hesitantly wrapped her arms around his midsection. She could feel the heat rising in her face, knowing all her friends must be making faces and whispering behind her back.

Jimmy whispered in her ear, "Are you okay, though? For real?"

Caught up in the moment, Hannah stammered, "Yeah, I'm fine."

"Are you sure? I saw how shaken up you were back there."

Hannah nodded her head, her chin brushing his shoulder. "Yeah, I'm sure."

"I'm here for you," Jimmy told her before pulling away. He hesitated, his face lingering near hers; he seemed to have lost himself in her eyes. Hannah saw the precise second that he snapped out of whatever trance he had let his mind wander off in. Jimmy retreated from her, joining Brad on the floor in front of the projection screen. Hannah turned to see Katie and Jenny gaping at her. They waved her over to sit on the couch with them.

Katie mouthed to her, "What was *that*?"

Hannah pulled her phone out of her back pocket to type out a message to show them instead of trying to mime it all: *He was outside the police station when I was leaving for my exam and when*

I went back to get my stuff. He said he wanted to make sure I was okay.

Katie and Jenny glanced at one another, exchanging surprised looks as Hannah typed some more: *I didn't get a chance to tell you, but he showed up at my work the other night for no reason. We spent my whole break just talking.*

Jenny and Katie stared at Hannah in disbelief, who simply bit her bottom lip and shrugged at them. Just then, Jimmy shifted from his spot on the floor, pushing his back against the bottom of the couch between Hannah's legs and Katie's. He rested his arm across Hannah's knees and settled against her legs. Hannah didn't need to look over at her friends to know what their faces looked like.

H annah didn't see Jimmy around campus after the bomb threat incident, and he had missed the next newspaper meeting that Monday. No one had mentioned him, which Hannah found odd. She caught herself sitting in that classroom, searching for him like a phantom whose presence she seemed to tangibly feel.

She had secured ad space from three other businesses when that meeting had come around: a coffee shop, the diner next to campus, and an adult novelty store. The latter had not been her idea, and the shop manager was just as creepy as she imagined he would be. Having those ads secured meant they had the necessary funds to print their first issue; the excitement in the room was palpable with the news. Joe wrapped up the meeting quickly so those who needed it had extra time to work on their articles or artwork.

Hannah pretended to organize her backpack, lingering longer than necessary to catch Brad before he left. When she spotted him approaching the door, she yelled, "Brad! Hey!"

He turned to see Hannah smiling at him. "Hannah! What's up?"

She shrugged. "Nothing. I'm not really sure what to do with myself—I don't have a class for a while, and I've got nothing to work on. What's up with you?"

"Not much. I was just going to head to the library to finish up this comic I'm working on for the issue," he told her, watching the last remaining contributors file out the door.

"Cool," Hannah said, gently clasping her hands in front of her. "Hey, um, have you talked to Jimmy? I thought he'd be here today. I know he was writing an article for the issue."

"Oh, yeah. He's just—he's not feeling well. He's been out for a few days, actually. I brought his final draft in for him today, so at least it'll get into the issue," Brad stuttered, obviously holding back from saying more than he should.

"That sucks. He's okay, though, right?"

"He will be. Been here before with him," Brad replied. Hannah noted the regretful look on his face over the cryptic response he gave her.

Hannah nodded slowly, dragging out her words. "Well… if you talk to him again, tell him I hope he feels better."

"I'll do that," he said, motioning toward the door in front of them. "I should get going."

"Oh, sure." Hannah politely smiled as she watched him walk out the door.

Slinging her backpack over her shoulder, Hannah entered the crowded hallway when her cell phone buzzed in her back pocket. She took it out without a thought, only to see it was a text from Manny. She flipped open the phone to read the message: *Hey, can I call you?*

Hannah grunted and quickly typed: *What do you want?*

Another message: *You haven't been answering my messages. I've been calling and texting. Why won't you talk to me?*

She scoffed and typed back: *Are you for real? You broke up with me, remember? Why can't you understand that I don't want to talk to you?*

Manny replied: *Can we just talk?*

Before Hannah could finish reading the message, her phone buzzed with an incoming call from him. "What?" she answered sharply.

Manny ignored her annoyance, greeting her happily. "Hey, baby. It's good to hear your voice." Hannah could hear his smile on the other end of the phone, but it only fueled her anger as she quickly lost her patience.

"Don't call me that—I'm not your baby anymore. What do you want, anyway?"

"I just want to talk. I miss you," Manny confessed. Hannah had found her way outside the Student Center and sat on the red brick wall dividing the sidewalk from the front parking lot. Manny continued, "I've just been thinking over the past few weeks that maybe it was a mistake to break up. I can't stop thinking about you and want to give it another shot." There was a long pause. "I love you," he said finally.

Hannah had completely tuned Manny out, missing out on his first admission of love for her. Instead, Hannah considered all the possibilities of what Brad had held back from telling her about Jimmy.

"What do you think?"

"About what?" she asked absentmindedly.

Manny laughed, seemingly unbothered that Hannah hadn't been paying attention to him. "About getting back together!"

"You want to get back together?" Hannah asked incredulously. She looked around at the students walking past her to see if she had drawn their attention, but they all seemed tuned into their headphones. Hannah only noticed Brad once he was a distance away from her. She was unaware that he had overheard her exchange with Manny and hadn't seen the questioning look on his face as he processed what he thought he heard.

"I don't know, Manny. I mean, it's been a little bit. What if there's someone else?" she asked with weighted implications.

Manny spoke fast, a hint of anger in his tone, "Is there?"

"I don't know. Maybe?" Hannah hadn't seen or spoken to Jimmy in almost a week, and she wasn't sure what to make of everything that had happened between them up to that point. Hannah chewed on her lower lip, mulling over the thought that she was again making this thing with Jimmy something more than it was. "I don't know, Manny. I need time," she said as she hung up without hearing another word from him.

Hannah lingered on the wall a while longer, biting at her cuticles and staring off at nothing in particular.

The thing with going to a predominantly commuter college was that parking demanded expert-level strategy, even on the last day of the semester. To make it to any late morning class on time, a student must arrive by 8:00 A.M. just to park, or they would risk driving around in endless circles looking for a spot. Hannah learned that lesson on her very first day at SHU, having done just that. Because of that, though, Hannah and Katie had a standing breakfast date on Wednesdays at the cafe on the secondary campus. Hannah liked that cafe more because it was much less crowded than the one in the Student Center, and they served the best bagels at SHU.

"You okay, dude?" Katie asked, noticing that Hannah seemed extra quiet and moody that morning.

"Eh, not really. Manny called me the other day and said he wants to get back together," Hannah said flatly.

Katie nearly choked on her latte. "You're joking!"

"Nope!" Hannah sighed loudly, staring at the coffee cup she spun slowly between her hands.

"You didn't, though, right?" Katie leaned forward on the table with her hands balled into a fist under her chin, all in on the conversation.

"No!" Hannah couldn't believe Katie would ask, even though she had considered it. She chose to leave that part out, though.

"Well, do you want to?" Katie asked.

Hannah should've figured that would have been a follow-up question. She sipped her coffee to buy more time to answer, "I don't know. I guess I'm not sure if I miss *him* or the *idea* of him. Does that make sense?"

"Yeah, I get that," Katie said. "What about Jimmy, though?"

"What about him? Where is he?" Hannah's voice grew louder and more intense. "I haven't even seen him since he showed up at Chris's after the whole bomb threat thing. And my job a couple of days before that! But now he's just gone! I can't have just imagined it all, right? It's not like I have his number to call him or anything, so I guess that's that. I mean, I really like him, but am I being stupid here to think he likes me back?"

Katie's face tensed in thought. "From what I can tell, it seems like he does like you. I don't think you're making it up, but I don't know what's going on with him."

"I'm kind of worried about him, honestly. I asked Brad if he was okay, and he was just so weird about it." Hannah took another bite of her cinnamon raisin bagel.

"Really? Why? What did Brad say?" Katie questioned, picking her head up off her fist.

Hannah shrugged. "Something about how, whatever it is, had happened to Jimmy before, and that he 'will be okay.'"

"Weird," Katie muttered.

After a few more bites of their breakfasts, Katie changed the subject to discuss a chemistry lab experiment that had gone wrong earlier in the week; Katie felt sure that she had failed that portion of her final. Hannah welcomed the change in topic, having spent the night before tossing and turning, as she tried to nail down her feelings. She felt utterly exhausted.

As the clock approached 11:00 A.M., Katie and Hannah boarded the shuttle bus back to the main campus for their classes. When they arrived five minutes later, they walked up the sidewalk that ran through the heart of the school. As they were about to branch off in opposite directions, some guy on a skateboard nearly plowed into Hannah.

"What the hell!" she yelled before registering who it was. Jimmy hopped off his skateboard, kickflipping it into his hand, and jogged back toward her. Hannah could hear a quiet gasp leave Katie's lips.

"Banana! I'm so sorry! Are you okay?" Jimmy asked, slightly breathless.

Hannah's face flushed with emotion—anger, surprise, just to name a couple. She merely nodded while her brain-to-mouth connection short-circuited.

"I'm so sorry. I didn't see anyone coming, so I just went for the trick," he explained as he looked at something over Hannah's shoulder, becoming flustered. "Are you sure you're okay?" he asked again, touching her arm.

"I think so," Hannah squeaked out. Jimmy stared over Hannah's shoulder, a look of alarm now appearing on his face. She turned around to see what had his attention. A tall girl with long, fiery red hair pinned back with a headband approached them.

The girl laughed and gave Jimmy a flirtatious punch. His hand dropped from Hannah's arm on impact. "You ass! You almost took the poor girl out! Are you okay?" she asked Hannah.

"Um, yeah," Hannah looked from the girl back to Jimmy, confused about what was happening.

"Hi, I'm Kelly," the girl said with a tilt of her head and a wide smile. "I'm Jimmy's girlfriend."

"Oh," Hannah managed to say.

Jimmy stood staring at Hannah, his eyes wide and chest heaving with each breath.

Kelly nudged him with her elbow. "Aren't you going to introduce me?"

Jimmy cleared his throat. "Oh, right. This is my... friend. Hannah."

Hannah pursed her lips into a forced smile. Kelly wrapped her arms around Jimmy's midsection, outwardly claiming her territory, while his arms just hung limp at his sides.

"Well, it was nice to meet you, Kelly, but I have to get to class." Hannah quickly turned on her heels and marched away from them, feeling herself beginning to crumble; there was no way she would let Jimmy or Kelly see her fall apart.

Katie called after her, "Hannah! Wait!"

Hannah waved her hand without turning around and choked out, "See ya later!"

"You idiot! Are you really that stupid? Or just that blind?" Katie snapped at Jimmy before turning to leave in the opposite direction. Jimmy lowered his eyes to the ground, feeling stupid for not seeing what had been in front of him the whole time.

Hannah could barely hold back the emotion as she hurried into the Humanities building, making a beeline for the bathroom. She rushed into a stall, slamming the door shut. Sitting on the toilet seat, she propped her elbows on her knees and let her face fall into her hands. She had tried mightily to hold it in, but she could feel the warm tears starting to spill from her eyes. Hannah couldn't believe she was so dense, letting herself think that Jimmy had ever liked her or that the attention he gave her meant anything. The voice inside reminded Hannah that she was nothing more than a waypoint, a rest stop, until the people who surrounded her found their final destination in someone better. That there would always be someone better.

Hannah took a deep, shuddering breath in an attempt to pull herself together. Wiping the tears from her face, she gave herself an extra minute before exiting the stall. She arrived a few minutes late to class and didn't bother to apologize to her professor.

Once seated at her desk, Hannah took out her cell phone and texted Manny: *Okay, let's give it another shot.*

S till sitting on the splintered floor of the musty attic, Hannah giggled softly about the ridiculousness of young love. What she wouldn't give to go back and shake the shoulders of her younger self, try to talk some sense into her, or maybe just scream in her face. After all the years since then, she knew that she had loved Manny before their breakup that semester but that it had been lost the day he had pushed her aside to have some fun at that Halloween party. He never admitted to it, but Hannah was sure he hooked up with someone that night. She knew now that she had held onto that relationship so tightly simply because Manny had been her first everything. Holding on didn't make the relationship any less toxic, though. There were so many things her younger self left out of these diary pages. Had it been shame? Disappointment? Maybe it was just that she wanted to be able to look back and only remember the good things. Perhaps it was a little bit of all three.

Manny and Hannah had broken up once before this momentary hesitance about their long-distance relationship, but they had gotten back together within a day. If she remembered right, it was over some stupid fight about who would travel to see who.

Throughout that relationship, Hannah had learned to look past the person staring back at her in the mirror every morning, the one who kept asking what she was doing with her heart. She had learned to look past so many things: the little fights that were red flags, fielding questions about why she was still with Manny or why she even started dating him to begin with. People would tell Hannah she could do so much better, but she never believed it and doubted they did either.

In some ways, Hannah longed for those days when anything was possible. She missed the hope and excitement of new love about to spring forth. Hannah missed them now that they were long gone, but she didn't miss the messiness of its highs and lows.

She shifted her body around to get comfortable again, using an old blanket to prop herself up on her elbow. Hannah dove head-first back into her memories, bracing for the rollercoaster ride ahead.

Hannah met Whitney, Jenny, and Katie at Sunset Cove, a mall a few blocks from SHU. In late January, the weather had turned bitterly cold, leaving Hannah with little motivation to leave the house. The four of them were huddled around a table in the food court, listening to Jenny complain about her strict parents not allowing her to attend a concert with them. Whitney, Katie, and Hannah nodded and cursed Jenny's parents in agreement with her grievances.

Hannah often felt sorry for Jenny, having to hide so much of herself from her family: her art, her sharp wit, even her sexuality. Despite that, Jenny maintained a normal social life and a raunchy sense of humor, surprising nearly everyone she met with her dirty jokes.

At that moment, Hannah looked around at her friends while a sudden jolt of pure happiness washed over her. It had been a long time since she had a group of friends with whom she harmonized so well. If she ever had at all.

Something was still gnawing at her about Jimmy, though. He popped into her thoughts here and there when she entered the Student Center or when she caught herself singing along to the radio at work. Hannah had learned to push it down, trying to focus on Manny. It was easy, mostly because she hadn't seen Jimmy since that day he nearly ran her down on his skateboard; he had stayed away from Chris's house for the entirety of their Winter Break.

Jenny broke Hannah's thoughts, asking, "Hannah, how are things going with Manny?"

"I actually went down to his school last weekend for a visit," Hannah told them.

"Did you guys do anything fun? Outside of his dorm room, I mean," joked Jenny.

Hannah shrugged. "Eh, not really. He wound up being busy with football most of the weekend."

Jenny winced, "That sucks, girl. I'm sorry."

Hannah didn't want to bring down the mood, so she put on her best smile. "It was good, otherwise. I was just thankful to spend what time I could with him, I guess."

Katie met Hannah's eyes, giving her a sad smile. "Hey, don't we have a meeting coming up soon?" Katie asked in an attempt to change the subject.

"Friday!" Whitney, Jenny, and Hannah shouted in unison, causing them all to crack into some laughter.

Katie could hardly remember the dates and times of their meetings or even her class schedule. They often joked with her that they were impressed she could remember her own name.

"Are you all going?" Katie asked them.

All of the girls nodded their heads.

"I'm surprised you're going, Hannah," Whitney snorted.

Hannah glowered at her, knowing Whitney was dying to bring Jimmy into the conversation somehow. "Why wouldn't I?"

"Jimmy?" Whitney asked.

"What about him?" Hannah's eyes darted between her three friends as they watched her expectantly. "Guys, it's fine. There was nothing there, obviously. He's back with Kelly. End of story."

"And you're back with Manny," Whitney reminded her.

Hannah momentarily leaned forward and stared at her, wondering why that wasn't her first thought. From the look on Whitney's face, she was thinking it, too. "Well, yeah, of course. The whole thing is done, so can't we just leave it alone?" Hannah dropped her hands heavily onto the table.

Whitney sat back in her chair and crossed her arms. She smugly asked, "Why are you getting so uppity about it then?"

"I'm not!" she said forcefully.

Whitney rolled her eyes. "Right. The only one you're fooling here is yourself, Hannah."

Hannah scowled. "What is that supposed to mean?"

Whitney leaned forward, bracing herself on the table. "*Please*, like you don't know that you're still hopelessly pining over Jimmy. That getting back with Manny isn't some ploy to try to make Jimmy jealous or something."

Hannah stared at her friend with an open-mouth frown, unable to formulate a sentence.

Whitney continued, "I can't stand girls like that. You walk around like some innocent little mouse, leading on all these guys, making people think you're so lonely. Boo hoo. Poor you."

"What does it matter to you, anyway?" Hannah questioned. "You don't want Jimmy—you don't even like him! You don't even know Manny. You don't know how hard this has been—"

"Right. Real hard! Don't act like you don't know what you're doing. We all see it," Whitney snapped.

Hannah looked to Katie and Jenny for backup, but they just sat with their heads down, afraid to get involved. "Screw you, Whit," Hannah sneered. She turned to Katie and Jenny, "And some friends you are."

Just like that, her head-in-the-clouds, grateful-to-be-alive attitude had vanished. Hannah stood up quietly, gathered her things, and walked out on them without another word.

She huffed on the walk back through the cold, holding her coat tightly closed around her. Hannah was angry at Whitney for what she had said, but she was even more furious at herself because she knew Whitney was right. She had questioned her own intentions about getting back together with Manny, if it had been the right thing to do or if she was trying to get back at Jimmy somehow. She also hated how just the mention of his name was enough to cause her heart rate to climb still.

The newspaper crew met Friday morning so writers and artists could turn in their final drafts and review the layout for the first edition. Publishing had been delayed because of finals, Winter Break, and several snow days. Hannah arrived at the meeting a few minutes late, having planned it that way to avoid talking to Whitney, Jenny, or Katie. All three were already seated next to one another in the circle when Hannah strode into the classroom. She knew they were all still mad at each other, but she was nevertheless surprised that they didn't save her a seat. In fact, the only open desk was directly next to Jimmy.

Hannah sighed. "Sorry I'm late, Joe," she quietly said as she cut in front of him to get to the empty seat.

She could feel everyone's eyes on her and instinctively shrunk into herself, wondering how many of them knew about her fight with her friends. She was sure Whitney had blabbed about it to anyone who gave her the time of day. Hannah glanced up, noticing Jimmy watching her approach with a slight smile edging at the corners of his mouth.

She dropped into the chair beside him, letting her backpack fall to the ground with a loud thud. When Hannah bent down to search through it for a notebook and pen, she felt a sudden warmth come close to her.

"Hey, Banana," Jimmy whispered.

Hannah inhaled sharply. "Don't call me that," she whispered back before turning back to Joe.

Hannah could feel Jimmy's eyes on her and the tension that drifted between them, but she refused to give in to the temptation to meet his gaze. She felt played by him and so angry, even if she didn't have much of a right to be. Jimmy eventually gave up and started to work on a doodle of a stick figure on a skateboard.

Joe concluded the meeting, saying, "All right, we'll meet on Monday to review the final layout as a group because it *will* be going to the printer that night. Chris and I will work on it this weekend, and we'd love everyone's input. See you then!"

Hannah attempted to bolt out of the classroom without even putting her stuff back into her bag; she felt suffocated being in the same room with her three best friends she wasn't speaking to and a guy who had disappointed her. As she stood up, a hand quickly found her wrist, gently holding her to the spot. She looked down to see Jimmy's scarred knuckles wrapped around her forearm. "Hannah, do you have a minute?" he asked.

Hannah lost all strength in her legs and hit the chair with a thump. "I don't know," she said nervously. "I have to get to work early today." It was a lie, but she needed an escape.

"Just one minute. Please," Jimmy pleaded. Out of his periphery, Jimmy could see Brad approaching. He looked away from Hannah briefly to tell him, "I'll catch you later, man, yeah?"

Brad instantly stopped, nodded, and walked out of the classroom.

Hannah could almost see the walls slowly closing in around her, feeling more trapped than ever, with Jimmy's hand still holding her. She noticed that the whole room had emptied around them, and the voices in the hall seemed so distant. Brad could've been her lifeline out of there, but he was long gone, too. She could only stare at her cold feet in black ballet flats, tapping anxiously against the linoleum floor. Hannah tried to ignore what felt like a surge of electricity pulsing through Jimmy's hand into her body, but she was failing.

Jimmy cleared his throat, searching for the right words to say, but he kept it simple. "Listen—I wanted to say I was sorry for the other day."

Hannah tried to act like she didn't know what Jimmy was talking about, flashing him her best fake smile. "Oh, why? I told you—I wasn't hurt. It's fine."

"Not that. I mean, I am sorry about that, but I meant with Kelly," he said with conviction.

Hannah shrugged, still trying to play the cool, uncaring girl; she didn't realize how her carefree attitude was throwing him off. "Okay…" she said and let her voice trail off.

"Well, it's just that—I don't know—I thought we, ya know— maybe I had it wrong, though. I don't know. You just seemed so upset—." Jimmy tripped over his words, unable to figure out what to say.

"It was nothing, right? I mean, obviously," Hannah interjected.

Jimmy looked at her, stunned by how she was acting. "I just thought you and I—"

Hannah did her best to sound reassuring, telling him, "It's fine. We're good. Really. I have to go, though. I told my boyfriend I would call him before I had to get to work."

It wasn't true. She didn't have a phone call scheduled with Manny. She didn't have to say that, but she did. Hannah wanted Jimmy to feel hurt, just like she had felt hurt. She watched his face fall, realizing that her retaliation did nothing to make her feel better. He released his hand around her wrist and let her go.

Hannah rushed down the hallway and turned the corner before stopping to catch her breath. She leaned her back against the cool cinder block wall, taking fast, shallow breaths; she could feel the anxiety attack rising within her. Hannah slid down the wall until the tile floor was underneath her. She looked down at her forearm where Jimmy's hand had been, still feeling the warmth and weight of his fingers there. She knew she'd again been swallowed whole into the sea that was Jimmy Taylor. Overwhelmed, she crumpled up into a ball and cried silently.

Hannah's body suddenly tensed when she heard what she thought were fast, heavy footsteps coming down the hall in her direction. She kept her head down so that her hair fell across her face, hiding it, and shrunk her body even more to make herself invisible. The footsteps stopped a few feet from her, assessing whether they should intervene or leave her be. Hannah picked up her head just in time to see a pair of black Airwalks retreating around the corner in the same direction they had come. She leaned her head back against the wall again, knowing it had been Jimmy who saw her falling to pieces.

Hannah hadn't noticed the footsteps stop only a few feet around the corner as Jimmy took pause over what he had seen. The two mirrored one another as they stared at the ceiling, each trying to catch up with their racing thoughts. Each feeling a little bit broken inside over yet another missed connection.

The adrenaline dump of the panic attack had left Hannah tired and hungry, so she opted to have lunch in the Student Center rather than going to class. She wanted nothing more than to hole up at a table in a far-off corner for a while. She grabbed the most perfect underbaked chocolate chip cookie and a Cherry Coke from the food line and found an empty table at the far end of the cafeteria. It wasn't the lunch of champions, but sometimes Hannah just needed to feed her soul more than her stomach. She buried her nose in one of her textbooks, savoring the cookie's sweetness.

She had read about half of the chapter when her phone buzzed with a new text message from Katie: *Hey! I know things are a little weird right now, but I just wanted to make sure you're okay. I wasn't sure what happened back there, but you didn't look good when I left.*

Hannah was still upset with her three friends but needed someone more than her anger, so she found a way to let it go. Besides, having someone check in on her like that felt nice; it was something she had been without for a while.

Hannah typed: *I'm okay.*

Her thumb hovered over the "send" button, but she knew she was not okay—not even a little bit, and she was sure Katie knew it. Hannah erased the message. She knew that, in building this new version of herself, she would need to learn to trust people and let them in on how she felt.

She texted Katie: *Not really. I skipped class, just couldn't do it today.*

Katie replied: *Did you go home?*

Hannah typed back: *At the cafeteria for now.*

After that, Katie didn't answer, so Hannah returned to her homework.

Within ten minutes, Katie entered the cafeteria and looked around the room frantically. She spotted Hannah at a corner table, sitting alone, looking like some sad origami figure all folded in on itself. She pulled a chair out from the table, screeching it loudly against the floor. Hannah shot up with a start, surprised to see Katie sitting there in front of her.

"So what happened?" Katie asked.

"Wait—weren't you just in class?" Hannah blurted out.

"I was, but I said I had to leave because I wasn't feeling well. This is more important than that. So, talk to me—what happened?" Katie asked again, pulling a water bottle from her backpack and taking a long drink.

Katie's words echoed in Hannah's mind, saying that she was more important than a class. It was all she had wanted to hear from Amanda, and it felt weird coming from this person she had only known for a few months.

She told Katie about Jimmy's weird apology and how he had stuttered through the whole thing. She had soon found herself spewing everything that had been on her mind in recent weeks. She told Katie that what she felt for Jimmy was more than just a crush. She had this crazy attraction to him that she couldn't shake. It was a feeling so profound that she couldn't explain or rationalize, like they had known each other forever. Whatever it was, Hannah admitted that it confused her about her relationship with Manny and whether she even loved him anymore.

"How can I possibly be in love with him when I am so obviously smitten with Jimmy? I can't be, right?" Hannah asked Katie.

"First, dude, take a deep breath," Katie started. "But, I would say that if you're questioning it, then I think you already know the answer."

"I know," Hannah whined. "I'm sorry just to vomit all of that out." She propped her elbow on the tabletop, resting her face in the palm of her hand.

"Is there anything I can do?" Katie asked.

"Just tell me what I should do. Make this easier," Hannah replied.

Katie pouted at her while the two sat silently for a few seconds. Katie reached across the table and grabbed Hannah's free hand. "Hannah, I'm sorry. I shouldn't have let Whitney say those things to you. I should have defended you, and I didn't. I panicked," Katie replied.

Hannah smiled at her weakly. "It's okay," she said. "I guess everyone is still really mad at me, huh? You guys didn't even save me a seat at the meeting today…"

Katie let out a sharp exhale. "Oh, well, they'll get over it."

"Thanks for being here now, though," Hannah said as she squeezed Katie's hand, and the two friends started complaining about their classes as if nothing had happened between them.

Later that night, Katie started a chat with Hannah over Instant Messenger:

(Katie) *Don't be mad at me.*

(Hannah) *Maybe don't start out a conversation that way, then? What did you do?*

(Katie) *I have to be honest with you about something.*

(Hannah) *Okay…*

(Katie) *I saw Jimmy the other day, and he told me that he wanted to talk to you so he could apologize. I told him you probably wouldn't want to talk to him. He kind of figured the same and asked for my help. So we planned it that the only open desk would be next to him at the meeting so that you would have no choice but to sit next to him and would have to talk to him.*

(Hannah) *What the fuck, Katie?*

(Katie) *I know, I'm sorry. I know it seems bad, but at the mall the other day, you seemed so let down about your visit with Manny, and then Jimmy really felt terrible and wanted to say sorry. I thought it might be something good for you, but I didn't know things would go so badly.*

(Katie) *And then I saw Brad when we left the Student Center after lunch today, and I stopped to talk to him…*

(Hannah) *And?*

(Katie) *I started asking about the comic strip he was working on, and then we started talking about Jimmy. I can't even remember how we got there.*

(Hannah) *Oh my god, Katie.*

(Katie) *Jimmy broke up with Kelly again.*

Hannah's heart skipped a beat.

(Katie) *Brad just unleashed all of this information. He didn't think Jimmy wanted to get back together with her in the first place, and that he only did because Kelly was really laying it on thick with him to get him to cave to her. I guess Jimmy told Brad that you were giving him mixed signals, so he wasn't sure where you guys stood.*
(Hannah) I *was giving* him *mixed signals? What?*

Hannah took deep breaths, trying to steady her heart rhythm.

(Katie) *I know, dude. Apparently, Jimmy talks to Brad about you a lot! Like how he wanted that day at the comic book shop to be just the two of you because he had feelings for you then. Brad said he felt so dumb for not seeing it before you guys left SHU. He said Jimmy felt really bad about that day on campus with the skateboard and Kelly because he saw how hurt you were. He called it off with Kelly right then and there. Like, literally, broke up with her on the sidewalk. Jimmy went looking for you, too, but he couldn't find you. I guess that's what he really wanted to talk to you about after the meeting today.*

Resting her hands gently on the keyboard, Hannah hoped for the words to come. They didn't, so she set an away message and walked away from her laptop. Hannah wasn't sure it was possible for things to get even more complicated—until they had.

Hannah skipped the layout review meeting the following Monday. She just sold the ad space, anyway, so what did it matter if she was there? She had hidden herself away from everyone that week, answering messages with one- and two-word answers before she stopped responding altogether. She simply went through the motions of attending class and going to work. The repetition of folding and arranging clothes, scanning and bagging merchandise was oddly soothing. Hannah had even picked up a few extra shifts for the mind-numbing effects of the routine.

Hannah spent the rest of her time wrapped up in her feelings, letting herself be pulled in two different directions. In her sleep, Hannah watched night after night as her arms slowly tore away from the rest of her, with Manny on one side and Jimmy on the other. Manny was the comfortable choice, and he had finally said he loved her. Hannah believed him, for the most part, though part of her questioned whether he meant it. Jimmy, though, was a wildcard—a complete unknown. Did he even like her?

It should have been simple, but it just wasn't. The reality was that while Hannah was dating Manny, she was also utterly infatuated with Jimmy. She worked hard to push aside daydreams of what it would feel like to kiss him, to have his hand in hers. Whatever it was she felt for him, it was so much stronger than what she had ever felt for Manny. Her rational mind couldn't process what her heart already knew to be true.

No, it can't be love, she would tell herself. *Don't be stupid. We're practically strangers.*

Hannah hopelessly tried to convince herself that it was just an infatuation, a silly schoolgirl crush. It would be over soon enough. She just had to wait it out, was all. Besides, for all she knew, Jimmy had run right back to Kelly thinking Hannah absolutely hated him by then. Hannah told herself there was no sense in mulling it over like she was, yet her fixation with Jimmy continued to live on.

Hannah walked quickly back to her car after she left class on Thursday when her phone buzzed with an incoming call from Manny.

"Hey!" she said, sounding cheerful when she felt anything but.

Manny did not try to hide how down he was feeling. "Hey, baby," he said.

"You sound weird—everything okay?" she asked.

"I'm at the hospital," Manny said flatly.

"Oh my god! Are you okay?" Hannah stopped walking in the middle of the sidewalk, causing the person behind her to walk right into her. They exchanged apologies as the other person kept walking on their way.

Manny hesitatingly told her, "Not really. I had pain this morning. Down there."

Hannah wasn't sure what he meant. "Did you get hurt at practice or something?"

"No. They did some tests, and I have some kind of infection," he told her.

"Oh, like a UTI?"

Manny let out a long breath, obviously annoyed. "No, like, an STD."

"What? How?" Hannah shrieked.

"Well, that's why I'm calling. You tell me," Manny said cooly. Hannah sensed the unspoken accusations sitting heavy on his tongue.

"Excuse me?"

Manny raised his voice. "Oh, come on, Hannah! Don't play so innocent now. You're the only one I've been with, so don't bullshit me here."

Hannah laughed just then but promptly forced herself to stop. She had always had a bad habit of laughing when her anger started to rise beyond where she knew she could control it. "You can't be serious," she said more severely.

"I can't believe you're fucking laughing right now. I *am* being serious, Hannah. You're the only one I've been with," he repeated through gritted teeth. "Besides, you were the one who said you might have something else going on over there before we got back together!"

"Yeah, but I haven't slept with anyone, Manny! You're the only one I've been with, too!" Hannah raised her voice to match his, indifferent to the attention she drew from passersby. "You were the one who went to that Halloween party! Which of those little sluts did you hook up with? Or were you too drunk to remember?" Hannah questioned.

"Oh my god, Hannah! I *told* you—I didn't hook up with anyone! It's only ever been you!" Manny's anger was getting the best of him. "I don't know what you're doing up there. I've never visited your school or met your friends."

Hannah interrupted him, pointing out the obvious, "Because I don't live on campus like you do, Manny! None of my friends do, either! We all commute!"

"Well, maybe you're hooking up with one of them! Or all of them! What do I know?" Manny continued.

"This is fucking ridiculous," Hannah muttered.

"Is it, though? Stop lying to me, Hannah!" Manny yelled. "I feel like I don't even know you anymore."

As calmly as she could muster, Hannah said, "Manny, you know me! I'm not lying to you, and I resent the fact that you think I would cheat on you. I would never do anything like that to you." Hannah took a deep breath, pausing as the truth became glaringly obvious. "We should've never gotten back together."

"Maybe you're right," Manny replied.

"I sincerely hope you feel better, but we're absolutely done. Have a nice fucking life," Hannah seethed. She hung up on him, not caring what else he might have to say.

Hannah stood on the spot, looking at the world around her, trying to calm the fury raging within. She fought the urge to punch something, but then she realized it wasn't anger, sadness, or disappointment she felt. The decision had been made for her, and Hannah only felt at ease.

Hannah closed the journal and chuckled about these crazy moments that felt so big and intense as they were happening to her back then. Manny had reached out to her a week after that fight to let her know that he didn't have an STD after all; he had gotten an infection from not washing his underwear often enough. The very thought grossed her out even now. It had been the emergency room doctor who had suggested to Manny that Hannah was cheating on him since he denied sleeping around when they asked about his sexual habits during the exam. Manny apologized to her, thinking it would make everything right between them, but Hannah had stood her ground. She recalled throwing her phone across her bedroom after that conversation, resulting in a long crack on the phone's screen. Her mom had been so angry with her about it.

At least I finally came to my senses, Hannah mused.

She still harbored some anger over that situation. Not necessarily toward Manny, though. She was angry at the doctor in the hospital, who blamed Hannah before even having answers about Manny's health. She also held some anger toward herself for dealing with so many mistreatments for so long. It had been because of the lonely girl within her at that time of her life, the one with a hole in her heart that she so desperately wanted to fill. She had always been a girl who just wanted to feel loved and connected to someone meaningfully

Still, she was proud of her younger self for realizing she deserved so much more than she had gotten from Manny.

Hannah stood to stretch before climbing the ladder back down to the main level of the house for another cup of coffee. She had gotten an early start to the day, having gone right into the attic as soon as she had rolled out of bed. She stood at the coffee pot, waiting for the sweet aroma to fill her nose as Jake padded into the kitchen.

He sat at the table and asked, "How long have you been awake?"

"Since about four o'clock," she told him. "Been up in the attic."

Jake glanced at the clock. "Geez, honey. You've been up there this whole time?"

Hannah rubbed the sleep from her eyes. "Yeah, I just couldn't sleep anymore."

"How it's going up there, anyway?"

"It's going," she answered. "It's been a lot to go through some of that stuff. It's just bringing a lot up, ya know?" Hannah could feel that familiar lump growing in her throat. She turned away from him to stare at the coffee pot, hoping the wave of sadness would dissipate.

"I can imagine. Do you want to talk about it?" Jake asked hesitantly.

Hannah took a deep breath, tears beginning to flow, and divulged details about all that she remembered of her early days in college, with *The Inkwell* and Jimmy. "In some weird way, I loved him even when I didn't know him. There was always love there. I guess there always will be," she admitted. Hannah poured two cups of coffee for them, handing Jake his while she added sugar and milk to hers.

They sat silently across from one another for a few beats before Jake finally spoke again. "Well, I do believe in the idea of soulmates. I think you and I are proof of that, but I am not naive enough to pretend that out of eight billion people in the world, only one would be the perfect match for just one other person. I think we all likely have, maybe, a small handful of people out there. It's just a matter of the twists and turns we take in life if they cross our path or not."

"Yeah," she said, mulling over the thought. "Like, even if it's not romantic love, maybe it's friendship or a family member—even a pet or something."

"Exactly," said Jake. "Maybe Jimmy was that for you—a true soulmate. But how lucky for me that you and I crossed paths at the right time? I think if we had met any sooner, this would've never happened." He gestured his hand in the space between them at the table.

"You know," Hannah said, "I had the same feelings, the same… recognition when we first met. I knew you would be such a special person in my life. I just didn't know how at the time."

It was unbelievable how long Jake and Hannah had swirled the drain of each other's lives before they ever met. They had literally bumped into each other at a local bar one night. Things had been so easy between them from the first 'hello.' It was Jake who made it easy; he was outgoing, loud, fun, and funny. He was the complete opposite of Hannah, which was typical of the men she had been attracted to over the years. They eventually realized they knew some of the same people and visited the same places. They also discovered that Jake had worked across the street from her all those years she had been employed at the thrift store.

Hannah's mind drifted to various teachings she had learned about in a World Religions course she had taken as a requirement at SHU. It was that or Philosophy, which seemed a lot more boring. Ideas of reincarnation and karmic relationships danced around her thoughts, and how souls sometimes return to a new form to fulfill some lesson or destiny that hadn't been completed in their prior life. That, at times, souls were bound by some invisible string or contract. Their meeting on Earth preordained. Inevitable.

Hannah wondered if her and Jimmy's souls were bound together somehow, fated to meet all those years ago. Had something deep within them recognized each other from another time and place? Maybe the cavernous aching inside her that Jimmy's death had caused was really because the cord that held them together had been cut, as if she had lost a part of herself. Hannah hoped their souls were still connected, bound to meet again someday.

C hris hosted a party at his parents' house for the newspaper crew to bring everyone together while the first edition was still at the printer's. There had been a mechanical fire at the printing shop, which had delayed delivery significantly. The most recent update from the last week of March was that it would be completed any day. It was hard to feel like the first issue wasn't doomed, with the delays in getting it to the printer and everything else that happened after that; morale was definitely low.

When she arrived, Hannah was met with a collective, "Hannah!" She laughed and waved at no one in particular.

Whitney, Jenny, and Katie were huddled on a couch in front of the projection screen, watching Chris and Jimmy play Rock Band. Hannah could tell the game was intense just by looking at Chris. His hair was plastered to his forehead, and the collar of his T-shirt was darkened by the sweat pouring down his face. Her eyes assessed Jimmy from head to toe, her stomach instantly tying in knots from just being in the same room with him again. He wore a black zip-up hooded sweatshirt from the record shop he worked at, light denim jeans with a studded belt, and the same bulky, black Airwalk sneakers. His dirty blonde hair was an unstyled, wind-swept mess. There was no hint of sweat or stress on him, taking the competition in stride. Hannah noted that he didn't even bat an eye at the mention of her name or react as she swept past him just a little closer than necessary. She inhaled deeply when she passed him, breathing in that familiar smokiness.

Hannah would be lying if she said she hadn't looked for Jimmy in every corner of campus, sniffing out any nicotine smoke trail like a bloodhound, hoping to find him at the other end of it. She had spent a lot of time loitering in the Student Center, the cafeteria, and the library. Whenever Hannah found herself in Stonebridge, she thought that maybe he'd walk by the diner window she sat at or that he would be casually browsing the local bookstore's shelves. He was never there, though, having become like a ghost or maybe just a figment of her imagination.

Hannah sat on the arm of the couch, leaning with her hand pressed on the headrest while she talked to Whitney, Jenny, and Katie. The girls told her that Jimmy was crushing Chris in their Rock Band battle. They then booed and laughed at Chris, taunting him playfully. The booing distracted him enough to cause a few missed notes, pushing Jimmy further into the lead. Hannah laughed at her friends' silliness while her eyes remained fixed on Jimmy's back, watching his muscles dance under the tight sweatshirt. She tried to telepathically break his concentration, willing him to turn around to face her. Hannah's gaze was broken only by Chris shouting a few choice words at the girls. At the end of the song, Jimmy lightheartedly pestered Chris about his defeat, careful not to turn around too far and see Hannah.

Chris and Jimmy gave up their spots to two others who had been patiently waiting their turn, while Katie told the girls about a conversation with Joe the night before. She had confessed to them in a late-night pow-wow earlier in the week that she had a massive crush on him. To keep the information out of prying ears, Katie whispered so quietly that Hannah had to lean over Jenny to hear her better. "He called me to talk over some edits to my article, and then we ended up staying on the phone for, like, two hours!"

When the conversation waned, Whitney asked Hannah if she had heard from Manny recently. They hadn't spoken much since their fight at the mall, especially avoiding topics like Hannah's love life. Whitney was just too nosy for her own good, though, and had an insatiable itch to create drama for her own entertainment, which had been easy for her to do with Hannah.

"Oh god, no!" Hannah exclaimed. "I swear I'd still probably try to reach through the phone to choke him if he did try to call me. I still can't believe he had the nerve to think I'd take him back!" Hannah had already told them about the origins of Manny's infection, which they had collectively gagged over.

"I don't blame you!" Jenny said with a scowl. "Men are the absolute worst! You're better off, Hannah."

"Definitely!" Katie agreed.

Jenny touched Hannah's thigh with a wink and suggested, "Maybe you should try switching teams."

Hannah playfully shoved her hand away. "Oh my god, Jenny!"

The four lost themselves in a fit of laughter. It made Hannah feel so good to laugh with those girls again; she missed it more than she realized. As the moment died down again, Whitney turned the conversation to herself, disclosing details of an encounter with another woman at a club the weekend before. None of them believed that it had happened, thinking that she was only telling the story to try to one-up Jenny's lesbianism somehow. Hannah and Katie exchanged looks, silently acknowledging that fact.

Soon enough, more of the newspaper staff and some additional tag-along friends had filed in, filling the basement with the most motley crew of kids. Some were trying to watch an obscure movie on a small TV, while others were chatting in groups and playing various games.

Hannah shifted uncomfortably on the arm of the sofa, searching the room for something more substantial to sit on. She spotted an empty chair across the room and stepped over several scattered bodies on the floor to retrieve it. She situated herself next to the couch, looking around the room at the faces of friends and strangers, enjoying the ease of just being with those people. Hannah felt like she genuinely belonged for, possibly, the first time in her life.

While taking it all in, Hannah realized that Jimmy was gone. She looked around more urgently, scanning each face, but none belonged to him. She felt a fear rise in her that he had left the party, worried that she had scared him off somehow. Hannah's eyes suddenly stopped on the basement windows, where she saw those familiar black sneakers pacing the driveway. They came to a rest in front of the window, and the body they belonged to lowered itself to the ground. A hand placed down a large Dunkin' Donuts coffee cup and then a blue pack of cigarettes. Hannah sighed in relief that Jimmy hadn't left, hoping they might have a chance to talk. Maybe it would just be weird small talk, but she wanted to resolve the situation between them more than anything. What she really wanted was to start over.

It doesn't have to be this uncomfortable, she thought. *No matter how things turn out.*

With the chaos of the noise around her, Hannah hadn't noticed Jimmy and his belongings move away from the window until she heard his heavy feet jogging down the steps again. Jimmy stopped at the bottom of the staircase, scanning the crowded room. When his eyes found Hannah, he tilted the large, white styrofoam coffee cup toward her—an olive branch. Hannah smiled in response.

Was he looking for me? Hannah wondered. *Should I go over there?*

Before she could decide what to do, Jimmy sauntered over and squatted beside her chair, balancing himself on his toes. He still wouldn't look at her, instead focusing his gaze in the direction of the movie playing on the small TV. Hannah looked down at him, only then noticing a black pair of wayfarer sunglasses hidden in his disheveled hair. She noted how Jimmy clenched and unclenched his jaw in a fast rhythm. She had seen him do that before, which meant that he was ruminating on something. Hannah wondered what was on his mind and if they were thinking over the same thing.

Jimmy suddenly turned toward Hannah, catching her staring at him again. It reminded her of the first time they met when he had seen her staring at him in the same way. Hannah could feel the heat of embarrassment rising in her face.

Jimmy smirked from the corner of his mouth. He whispered to her, trying to avoid annoying the movie watchers, "Hey, Banana."

"Hey," she whispered back. "I thought you left."

"Nah, I walked down to get a coffee. Besides, I just needed some fresh air and a smoke."

Hannah snickered. "Doesn't the cigarette defeat the purpose of the fresh air, though?"

Jimmy laughed, considering what she had said. "I mean, yeah, I guess it does." The smirk on his face grew into a big grin, knocking the breath out of Hannah's lungs; it was difficult not to swoon over Jimmy's boyish charm when he smiled like that. "So you were looking for me?" he teased as his eyes widened in anticipation of her response.

"I never said that," Hannah quipped smugly.

Jimmy turned back toward the movie, still smiling because he knew she was lying. After a long pause, he turned his whole self to face Hannah, falling to his knees with his feet propped under him. "Listen. I'm sorry that I freaked you out after that meeting," he said quickly.

"No, it—"

"No, I was a little intense," he interrupted. "I can get like that sometimes, and I don't even notice until it's too late." Jimmy shook his head and looked down at the floor, his jaw tensing again. "Ya know—I felt so stupid for how I acted. Not just that whole thing with Kelly, but in the classroom, too. Especially when I saw you crying in the hallway. I never wanted to do that to you."

Hannah knew how he felt, having been told so many times that she was "too much." Too emotional, too honest and open, too anxious, too whatever. That she made people uncomfortable. She hated that Jimmy had been told that, too, and that he believed it.

He suddenly got up and walked away, leaving Hannah confused. He returned with a chair, butting it right up to hers, close enough that their arms and legs touched. Jimmy put his arm around the back of her chair and leaned toward her slightly, the weight of his body pressing against hers. Hannah could feel his breath on her ear as he spoke, "There's a lot I wanted to tell you that day, Hannah. A lot that I still want to tell you."

Hannah felt her chest tighten as Jimmy rambled on about how he felt this deep affection for her that seemed to come out of nowhere. That it was as if they had grown up together riding bikes through the neighborhood or sharing secrets in some tree fort in the woods. Jimmy admitted that he looked for any opportunity to be alone with her: the comic book shop, at her job, even the campus police station. He acknowledged that the tension between them from day one had been so overwhelming that it eventually got in the way of his relationship with Kelly.

"But what she and I had was dead for a long time, and my feelings for you were finally enough of a reason for me to stop the endless CPR," he said. "But you're back with your boyfriend, I guess, and I know it's not fair of me to say all of this to you. I was pretty sure I'd literally explode, though, if I didn't. Like, just spontaneously combust on the spot." Jimmy made a sound effect like a bomb detonating, gesturing his hands to demonstrate the path of the mushroom cloud. "I'm sorry. Is it still too soon to joke about bombs?"

They both suppressed a laugh, grateful for the brief respite from the heavy conversation. While she had wanted to hear all that, the affirmation that she had not just created this entire narrative in her mind, Hannah was acutely aware that Jimmy had captured the attention of her friends nearby. Her tone changed to one more serious, suggesting, "Why don't we take a walk or something when this is over? We can talk this all out then, okay?"

Jimmy's face dropped, thinking the worst. He nodded in response and looked away from her again. Hannah sensed his attention floating away, watching him repeatedly clench and unclench his jaw. He suddenly shifted his body away from her, removing his arm from the back of her seat. Hannah watched as Jimmy turned to the opposite end of the room where Brad sat. There was a look of confusion on his face as he looked from her to Jimmy. Hannah shrugged her shoulders at Brad, just as confused.

She watched Jimmy shake his head at Brad and make a slashing motion across his throat.

Hannah touched Jimmy's arm so he would focus on her again. "I want to have this conversation with you, but just you and I. Not with an audience," she told him as she gestured to the crowd before them.

Hannah didn't want this chance to slip through her hands after all the months of back-and-forth. She leaned into him gently and rested her head on his shoulder, trying to show him she was all his. Jimmy's body stiffened at her touch but then cautiously relaxed muscle-by-muscle. He delicately leaned his head against hers. It felt right, and she instinctively melted a little deeper into him.

The movie ended only a few minutes later with a lackluster conclusion, not that either Hannah or Jimmy had paid much attention to it. Hannah was more focused on the points where their bodies connected.

Jimmy whispered, "C'mon." He stood fast, knocking her head off him without a second thought. She sat there, surprised by his quick exit, thinking he looked more like someone needing an escape from her rather than with her.

Hannah took a few moments to find her legs underneath her before following Jimmy out of the house. Like a twisted dream, the last ten minutes had felt surreal, overwhelming, and unnerving all at once. As she walked past them, the girls tried vehemently to get her attention, having witnessed the exchange between Hannah and

Jimmy. She pretended not to notice them, wanting that moment to be just for them.

Hannah rushed up the stairs, pushing open the door to the outside. She hadn't realized how stuffy the basement had become until the early evening air hit her face hard as she stepped onto the back porch. It was surprisingly warm for that time of year, leaving Hannah comfortable in the light sweater she had worn.

Jimmy was pacing the driveway up and down, puffing on another cigarette. The door slammed shut behind her, causing Jimmy's pacing to cease. He fixed his eyes on Hannah as she froze to the spot with several feet of macadam separating them. They were alone finally, away from prying ears and eyes. She felt determined but didn't have a clue how to start.

"What was that up there?" Jimmy asked suddenly, his tone riddled with anxiety. He stepped forward to bridge the gap between them. "Don't lead me on—"

"Manny and I aren't together anymore," Hannah blurted out. "I broke up with him a few weeks ago."

Jimmy looked dumbfounded by the news, his eyes unblinking. He visibly shivered, seeming to come back into his body again. "Oh, I see," Jimmy said in a near whisper as he flicked ash from the cigarette between his fingers. Hannah looked down to see him wiggling the fingers of his free hand rhythmically, almost like how he strummed a guitar. "You didn't come to the last meeting. It was because of me, right? Because of what happened?" he asked.

Hannah only nodded in response.

Jimmy closed his eyes and sighed. "I have a bad habit of being too much sometimes, scaring people off." He opened his eyes again to look at her, and a certain sadness shone in them. "I feel like all I do is scare you, Hannah."

Her shoes scraped the pavement as she stepped forward, closing the gap a little more. Hannah laughed nervously. "I'm afraid of everything, Jimmy. It's just who I am. You do scare me. That day scared the shit out of me. I felt so trapped and didn't know what you would say. Honestly, I wasn't sure if I wanted to know because this will-they-won't-they thing was starting to get old." She took another step forward in the pause.

"Hannah, I know I shouldn't have dumped all of this on you like I did. I mean, I thought you had a boyfriend, so I didn't anticipate any of this. I'm not sure what I thought would happen, anyway, even if you were still together with him. I guess I thought I still might have a chance to get the girl somehow." He chuckled and breathed deeply, admitting, "I don't know where to go from here. I do know I'm scared of this, too. I know I feel it so deep in my bones, more than anything I ever felt with Kelly. I don't know if it's love or what, but it feels like it could be. Which sounds crazy—I know—because I hardly know you. It's just that being near you, Hannah, makes me feel so overwhelmed, like I can't breathe or think. I never thought you could feel the same way about me, that I'm just misreading all the signals. I just—I don't want to be afraid anymore. I wanted to tell you all of this to at least try to see where this can go." Jimmy stepped forward again, leaving only about a foot separating them. "Please, *please*, give this a chance. Whatever this is, or could be. Give *me* a chance."

Hannah nodded and squared her shoulders. "I get it," she said. Jimmy stared blankly at her as she continued, "I get everything you said. I've always been too much. I've always been scared. I'm fucking terrified right now, Jimmy, because—because I think I might love you, too." Hannah surprised herself with how freely the confession flowed.

Jimmy flinched suddenly, throwing his cigarette to the ground. Hannah wasn't sure if it was because of her words or if the forgotten cigarette had burned him. Jimmy squashed it with the toe of his sneaker. "So now what do we do?" he asked.

Hannah reached out a hand to him, which he promptly took hold of. She noticed the roughness of the calluses on them from plucking at his guitar strings for hours. "How about we take that walk? We can just take it slow and really get to know each other."

"Sure," Jimmy agreed. He wriggled his hand out of hers and wrapped his arm around her shoulders to pull her into a quick side hug.

Hannah and Jimmy left the driveway and walked side-by-side, bumping shoulders every other step. They created a circular path through the dense neighborhood, continuing to trace it again and again as they strolled. They talked about their families and what life had been like growing up. Hannah was an only child, whereas Jimmy had a much older brother—he made a joke about being a "whoopsie" kid. They found common ground in the complicated relationships they had with their parents, but Jimmy told her he was at least close with his mom. He admitted that it was hard for him to be around his dad, though. Jimmy didn't elaborate on that other than to say he would never be as great as his brother in their dad's eyes.

Curiously, Jimmy asked, "Can I ask what happened between you and Manny?"

Hannah's lips sputtered. "Pfft. That's a loaded question, but the final straw was him accusing me of cheating on him. He, um, got this infection he thought was an STD. It wasn't, though. He was just gross and not keeping up with cleaning himself or his clothes often enough—"

"Oh, what? That's disgusting!" Jimmy shuddered.

"Yeah, it's super disgusting," Hannah agreed. "There were just so many things wrong in our relationship, but there was no coming back from that one."

"Well, I promise you I do my laundry a couple of times a week and always put on clean boxers. You won't need to worry about that again," he joked.

"It's your turn now! Tell me what happened with Kelly," she said.

"Well—kind of the same thing as you, I guess. I could spend the rest of the night telling you all about our problems. She and I were just like oil and water, ya know? We'd get along for a while, and then we just ticked each other off to the point of breaking up. She'd always known what to say to win me over again. It was a vicious cycle, but I didn't think there could possibly be anything better out there for me."

"I can relate," said Hannah.

Jimmy huffed. "I guess I started to see that maybe I was wrong, thinking that love was just being able to tolerate someone enough. I've watched my parents do it for years, and I did it with Kelly. Honestly, I think she just tolerated me enough, too. But when I met you, I realized I didn't have to just tolerate being with someone. I could really want it."

The conversation became lighter as they poked fun at one another's interests, eventually discovering they both had a deep love for music. Hannah and Jimmy dished about their favorite bands and all the concerts they'd attended. They walked for another hour before their feet finally got too tired to continue. Before getting in the car, Hannah scribbled her number on the back of Jimmy's hand and kissed his cheek sweetly.

She took the long way home that night, rolling the windows down to allow the night air to circulate through the car's interior.

Hannah felt the weight of the last few months floating away. She sang her heart out as music blared through the partially blown-out speakers. Some nights were made for long drives and singalongs, and that had been one of them.

I n the weeks after Chris's party, Jimmy and Hannah became inseparable, spending as much of their time together as possible. Jimmy would call her every night until she inevitably fell asleep. Sometimes, he would stay on the phone a little longer just to listen to her soft snores, which reminded him of the kitten he had when he was small. Jimmy would close his eyes and imagine Hannah lying beside him in bed; it was a dream that would slowly lull him into a comfortable sleep.

They would drive out to the local beaches, spending hours sitting on the trunk of his car, gazing up at the stars. Jimmy spent so many nights teaching her more about constellations, planets, and galaxies. Hannah didn't mind that Jimmy often repeated the same stories to her or pointed out certain stars as if it were the first time.

Sometimes, they would stroll up and down the shoreline, picking up shells and sea glass.Hannah had always seemed to come alive near the water, a place Jimmy would bring her back to just to watch the spark in her ignite. One night in particular, at the bay beach, the two of them were skipping stones to break the stillness of the water. Jimmy watched Hannah from a distance, completely bewitched, as she excitedly cheered herself on when she succeeded with a good skip.

Jimmy ran up behind her, hugging her tightly around the waist and lifting her into the air. Hannah kicked her feet, cracking up with laughter. When Jimmy returned her back to the sand, he spun her around to face him and kissed her so deeply that he nearly knocked her off her feet again. He cupped her face tightly while Hannah wrapped her arms around his neck, never wanting the moment to end. She had been impatiently waiting for their first kiss, but it didn't feel right until that night on the beach under the stars.

As they walked back to his car, Jimmy realized that his North Star was there before him, walking just a few feet ahead.

Hannah spent a lot of time at the record shop, where Jimmy worked most days of the week. Jimmy was so passionate about music, which was something he and Hannah had bonded over. They listened to albums on the store stereo, picking apart lyrics and chords, and discussing the deeper meaning behind each song.

One Saturday morning, Hannah met Jimmy at the store when he opened it and stayed with him through the day. The store had been busy, but Hannah loved to watch Jimmy talk with the customers who came in and out. Witnessing him interact with people was like watching your favorite movie on repeat—it never got old, and you always saw something new you hadn't noticed the first hundred times you watched it. She loved being a fly on the wall of his life. Jimmy seemed to know something about every album the store's customers bought, excitedly miming guitar riffs or philosophizing with them about the bands' musical stylings.

She kept a steady supply of light and sweet coffees and sodas coming in for him, joking that he should consider drinking water sometimes.

Jimmy bantered back with her, "It'd be like putting water in your car's gas tank, Banana—you'd maybe get out of the parking lot, but you'd absolutely ruin the system. You don't want me to die, do you?"

Hannah leaned over the counter and whispered, "No, because I'd probably die, too. And I want to live, so caffeine it is!" She leaned over far enough to kiss him.

Once it was closing time that night, Hannah and Jimmy were off to a VFW in Stonebridge, where his band was scheduled to play a show. Jimmy started his punk band, Cat Hair, with Brad and some other friends in high school. She had considered inviting the girls but eventually decided against it. She didn't involve her friends in the early days with Jimmy, especially Whitney, who she was sure would try to start unnecessary drama.

Hannah had stood alone, leaning on the far wall of the event space, trying to blend into the beige paint and desperately avoiding the smelly teenage boys that filled the room. Jimmy worked the crowd, calling out people who were moshing too dangerously or not hard enough. Between songs, he had pulled Hannah onto the floor, announcing to the room that his girlfriend was in attendance. It was the first time he had ever called her that, but she didn't mind. They had never talked about what they were to one another. They just kind of knew, and Hannah liked not having to guess where she stood with him.

Jimmy and the band started the next song as he twirled her around in the middle of the mosh pit, kicking away anyone who got too close to her. Hannah seemed to forget who she was then, smiling and laughing so freely, her hair fanning out around her as she turned in circles like a ballerina. After that, Hannah stood further off the wall and bopped her head to the music. She sang along with songs she knew from listening to Cat Hair practice in Brad's garage.

Most of all, though, she watched Jimmy with awe all night. His body writhed with the rhythm of the music as if it had utterly possessed him. She wished she could be more like him in that way, hoping that one day she could learn how to be wild and free like him. That she, too, could have something in her life that lit her up so that stardust shined through her pores. Something that made her feel alive, like how music made Jimmy feel.

Continued

Hannah beamed as she flipped through a few pages of pictures of them together back in those early days. They had captured so many moments on Hannah's digital camera, including some video recordings that had been lost to time. She loved to walk in the park near his house and swing away their afternoons on the playground. Jimmy would swing so high that Hannah swore he could touch the clouds if he could only reach his hand out far enough. He would jump off at the very top, backflipping his way down to Earth. He didn't always land on his feet, sometimes purposefully, so Hannah would kiss his wounds better.

Hannah remembered how Jimmy visited her at work at the thrift store. He loved digging through the racks to see the random assortment of clothes and housewares that had been donated or bought for dirt cheap from stores that had gone out of business. Her manager despised how he hung around the store, following Hannah around. Jimmy eventually took to hiding in clothing racks when Hannah's manager appeared so that she wouldn't kick him out of the store. On other nights, Jimmy would just come by when Hannah was on break, and they would sit on the trunk of his car listening to music while sharing whatever fast food he had brought for her.

Hannah and Jimmy practically lived inside an imaginary bubble, just the two of them. They protected their relationship from prying opinions; nobody was ever allowed close enough to get between them.

She ran her fingers around the edges of each photo, riding the high of the happiness and love captured in them as if they had only been taken yesterday. There was a picture of Jimmy walking around the lake in the park with the sunset glowing red and orange behind him, his crooked smile in full focus. There was another of Jimmy swinging so high on a swing that Hannah had captured him upside down, defying gravity. Hannah kissed his cheek softly in another photo, unable to remember the time or place. The last in the series gave Hannah pause—she was pictured with a flushed face in a sea of cotton bed sheets. She recognized it to be from Jimmy's old bedroom back in Stonebridge.

Her gaze lingered on the last photo, remembering that day in particular: the first time she and Jimmy had slept together. As cliche as it was to think, Hannah felt like the experience was something out of a movie in that it was so utterly life-changing. They had both only ever been with one other person: Hannah with Manny and Jimmy with Kelly. Hannah's experiences with Manny were often rushed, erratic, and clumsy. They were intimate moments typical of two young people trying to figure it all out for the first time.

Jimmy, though, had taken Hannah by surprise. She often thought of Jimmy as a car that traveled only a hundred miles an hour, with its brakes completely disabled. So when he approached her so gently and thoughtfully, Hannah was dumbstruck. She thought about how Jimmy detailed every angle of her curves, stopping to memorize each freckle and outline the stretch marks that had appeared on her thighs the summer she grew taller than every boy in her class. He looked at her as if she were a piece of art, and it changed her.

*T*he *Inkwell* crew had rushed two more issues of the newspaper before the end of the Spring semester. The group had grown closer, though, meeting more often because of the rushed deadlines and to simply hang out together. The creative energy had been almost tangible during those meetings, with a certain magic that seemed to fill the room when they were together.

Jimmy and Hannah tag-teamed newspaper drop-offs to each business that had sponsored ads. A couple of store managers had told them how popular their newspaper was with patrons and that they saw an uptick in students coming through their doors. *The Inkwell* had also been well-received by SHU students, who were anxious for new issues. Hannah found a strange sense of fulfillment for her work on *The Inkwell*, like she was contributing to something that mattered.

On a warm Spring afternoon, with a stack of newspapers in the backseat of Hannah's car, she and Jimmy drove around distributing the third edition issues.

"How about I go in there with these?" Jimmy suggested to Hannah as she pulled into the adult novelty store's parking lot.

"I am not gonna argue," Hannah laughed. She watched Jimmy disappear into the store's blacked-out front door as she drummed her fingers on the steering wheel in time with the radio.

When he returned to the car, Jimmy eyed Hannah with a look of disbelief. "That dude was fucking creepy. Even to me."

"I told you!" she shouted playfully.

"He asked me where you were," Jimmy told her with a devilish grin.

Hannah gasped. "No, he did not! Ew!"

Jimmy nodded. "He did! I told him you were waiting in the car for me, so maybe we should get out of here before he comes out looking for you."

Hannah swiftly pulled out of the parking lot, kicking up a small cloud of dirt as her tires spun out. They returned to campus to hand out their last stack of issues. Hannah paced the sidewalk between the back parking lot and the Student Center, passing out issues to students as they came and went. Jimmy had brought his skateboard from the car and spent most of the time doing tricks off the short dividing wall. Hannah didn't mind, though, because he had attracted more attention their way, so the stack of newspapers disappeared quickly.

Once their hands were empty, Hannah and Jimmy walked the few blocks down to the beach at the end of Chris' street. The sun danced in and out of the clouds that day, but the air remained thick and heavy with the approaching arrival of summer. They sat in the sand, watching the small waves lapping onto the shore. Jimmy was smoking a cigarette as Hannah slowly sifted sand through her fingers like an hourglass, counting down the seconds.

She broke the silence, saying, "Ya know—we could never have a cute celebrity couple name." Hannah had a way of letting the most random thoughts slip from her brain right through her lips without a second thought.

Jimmy laughed, choking on a puff of smoke. "What?"

"We'd never be able to have a cool celebrity couple name," she repeated.

"What is a celebrity couple name?" Jimmy asked, confused.

"Where they mash up their names to make one name for the both of them. Like Jennifer Lopez and Ben Affleck—Bennifer," she explained. "Or Angelina Jolie and Brad Pitt—Brangelina."

"Who are those people?" Jimmy asked.

Hannah gawked at him. "You're kidding!" Jimmy's expression remained blank. "They're famous actors. Well, one was a singer who tried to be an actor. I don't know how well that worked out for her, though."

"Oh, okay. I think I get it," Jimmy said. He sat with a thoughtful look, taking long drags from his cigarette. "Um, let's see… Jimnah? Jinnah?" he suggested.

Hannah started to giggle, her laughter becoming increasingly louder. "Himny? Himmy?" she squeaked out.

"Hammy!" Jimmy shouted excitedly; she could tell he was beginning to like this game.

Hannah fell backward, grabbing her abdomen, which had gone sore from laughter. Jimmy extinguished his cigarette in the sand, laying back to let the belly laughs consume him, too.

When both of them eventually quieted down, Jimmy suggested, "I mean, you could use my real name—James. Maybe that's something to work with?"

"Oh yeah, I forgot about that!" Hannah declared.

Jimmy laughed in disbelief. "How could you forget that?"

"I don't know!" She eyed Jimmy, evaluating him. "You're just not a James. You're definitely more of a Jimmy." Hannah paused, nodding in agreement with her assessment. "I never asked, but were your parents fans of James Taylor or something?"

"My mom is, but my dad is *definitely* not! He hated the idea, but I guess she won the argument. My dad hates my name, but I think he hates it more that everyone calls me 'Jimmy.' So there's that," he said sarcastically. Jimmy abruptly became quiet and reflective as he stared out over the water. "Anyway—what about Hames? Or Jannah?"

Hannah smirked and said, "Eh, Jannah is a normal name. My vote is still for Hammy."

T hings were great between Hannah and Jimmy until they suddenly weren't. Ever since the summer had unofficially started with Memorial Day weekend, he retreated into himself more and more, hiding away from everyone—even Hannah. Jimmy didn't pick up calls, respond to texts, or instant messages. Not that he was ever online, anyway. Hannah had even tried posting on his Facebook wall, but he ignored that, too. Hannah desperately reached out to Brad one night, but he told her to give Jimmy some time and didn't offer anything beyond that.

Hannah found herself withdrawing, too, scurrying back into her shell. She spent her days obsessing over what she had done and said in recent weeks, trying to figure out what she had done wrong to cause Jimmy to flee from her. She diligently beat herself up, trying to make penance for some indiscretion she couldn't quite identify.

Hannah sometimes drove by Jimmy's house to see if he was home. He always was, but she didn't stop to knock on the door. As much as the separation hurt, Hannah didn't want to face all the ways she had undoubtedly wrecked their relationship. She sometimes lingered in the park down the street from Jimmy's house, hoping he might skate on through. He never did, though. Whenever the front door chimed at the thrift store, Hannah would perk up, hoping to see him walking in. She had even started to make frequent trips to Dunkin' Donuts, anything just to feel connected to him again. She'd opt for her coffee to be light and sweet like Jimmy preferred, sipping slowly with her eyes closed in a daydream. Jimmy had become a ghost, the whisper of someone she used to know.

Hannah tried to focus on her friendships with Whitney, Jenny, and Katie. They spent their nights driving south, attending concerts at seedy bars in neighboring beach towns. Hannah danced and sang, trying to shake off the invisible cloak of sadness she was wrapped up in. They spent countless days soaking up the sun on the beach, which turned into bonfire nights when the sun sank below the ocean waves. They talked and laughed, drinking too much on those sticky summer nights.

The girls didn't know what to do for her, but they tried desperately to help heal her broken heart. It worked sometimes, but it was always just temporary. They tried encouraging her to talk to other guys or drunkenly make out with someone at a beach party, but Hannah wasn't interested. She felt Jimmy everywhere. She saw his face in strangers she passed on the street, and thought she heard his booming laugh or raspy voice in crowded rooms. She always let herself get excited, only to be let down when he was still nowhere to be found.

Most nights, Hannah felt like she couldn't breathe, as if the walls of her bedroom were slowly creeping in around her. She would climb out of bed and sit on the back porch for hours, trying to convince herself that the world was not imploding around her. Hannah would look up at the stars, imagining Jimmy doing the same on the front porch of his house with a cigarette glowing brightly in the darkness.

On other nights, she would play "The Sims" on her laptop until the sun kissed the horizon in good morning. Hannah found comfort in losing herself in a fictitious life where she really could be anyone she wanted. She didn't have to only be the girl so often abandoned by the people she poured her love into. It was easy in that pretend world to get people to like you and to stay.

Despite her broken heart, she did worry if Jimmy was okay. No matter how hard she tried, Hannah couldn't stop her heart from loving or caring about him. Deep down, a part of her knew something must be terribly wrong with him; she just couldn't believe he would vanish like that without a word. It just didn't seem like him, yet she always convinced herself that it was all because of her. She had to face it: there had always been a common denominator in her failed connections, romantic or otherwise. It was her.

When her birthday rolled around in late July, Hannah had stopped attempting to contact Jimmy altogether. After several weeks of trying to reach him, he seemed to be totally off-grid. Hannah didn't want to give up on him, or their relationship, but she also had to face the truth that she wasn't wanted anymore. It was time to move on, even though her heart still lingered.

The girls had taken Hannah to the beach for her birthday and had surrounded her as she blew the candles out on her cake that night. As she leaned over the tiny, dancing flames and closed her eyes, Hannah wished only for Jimmy.

It was nearly midnight when a new instant message box appeared on her laptop screen. Hannah had been lying on her bedroom floor, staring at the ceiling, when she heard the notification sound over the music playing through her headphones. She almost ignored the message, wanting to be left alone to wallow in her self-pity. Something in her, though, told her to pick herself up off the floor.

Hannah nearly fainted when she saw Jimmy's screen name in the flashing box.

(Jimmy) *Banana? Are you still awake?*

Hannah wasn't sure she wanted to engage with him, but the temptation to pick at the scab of her wound was strong. After all, it had been what she wished for over her birthday cake only a few hours earlier. Another ping sounded.

(Jimmy) *Are you there?*

Hannah sat in her desk chair, thinking about what to say. All the heartache that had built up over the last two months began to come forth. Then, a third ping.

(Jimmy) *I need to see you. We need to talk.*

Screw it, she thought.

(Hannah) *I'm on my way.*

Before she could think twice, Hannah was out of the house and in her car, driving through the dark streets toward Jimmy. Having made the trip so many times by that point, she no longer needed a GPS to guide her to his front door.

Hannah pulled up outside his house, spotting the outline of his thinner-than-she-remembered frame hunched over on the front steps. Piercing through the darkness was the cherry-red end of a cigarette; he was just as she had imagined all those nights she spent sleepless on the back porch. Hannah steadied herself with a deep breath before getting out of the car.

With her hands balled up into fists, Hannah strode up the front walk, ready for a fight. She noticed that Jimmy was wrapped in a light blanket, even though the night was far from chilly. He stamped the cigarette out on the step before moving from his perch to meet her halfway. When they were merely a foot apart, he opened his arms, quickly wrapping Hannah up into the blanket with him. Hannah's arms remained at her sides, simultaneously feeling love and contempt for him. They stood like that for several minutes as tears streamed down Hannah's cheeks.

Jimmy pulled away from her, holding her at arm's length. A look of sadness crept across his face when he saw the glistening streaks of wetness running down her face. Hannah instinctively wiped them away, embarrassed at the show of emotion, but quickly stopped herself. There was no point in hiding it; besides, maybe he needed to see the damage he had inflicted on her.

"Banana," he whispered with a frown.

"Don't call me that," Hannah said sternly, shaking his hands off her shoulders.

His hands fell stiffly to his sides. "I missed you, Hannah," Jimmy told her.

Something shifted to anger inside of her just then. "You missed me? That's all you have to say? As if I'm just supposed to believe it?"

Jimmy was stunned by her reaction, but he knew he deserved it. "I know I hurt you. I'm so sorry." He shifted his weight between his feet in the uncomfortable silence that followed.

Hannah spoke fast, her voice rising in distress. "Hurt? You did more than hurt me, Jimmy! You crushed me, and all you can say is 'sorry'? You made me feel like I was *nothing*! That what we had meant nothing!" She was really crying by then, letting the weeks of pent-up rage and grief overflow. Hannah's expression softened, though, at the sight of tears welling up in Jimmy's eyes; he had no longer been able to hide the shame and guilt that had eaten at him all summer.

"I know it's not enough," he admitted, looking down at his feet, afraid to look at her and face what he had lost. With a deep inhale, Jimmy found it in him to meet her eyes again. "I was hoping we could talk and I could try to explain everything. If you would let me, anyway," Jimmy choked out. "Maybe we can take a walk or something?"

Hannah sighed and slumped her shoulders as she considered her options. "Sure," she said in surrender.

Jimmy dropped the blanket in the grass as they turned left onto the sidewalk. Hannah had so many questions she wanted to ask him, but she waited for Jimmy to say something more as they walked together through the quiet night.

Jimmy began to carefully tell her, "So—I, um—I've been dealing with a lot this summer."

"So have I, Jimmy," Hannah snapped.

He kept his eyes trained on their feet moving along the concrete. "I know, and that is all on me. I really am so sorry," he repeated. "Remember when I kind of dropped off from the newspaper for those couple of weeks? In the fall?"

Hannah crossed her arms. "Yeah… ."

"Well, I had a bad fall while I was skateboarding, and I got a concussion," Jimmy told her.

"Okay… ."

"It's not the first, but I had difficulty recovering from it. Migraines and dizziness," he explained. "It really affected me. Like, it completely fucked me up. I got pretty depressed, being stuck in bed for a couple of weeks with my room spinning all around me."

Hannah nodded in understanding. "I could see that," she said.

"The thing is—I was having a similar hard time when I was younger. Mentally, I mean. I saw a bunch of doctors, and they said that I was Bipolar." Jimmy said it so quickly that Hannah barely caught the last part.

She screwed up her face. "Did you say Bipolar?"

Jimmy hesitated. "Yeah, but I never really believed it. Depression, sure. But the mania part?" He shrugged. "They've told me my behavior is 'risky' and 'impulsive.' Anyway—I've been fine for a while. Medicated and stuff, but that fall just threw everything out of whack. I was thinking some bad thoughts. Like, the worst kind you could think of." Jimmy motioned like he was placing the muzzle of a gun to his temple. "I wound up going to the hospital to get my meds adjusted and to just take a break from everything."

"Oh," Hannah mumbled as she let it all sink in.

"So that's why I was out of school those weeks. This summer—I don't know. I just fell into this depression again. I don't know what it was—the meds weren't right, I guess. I just was in the same place, and I was too scared to tell you. I didn't know what you would think of me if you knew."

Part of Hannah was still angry with Jimmy. He should have told her what was going on with him instead of just running away. The other part of her felt bad for him, wanting nothing more than to be his comfort. Everything she had been going through that summer felt minor in comparison, and she suddenly felt silly for how she was acting.

"So where are you at with it now?" she asked.

"Good," he said with a more hopeful tone. "I got everything adjusted again, and I've been feeling good the last, like, two weeks.

I wanted to call you when I started feeling like me again, but I was pretty sure you hated me by now."

Hannah stopped walking and punched him on the arm—not hard, but enough to make a point. She flexed her fingers in and out of fists and let out a guttural growl. "I want to hate you, Jimmy, and I am so mad at myself that I just don't. I don't know that I ever could hate you. I mean, I appreciate you telling me all of this now, but I deserved to know weeks ago!"

Jimmy inhaled sharply, patting at the pockets of his pants. "Damn," he whispered. "I left my cigarettes at the house. But you're right—you did deserve to know from the beginning. I just didn't know how to tell you. I was so afraid of scaring you off. I couldn't lose you like that."

"So you disappeared on me? Make it make sense," Hannah scoffed.

Jimmy started walking again. "It sounds stupid, I know. I just felt like, maybe you were better off without me. I thought I was doing the right thing, but by the time I realized I was wrong, I felt like the whole thing had gotten so far away from me. I just—I've always felt so ashamed about this."

"You shouldn't feel ashamed," Hannah told him. "You're not the only one who gets depressed sometimes or feels like maybe things would be better without you." Hannah looked at him anxiously as she opened up to Jimmy about her own struggles. "I've had a lot of long and lonely nights, Jimmy, so I get it. Probably started in middle school and, most recently, it was because of everything this summer. I've spent so much time thinking that I wasn't worth anything, that everyone would just be better off. So, yeah, I know how it feels to just want to crawl up and hope for the world to end so you don't have to do it yourself."

Jimmy reached a hand out to Hannah so she would stop walking and pulled her into a tight hug. Hannah's arms hung at her sides momentarily, still feeling conflicted in her resentment and affection for him. Eventually, the side that hadn't stopped loving Jimmy won, and she wrapped her arms around his thin waist. Jimmy kissed the side of her head.

When he let her go, Hannah started to walk again slowly. "On the bright side, at least your parents help you with it. Well, I guess your mom does. My parents have never even noticed, or they just choose to ignore it. I'm not sure which."

"It's my dad's biggest disgrace, having a son as fucked up as I am. Needing medication to just be kind of normal," Jimmy confessed.

Hannah frowned, wanting to hug him again. She thought if she could just hold him tight enough, she could fit the broken pieces of him back together, that her love would be enough. As they continued to walk silently for another block, Hannah wondered what this all meant for them. She could not deny that she felt whole once again just being next to him.

She saw the glowing Dunkin' Donuts sign in the distance, advertising that it was open 24 hours. Without a question, they walked in its direction. They couldn't risk tiredness now, not when they had so much to catch up on. Jimmy ordered his usual: a large coffee, light and sweet.

He looked at Hannah in surprise when she said, "Make it two." She had grown so accustomed to it, preferring it, in the space between them that summer.

As they walked back up the street toward his house, Hannah asked, "So now what?"

Jimmy took a long sip of coffee, trying to find the courage to tell her how he still felt about her. "I know I don't deserve it, and you have every right to say 'no,' but I'd like to figure out how to make this work again."

It was all she had wanted that summer, but could they really pick up where they left off? Hannah had always believed in second chances, often giving third, fourth, and even fifth chances. She was usually left disappointed, though, having given those chances to people who never really deserved them in the first place. She knew that Jimmy was genuinely sorry, and that this wasn't entirely his fault. Not all of it, anyway.

"It's okay if you don't want to. Or can't. I would understand," Jimmy stuttered, readying himself for the letdown.

Hannah puckered her lips in thought. "It's just that—I do want to. I really want to, but—I'm scared. I don't want you to do this to me again. You can't." Hannah was fighting back tears again. "I don't think I could survive it a second time."

Jimmy smiled, reaching a hand to her chin, and gently turned her head to meet his gaze. "Never," he promised. He put an arm around her shoulder as they walked underneath the long row of lampposts.

Back at Jimmy's house, they spread out the blanket he had left behind on the front lawn and laid on their backs to stare at the vastness of the night sky. They talked for hours, not wanting to stop, fearing they might fall asleep and miss those minutes with one another; the coffee had only done so much to stave off the crash.

Eventually, the streetlights faded as the sun rose on a new day. Before Hannah drove home, Jimmy kissed her deeply, like he had that first time on the beach when they were skipping stones. It felt right, like that night was their second chance at a new beginning. When Jimmy pulled away, he leaned his forehead against hers and whispered, "Happy Birthday, Banana."

Hannah closed her eyes and placed a hand over her heart, rubbing the spot where the invisible scars of that summer still lived. Hannah felt that pain as intensely as ever, remembering how far she had fallen into her own depression all those years ago. She recalled those lonely nights that never seemed to have an end, the overwhelming worry that consumed her, and felt the tears well up in her eyes without effort.

Hannah questioned if going through these old memories was the best thing for her right now amid such heavy grief. She had to accept that Jimmy was gone, and no amount of reminiscing would bring him back to this plane of existence. She could go through all these memories and photos, re-read his obituary and stories from friends, but no matter how much she remembered or learned, she knew that she would never find the answers she was looking for: the moment where it all went wrong.

In some way, Hannah always believed deep down in her bones that she and Jimmy would cross paths again, that their story wasn't over. That they would find each other in the world as acquaintances or friends. Maybe even lovers again if the timing had been right. But now, that was gone. Hannah's chest heaved as her cries turned to sobs. They would never have the chance to meet on a sidewalk somewhere on a random Tuesday afternoon to exchange hugs and pleasantries. They would never again look each other in the eye and feel the embers within reignite, feeling the calmness that comes when your soul is in the presence of one it recognizes. She would never see his smile again, the one that never failed to steal the breath from her lungs. She would never again hear him say her name, how it so easily rolled off his tongue in that husky melody.

It's not fair! she thought. *It's not fucking fair!*

Hannah angrily tossed aside the journal in her hands. She picked up the following two notebooks to skim through. With her eyes blurred from tears, Hannah could see how empty they were. Her life had become increasingly hectic as her time at SHU went on. Hannah had somehow managed to balance a full-time school schedule, a full-time work schedule, *The Inkwell*, a relationship, and her friendships. Looking back, Hannah wasn't sure how she did it back then, knowing the stress would break her down entirely if she had to do it all over again now in her mid-thirties.

Hannah and Jimmy jumped back into their relationship as if his summer disappearing act had never happened. Jimmy had started new medications to help improve his headaches and depression, which seemed to help.

The last days of summer were spent not in a constant flow of activity, but in a more subdued way. They often found themselves nestled into simple, quiet moments together watching old movies or swinging the days away in the hammock that sat catty-corner in the far end of his backyard. Most nights, they simply drove around, fingers interlaced, talking about their dreams for the future. Both Jimmy and Hannah were always careful not to include or exclude each other from their plans, leaving their relationship open-ended. Jimmy wanted to work in the music industry, telling Hannah, "I just want to be *in it*." He was so sure about his career path, something Hannah ultimately grew envious of. She could never nail down what she wanted to do with her life, having changed her major twice in her first year at SHU, most recently landing on Psychology; she still wasn't sure if that was a good fit either.

Jimmy continued to perform with his band, Cat Hair. He had promised to go a little easier with the moshing and headbanging, but he didn't; Hannah didn't think he could control himself when he was on stage with a guitar in his hands. Jimmy was known to throw his body down to the ground, contorting his limbs in crazy ways. He would thrash around in mosh pits, kicking and punching at the air or anyone who happened to get too rowdy. Hannah initially tried to remind him of his promise to take it easy but stopped bringing it up after a while. She didn't want to take away the one thing that genuinely made him happy.

Hannah started to consider herself Cat Hair's main roadie, having taken on the role of helping pack and unpack their gear as they traveled around the state to church gymnasiums, American Legion halls, and random suburban basements. She never complained, though. There was something so captivating about those nights—the sea of sweaty, dancing bodies and a chorus of voices all singing the same song. It was there in the drives home afterward, with the windows rolled down, the chatter of hoarse voices, and the ringing in her ears. Hannah wished she could press pause on those moments to savor them just a little longer.

At the start of the Fall semester, Jimmy managed to work his charm on a marketing manager for an alternative music magazine, landing a coveted paid internship position. Hannah wasn't surprised, though. People spent hours devouring self-help books to learn that secret something that Jimmy had seemingly just been born with. Hannah was so proud of him, of course, but she didn't love the idea that Jimmy would be spending most of his time in Highgate City for work, rather than SHU or at home in Stonebridge.

Hannah couldn't pretend she wasn't worried about what the time apart would do to their relationship, even if it felt stronger than ever. That voice in her head continued to haunt her with fears that Jimmy would disappear again, that it would be so easy for him to get lost in a big city like that. It told her Jimmy would surely meet someone new, someone better suited for him. As much as Hannah tried to fight the idea, it seemed possible. People loved Jimmy once they got to know him, so he had no problem finding a friend in anyone.

Hannah noticed a subtle shift in Jimmy that made him seem more serious and thoughtful. His wardrobe changed from dirty denim and band t-shirts to Dickie's pants and clean-cut sweaters pulled over button-down shirts. Jimmy had taken to straightening his hair more deliberately, letting it fall naturally rather than using a ton of product to hold it up in every direction.

The Inkwell had become a popular publication on campus, morphing into a kind of living, breathing life form of its own. The student body at SHU loved the honest and funny content. The administration, not so much, but that was the point. Hannah sometimes felt like a pseudo-celebrity when people on campus recognized her as a staff member, making socializing much easier. *The Inkwell* was something interesting about her, and Hannah had never been that before.

For the first issue of the semester, Hannah had been tasked with interviewing a comedian from Highgate City who had found temporary fame on the internet. She had tanked the interview miserably, finding it incredibly difficult to think of questions to ask that seemed relevant. Jimmy lent a hand by writing down a list of things to ask, but some seemed so off-the-wall that she just couldn't bring herself to use them. In the end, Jimmy helped Hannah ramble through writing the article, which found itself buried in the back pages of that issue.

E ven though *The Inkwell* consisted of six issues that year, its future had become uncertain with the departure of Joe, Brad, and Jimmy, who were all graduating and moving on to real jobs. Jimmy had been less involved with *The Inkwell* because of his internship. Joe and Brad both juggled intense courseloads and struggled to give their time to meetings, content, and editing. There was an overwhelming sense that things would never be the same after that year, and it noticeably dampened the mood of meetings and get-togethers.

Jimmy loved his internship position with the magazine, though. He took on more responsibilities almost immediately and earned himself a promotion, which was unheard of for an intern. He met all kinds of musicians and had an opportunity to see behind the curtain of the industry. He was really *in it,* just like he had wanted.

Hannah constantly worried about Jimmy, checking in with him nearly every day about how he was feeling. She incessantly urged him to rest and recover from the long, stressful days. Jimmy would get annoyed with her constant agonizing over his health, but he reassured her every time that he was taking care of himself. Hannah had no reason not to believe him, so she did.

With his graduation only two weeks away, Jimmy was offered a permanent position with the magazine. He had gladly accepted, treating Hannah to dinner at the University Diner to celebrate. Jimmy enthusiastically talked about the job, feeling like things were falling into place for him. Hannah toasted Jimmy with her soda, smiling and talking excitedly with him about it. Underneath it all, though, she felt uncertain about their future together, knowing that being in different phases of their lives would only make things more complicated. Obviously, taking the job was the right choice, but it meant even more days in the city away from her. Hannah tried to overlook the growing rift between them, focusing on her happiness for Jimmy, but it was useless. To make it even worse, Jimmy didn't even notice the ever-expanding divide. That, or he was better at ignoring it than she was. Nonetheless, Hannah held on tight to their relationship, fearing the impact of its ending was near.

Jimmy graduated with a double major and honors on an unseasonably cool morning at the end of May. Hannah couldn't have been more proud of him for overcoming so much to achieve what he had. She was disappointed that she couldn't watch him graduate; SHU students were only given three tickets for guests to the ceremony, and his family claimed all of them.

The day had been overshadowed by Jimmy's dad's passive-aggressive and, sometimes, outwardly mean comments. In his eyes, Jimmy could always do better, be better. He disapproved of Jimmy's career path, thinking a real job meant staring at a computer screen in a cubicle for eight hours a day. It hurt to see Jimmy yearn for his approval, even though he denied that he did. To Hannah, it seemed that nothing Jimmy did would ever be good enough or make his dad happy.

Jimmy endured a family graduation party that his mom had insisted on throwing, inviting all kinds of extended family he had rarely seen. Hannah suffered through it with him, having to introduce herself to new people about fifty times over. It had been her worst introvert nightmare.

They sat on the front steps of his house for a while, trying to dodge the crowd, lamenting about their families. Jimmy had also craved a hit of nicotine but knew not to smoke in front of his extended family, who would just sneer and make snide comments.

"They're all so self-righteous," Jimmy grumbled as he watched the flame from his lighter ignite the cigarette between his lips. "I hate stuff like this. We barely speak to any of them. It's just so exhausting."

"I know what you mean. Lucky for me, I guess, my family is so splintered I think the only thing that could bring them all together is a funeral. Even that's iffy, though," Hannah offered.

Jimmy took a long inhale. "I just feel like my friends are more my family than any of them. Even my dad and my brother—we've never been close. But my friends, even if it is a short list, and you—you're all my family. You're all who I got to choose to be my family."

Hannah leaned her head on his shoulder. "I like that," she said. "A chosen family sounds so much nicer than the real thing."

Jimmy nodded. "Tell me about it."

With his parents out of town for a long weekend away, Jimmy had secretly planned a party for his friends the weekend after his commencement ceremony and family obligations. It felt like every other night that *The Inkwell* crew gathered together, filled with laughter, games, music, dancing, and plenty of chatter. Jimmy and Hannah clung to one another and stole kisses all night under the outdoor string lights that zigzagged between the trees in the yard as if they were the only ones there.

The party almost felt like a goodbye to what once had been and what would never be the same again; it was both happy and sad at the same time. Hannah thought it almost felt like a funeral, but not quite. It was more like a celebration of the life they had all lived together that was at its end.

As the night wound down, Jimmy sat cross-legged in the grass, playing music on his acoustic guitar, the one he had painted in bright primary colors. The group drunkenly sang along with Jimmy to the songs they knew, not caring about the late hour or what his cranky neighbors would say. Hannah sensed some melancholy in his voice as he sang, thinking she heard it break a time or two.

Of course, he is sad, she thought. *This chapter of his life is closing, and it's bittersweet.*

As people began to filter out in the early morning, Jimmy invited them all to Cat Hair's final performance, which was scheduled for the following Saturday night. It was almost poetic that this would be their first gig at an actual music venue: The Junction in Stonebridge. Hannah was sad that it felt like the end of an era, but she knew Jimmy's future in music was only getting started; Hannah was sure that it would be something great.

Once the party had entirely dispersed, Jimmy and Hannah walked to the park. Hannah was so tired, wanting nothing more than to go home to sleep, but she was still too buzzed to drive. They walked and walked, waiting for the alcohol to work its way through their bodies. Finding a bench along the path, they sat down, feeling so at peace in the quiet stillness while the sun began to rise. Hannah laid her head on Jimmy's shoulder, wishing they could sit there forever and that the future didn't ever need to happen.

Jimmy inhaled deeply before his voice broke the silence. "We have to talk," he said. "I have some news."

"That's never good," joked Hannah.

"No, it is good. I'm moving," he announced.

Hannah picked her head up quickly. "*What?*"

"Yeah, I'm moving to Highgate City."

"What? *When?*" Hannah was having trouble processing what he was saying, thinking the alcohol was somehow distorting the words coming out of his mouth.

"Sometime this summer. I have to find a place still. It just makes sense since I'm done with school now. I spend a fortune commuting every day, and it would be nice to be away from my dad."

Hannah pouted, feeling a ball of emotion growing in her throat. "So you're just not gonna be around anymore?"

Jimmy met her eyes, a confused look on his face. "No, I still will be. My family is still here. *You're* here."

Hannah focused on the grass under her feet, remembering that voice in her head that had been telling her it was a matter of time before he left her behind for a new life in the city. "So, does this mean we're breaking up?"

"No! God, no!" Jimmy said, wrapping his arm around her shoulders and pulling her face into the warmth of his chest. "It's the complete opposite, Banana! I'm doing this to lay a foundation for us—"

"But when are we going to see each other?" Hannah interrupted.

"Every chance we get. All the time! It seems like a lot of time until you finish school, but it's not. It will be over before you know it, and then you can come to the city with me!" he proclaimed. Jimmy was forever the optimist, believing everything would magically work out for the best. Hannah was the exact opposite, always making a plan for the worst-case scenario. Plus, a backup plan for that—just in case.

Hannah's voice shook. "It's two more years, Jimmy! It is a lot of time! Anything can happen in two years."

"Banana, I can hear it in your voice. Don't cry. I know this isn't going to be easy for either of us, but we will be okay. I promise." Jimmy paused to kiss the top of her head. "I love you. I have always loved you, and that will not change just because I have a new address."

Hannah's grief kept her in a chokehold, stealing the words from her so she couldn't speak them. She wasn't even sure what to say, so she just let herself cry, wetting the front of the plain white T-shirt he wore. What she wanted to tell him was that with him was the only place she wanted to be. He was the only place where she felt safe and loved. It had always been him, even before she had known his name.

"Come on. Let's get you home," Jimmy said as he patted Hannah's shoulder gently.

"I don't think I can drive home still," Hannah moaned.

"Then stay with me tonight," he suggested.

They ambled back to Jimmy's house, where he guided her by the hand up the stairs to his bedroom. The two of them sleepily crawled under the covers, facing each other. Hannah nestled her face into the space between Jimmy's chin and chest as he wrapped his arms around her tightly, giving her a little squeeze as sleep finally washed over her.

That summer, the newspaper staff took a road trip out of state to experience a Waffle House restaurant, which they didn't have in New Jersey. Brad had the idea randomly one day, so he organized a trip for everyone to go with him. Ten people from *The Inkwell* piled into two separate cars early one Sunday morning; the boys rode in Jimmy's car after a heated debate about whether it would even make it there, while the girls rode in Whitney's car after she vehemently insisted that she drive. Hannah's friends relentlessly teased her, questioning if she could survive the two-hour drive without Jimmy. She didn't want their jealousy to ruin the day, so she turned the music up and coaxed them to sing along with her. Katie had found unused notebooks and pens in the backseat, spending time doodling musings about the other staff members.

The group gathered closely around a couple of tables they had pushed together, their emphatic chatter punctuated by loud laughter. That was the beauty of places like the Waffle House. Nobody batted an eye at them or their noise, not that the group would have noticed or cared. All that mattered was that moment in that restaurant, soaking in the last days of summer together—their last hurrah.

They shared forkfuls of food and passed plates around, ensuring everyone had a taste of everything on the table. Sitting there with her friends, Hannah thought it felt like a Thanksgiving dinner. There they were, the family she had chosen, breaking bread and rehashing all the moments together that they were all grateful for. Jimmy sat with an arm around the back of Hannah's chair the entire time, savoring being that close to her since they both knew it would end in the next week as he transitioned his life to Highgate City.

The group ate their fill, then strolled the streets around the restaurant, trying to walk off their bloated bellies before driving home. There was a park nearby where they congregated together on the worn-out playground with questionably safe swings. Brad, Chris, Joe, and Jimmy loitered near a rock garden while the girls chased each other in a chaotic game of Tag. When Hannah tried to approach the rock garden, she was quickly shooed away before anyone else noticed what they were doing.

When the project was finally complete, Joe called the girls over. Chris pretended to be Vanna White, unveiling their creation. "Ta-Da! Do you like it?" he asked.

Katie was the first to speak up, asking, "What's it supposed to be?"

Chris threw his hands in the air in disbelief. "Seriously?"

Joe chimed in, explaining, "It's our symbol: the ink pot and the quill sticking out of the top of it."

"It looks like a penis," Whitney said bluntly, causing several of them to bust out into laughter.

"No, it doesn't!" shouted Joe indignantly.

The group stood and stared at the rock art, some giggling and some scratching their chins, trying to decide if it looked innocent or more phallic.

"Nah, man," Jimmy said, smirking at Joe. "She's right. It's definitely a dick." He gestured his hands in a cupping motion. "The ink pot is, like, the balls. The quill is—well, the rest of it. I definitely see it, man."

His explanation created another round of giggles from the group, which Joe didn't find amusing.

"Fine, we'll fix it then," he said moodily.

Everyone talked over one another, begging him not to change it.

"Honestly, I think it's perfect as is," Jimmy said with a laugh.

Hannah chimed in, "Yeah, don't change it! I think we should take some pictures so we can always remember it!"

The group huddled around the symbol that had united them over the last two years, but Joe refused to smile. They left their design in the grass for whoever came next. Those organized lines of stones proved that they had existed together in that moment. That their lives had been intertwined, and all of them had been made better because of it.

At the beginning of her third year at SHU, Hannah had made a more concerted effort to look to the future, still feeling lost about what she should do with her life. She wrote list after list of thoughts on the topic, crumpling each one and tossing them haphazardly into the trash. She felt so behind the rest of her friends, who all seemed to have solid plans for their lives. It seemed so easy for them, but why wasn't it easy for her? She felt paralyzed by indecision, her mind spinning with all kinds of thoughts: *Should I go to graduate school? What would I even study? Should I just find a job and get some real-life experience? What would I even do for work? What's the best choice?*

Jimmy had moved to the city during the last week of August, becoming a whole adult overnight, complete with a real job and a studio apartment. Their relationship was enduring the distance well enough. Jimmy tried to come back most weekends, but he often had some work events lined up that took up all of his downtime. He would sometimes come back to see her on weeknights, but it didn't often work out that way with her work and school schedules, so they learned to rely on phone calls and texts.

When she was off work and had minimal homework, which felt like never, Hannah would take the train into the city to be with Jimmy for even a few hours. Their time together always felt rushed, though, with him having to get to work early or finish a project on a tight deadline. Sometimes, he would invite Hannah as his plus-one to certain events, but she wasn't always crazy about going. She relished the quiet nights in his apartment afterward when the two of them lay in bed, listening to the world continuing outside his window.

Hannah grew more concerned about how much stress Jimmy was under at work and how it might affect him. He still seemed utterly enthralled by the busyness that consumed his life, but Hannah continued to notice a trace of something in his smile and an edge of uncertainty in his voice. It never seemed to last, though, disappearing before Hannah thought to even ask him about it. She believed everything was okay because Jimmy always said it was. She never questioned him past that since her mind was consumed with all kinds of things, like her giant class load that year and the increased hours that she was working at the thrift store. So, Hannah let her mind forget her concerns about Jimmy, focusing on the stress of her own life instead.

B y the time of its fourth anniversary, *The Inkwell* was floundering. In all honesty, it had been limping along since last year, with only three issues to its name that year. Morale was down, and motivating anyone to work on articles or comics took increasingly more effort. The newspaper was still really popular among SHU students and had drawn a number of them wanting to join the staff, but none of them were ever really serious about it. The group had lost more members than it had gained and eventually devolved into a group of friends who just liked to hang out and occasionally write news articles.

During one get-together in Chris's basement apartment, Katie, Whitney, and Hannah sat in their designated places on the couch while the guys played video games. It was the usual after-class activity, except that some first-year girls had tagged along under the guise of wanting to be writers for *The Inkwell*. Whitney, Katie, and Hannah watched them giggle, flirt, and twirl their hair for the boys. Whitney made gagging noises loud enough to draw the attention of almost everyone in the room. Katie instinctively swatted Whitney's leg, disapproving of her behavior.

It had become more challenging to spend time with Whitney, who had been more irritable than ever. Neither Hannah nor Katie was sure why, but she seemed to always be in a crabby mood and constantly commented to Hannah about Jimmy and their relationship. Hannah brushed it off, knowing it had more to do with Whitney than it did with her or Jimmy.

Whitney grunted, letting her jealousy show. "I can't believe this! What is even happening over there? You'd think they were some boy band or something with the attention those snobs give them!"

"Pfft. I'm just glad Jimmy isn't here," Hannah joked. She hoped to make Whitney laugh again so they could return to having a good day together. Whitney rolled her eyes at the mention of his name, and Hannah knew she had made a critical error.

"Of course, it comes back to *him,*" Whitney scowled and crossed her arms. "It never fails! Not like it would matter—your boyfriend isn't anything special. He's like some grungy, smoked-out dirtbag."

By the look on Whitney's face, Hannah knew she wasn't trying to be funny in return; she was just trying to be mean. "You're not wrong!" Hannah quipped, again trying to lighten the mood even though she hated that Whitney always picked on Jimmy's appearance.

Katie jumped into the conversation to save Hannah from Whitney's impending wrath. "I know! We need a name! Something to say that we were the *original* girls!"

The trio contemplated the idea in silence for a few moments.

"I've got it! SBS!" Whitney shouted suddenly, nearly jumping out of her seat at the end of the couch.

"SBS?" Hannah and Katie asked together.

"Sassy Bitches Squad, duh!" Whitney replied as if they should've just known what it meant from the start.

Katie broke the silence with a loud snort after a couple of seconds. She elbowed Hannah in the ribs, whose lips reverberated in a forced exhale. Whitney smiled at them slyly, her icy attitude slowly melting away. The three of them leaned into a hug, their giggles growing louder. The new girls shot them dirty looks across the room, thinking the laughter was about them. Little did they know that they were merely a blip on SBS's radar after that day.

Hannah called out of work sick that morning to stay home and swim through her memories some more. Up in the attic, she pouted as she thumbed through the bare journal she had prepared for that year but barely even used. There were pictures of friends in random places she could no longer identify, long-gone pets, and other memories she wished she had some context for. Hannah recalled how her courseload had become nearly unmanageable during that last semester, how she barely kept up with her friendships and relationship with Jimmy; she barely had the time for anyone, let alone herself.

She flipped the page of her old journal to find a photo from that night of her, Katie, and Whitney sitting in a row on that old couch in bright-colored cardigans. Below the picture, Hannah had scribbled "SBS Forever" in purple marker with a heart.

Jenny was absent from the picture and from most of that year. Not only had her class load increased, but she was also tasked with helping to care for her sister's young daughter. Jenny's sister was in active addiction at that time and would go missing for days on end. Jenny's life seemed so foreign to the rest of them, who were still living out their college glory days.

Hannah thought back on her friendships with the girls during their time at SHU. They were now nothing more than memories, faded away into the pages of these journals, their images burned into glossy photo paper. Hannah wasn't sure what had become of Jenny. She hoped Jenny had found some happiness and could finally live her truth. Katie and Whitney went on to marry men they met in their graduate programs at SHU, both remaining good friends through the years according to their social media posts. They had both made successful careers for themselves and had a couple of babies each.

It was the most perfect era of girlhood, those years at SHU, where they lingered between their teens and adulthood. Hannah never quite had friends like those again. She leaned back against one of the boxes and closed her eyes, letting herself feel it all. She reminisced about the fun they used to have, the hours spent just talking and giggling with one another. Oh, the fights they would have! Dirty and scrappy, but always followed by heart-filled apologies. All the love they shared for one another.

Hannah felt an overwhelming sense of joy for the time they did have but was disappointed that life had taken them away from her. She hoped that one day, when going through their own photos and memories, they would tell their kids about those nights in that basement that seemed like they would never end. How it never felt as special in the moment as it did decades later. Maybe they, too, would wish they could go back for just one more night to relive some of those moments again, hoping to recapture a feeling. Hannah hoped they would remember her name, grinning big as they said it out loud, breathing her existence back into their lives once more.

J immy called Hannah on the night of St. Patrick's Day during the last Spring Break of her SHU career. She could hear a rowdy party happening somewhere near him in the city while she organized boxes in the stockroom at work. It had been a couple of weeks since they last had a chance to talk on the phone, and she missed hearing his raspy voice. She even missed listening to him inhale and exhale smoke from a cigarette as they spoke and how he mumbled his words as he balanced it between his lips to keep his hands free. Hannah closed her eyes, imagining every soft edge of his face, pretending he was in front of her instead of all those miles away.

After Hannah updated him about her classes, Jimmy dropped a bombshell of bad news. "I lost my job today."

Hannah's mouth hung open as she stopped unpacking one of the boxes. "They fired you? But I thought it was going great! Your manager even said so in your review last week!"

"Well, 'laid off', I guess. I'm just so pissed! Apparently, sales have been down for a long time, and the business has been going under for months. They never said anything to anyone until now, but they filed for bankruptcy and closed the doors today out of nowhere," Jimmy told her, inhaling and exhaling a long drag from his cigarette.

"Whoa," Hannah said with surprise.

"Yeah. I'm not entirely sure what to do now."

"Yeah, I don't know," Hannah said as she resumed unpacking boxes again. "Oh my god. I am such a jerk—I was talking on and on about my stupid classes, and you had this big news to tell me."

"Don't, Banana. I wanted to hear about all of that," he assured her. "Well, I guess I'll have to go online tomorrow and try to find a new job. Hopefully, I can find something in publishing or music. I'm just worried about bills and stuff."

"Yeah," Hannah said with a nod. "There's gotta be something out there. You'll find it."

"Well, maybe it can wait a day or two? I was thinking about coming home to see you," Jimmy offered. "I think my mom and dad are going out of town again this week."

Hannah's mood perked up at the idea. "Really?"

Jimmy laughed. "Well, yeah! I've got all the time in the world now!" His tone turned more serious, and he said, "I really miss you, Banana."

Hannah felt a deep sense of longing for Jimmy just then. She wanted nothing more than to be wrapped up in his arms and to feel his body pressed against hers. Hannah wanted to be pulled under into his tidal waves, suffocating in him, not caring if she ever breathed oxygen again.

"I miss you, too," she sighed.

"Anyway—" Jimmy said to change the subject, "You'll never believe who I ran into yesterday."

"Who?"

Jimmy chuckled. "Kelly."

Hannah nearly dropped the stack of jeans she held in her hands at the mention of her name. "Oh, how did that happen?"

"I was in the subway waiting for my train, and she happened to be on the platform! How wild is that?" Jimmy asked.

Hannah stammered, "Oh, yeah. That's wild. Did you talk to her?"

"Oh, yeah! She saw me and came over to sit with me. Apparently, she started a graduate program at one of the colleges in the city. I forget which one, though," Jimmy told her casually.

"Huh. What are the odds of that?" Hannah questioned, feeling her suspicions grow. She had only ever met Kelly that one time, but she knew enough about her from all that Jimmy had mentioned. Hannah was suspicious about her intentions with Jimmy, not putting it past her to try to steal back what she likely thought was still hers. "Are you planning to see her again?"

"Nah. I got off at my stop, and that was that," he said.

J immy drove from the city to meet Hannah at the SHU library the next day; it was the perfect middle ground between the city and their hometowns, and had remained open during the break. He applied for a couple jobs while Hannah worked on a paper for her Psychological Statistics course. They worked for about two hours before the pull to be together became too strong to ignore. The tension between them was evident in the flirtatious way they smirked at one another and the hand Jimmy placed on Hannah's thigh as he watched her typing feverishly.

As they returned to their cars, Hannah asked Jimmy about his job search, "You find anything worthwhile?"

He shrugged and smiled wearily. "I applied for a job at a record label in the city. I doubt I'll get it, though—they were looking for someone with a lot more experience."

"You never know," she replied, trying to sound optimistic but knowing he was probably right. Hannah reached for Jimmy's hand, giving it a little squeeze in encouragement.

Jimmy looked at Hannah and pulled her by the hand into him so that they were standing chest-to-chest. He gently touched her cheek, staring so intensely into her eyes that she swore he saw right through to the depths of her soul. She saw a noticeable sadness flicker in his eyes. Other students walked around them, but Hannah and Jimmy saw nothing other than each other. He pressed his dry lips against hers, leaving them there for an extended moment, letting the kiss sink in. Hannah melted further into him, tasting the familiar nicotine and coffee on his mouth.

Jimmy pulled back and rested his forehead against hers. "I love you so much," he said in a hushed tone.

She whispered in reply, "I love you, too, Jimmy."

They took their time strolling to the parking lot, figuring out where they could go until Jimmy's parents left for another extended weekend trip away. They drove their cars down the road to a small cafe that Hannah had come to love. She had watched Jimmy perform solo acoustic sets there during open mic nights more evenings than she could count.

The cafe was set up with eclectic furnishings and looked more like a rummage sale than a restaurant. The shelves were stocked with various books to peruse and board games for a bit of fun. The pair took up residence on a blue velvet couch nestled into a nook of bookcases. Hannah ordered coffees for the both of them while Jimmy grabbed a Connect Four off the shelf.

She noticed the energy shift as they focused on the game and asked, "Are you okay?"

"Yeah," Jimmy replied quickly. Hannah could tell he was lying in the way he didn't look at her when he answered, instead keeping his head propped on his fist as he considered his next move.

"Are you sure?"

Jimmy looked down at his feet, letting out a deep breath. "I don't know. I just feel like my life is falling apart right now. Everything I've worked for is gone."

"You mean with work?" Hannah asked.

"Yeah! Like—what am I even doing? I loved that job. It was everything I wanted. At least what I *thought* I wanted. It's weird, but

I felt kind of relieved when they let me go. All of it kind of sucked, honestly. It just wasn't what I had thought it would be. It was just so… " his voice trailed off as he tried to find the right words.

"Overwhelming?" Hannah offered.

"Overwhelming, yeah! This is the first day that I don't have to watch the clock to make sure I'm back in the city by a certain time, or meeting some stupid deadline, or that some freaking intern isn't blowing up my phone every five fucking minutes!" Jimmy was raising his voice now, exploding with stifled frustration. "And, did you know that musicians are such assholes? Every last one of them!"

Jimmy frowned so hard that all of his facial features drooped together, and tears welled up in his eyes. It caught Hannah off-guard, who had only seen Jimmy cry once like that two summers ago.

She reached for him. "Come here," she whispered, rubbing his back.

"I just spent four years working toward this one thing, and it totally sucked. My dreams are just dust now," he told her. Jimmy pulled away, wiping the wetness from his face before anyone else in the cafe had a chance to notice.

Hannah nodded in understanding as the conversation turned quiet again. She thought over his predicament and remembered a quote about how it was best not to meet your heroes. That sometimes, it was just nice to have the illusion that people, or even things, could be perfect. In reality, though, everyone and everything had flaws; there was no such thing as perfection. She wondered if all dreams were destined to fall apart, turn into dust, and die.

Hannah and Jimmy drove back to his childhood home well after they knew his parents were gone. They went straight upstairs to his bedroom, where Jimmy stripped down to his boxer shorts and climbed into bed. Hannah changed out of her clothes, putting on one of Jimmy's old T-shirts so the scent of him would seep into her skin. She followed his lead, laying under the covers, where they held each other for a while. It was nice just to know that the other was right there within reach. It was everything they had needed.

They spent a lazy evening in bed, exploring each other between the same three movies that cycled through the cable channels on the television across the room. When they eventually got hungry, Jimmy ordered a late-night pizza for them. He had nearly missed the delivery driver, though, too busy traversing Hannah's body to notice the doorbell ringing downstairs.

Before sleep finally came over her in the early morning, Hannah realized just how much she missed Jimmy after so many weeks apart. How much she needed him even, like she was missing a piece of herself. Like she had been parading around as only half a human being. Hannah thought that if she had any dreams for her future, it would be just like that night with Jimmy, envisioning the two of them idling together in their own apartment instead of just playing house like they were.

Out of nowhere, the image of a victorious Kelly wrapping her arms around Jimmy that day at SHU flashed in Hannah's mind. Her eyes shot open, and a feeling of dread crept in. It was a reminder that Kelly was so much closer to Jimmy than Hannah was, that she could so quickly slither her way back into his life again without Hannah even knowing. She rolled over toward Jimmy, staring at his outline in the dark. As she closed her eyes again, Hannah made a quiet plea to the universe for her dream of them to come true.

J immy and Hannah lounged around in the backyard the next day. The skies had turned cloudy with an impending storm, but it wasn't enough to chase them back inside. They soaked in the warm Spring sunshine, tangled up in one another in the hammock. When thunder finally roared, they ran for the screened-in patio off the back of the house.

Hannah and Jimmy sat, watching lightning dance across the sky. She noticed Jimmy's demeanor becoming particularly thoughtful as he watched the storm blow in. "Are you okay?" she asked.

"Just thinking about this fight I had with my dad the other day," Jimmy admitted.

"I didn't know you guys had another fight," Hannah replied. "What about this time?"

Jimmy shrugged. "The usual. How I've got no direction, and I'm just a lazy piece of shit. That I'm better off without the job because now I can 'buckle down and find a real job.' Whatever the fuck that means."

Hannah scoffed, "You worked your ass off at the magazine!"

"I thought it was a real job," Jimmy said. "I made *real* money and spent my *real* time on *real* projects."

"Don't listen to him, Jimmy. I know you'll figure this all out," Hannah said encouragingly.

Jimmy let out a long sigh. "I don't need my dad to love me, but I wish he could like me. I've tried for so long to be someone he would be proud of. I went to college and got a degree. Two majors and with honors! I landed a job before graduating, but it will never be good enough for him. I'll never be the person he wants me to be. I'll never be my brother. I lie to myself all the time that I stopped trying long ago to impress him, but I don't think I ever did stop."

"Fuck him!" Hannah exclaimed defiantly, causing Jimmy to crack into spurts of laughter. "What's so funny?" she asked.

Catching his breath, Jimmy shook his head. "Just you, Banana. You always surprise me with what comes out of your mouth."

Hannah grinned. "I'm serious, though, Jimmy. Fuck him! You should just focus on making yourself proud. You need to make you happy, not him. Chase your own dreams, not his. He's just a cranky old man who wishes he could have had the opportunities you have, that's all."

"He's the reason I've never wanted kids. I've never wanted to be someone's dad," he told Hannah. Jimmy looked at her, trying to gauge her reaction to what he said. They'd never discussed a future together, but they both secretly hoped there might be one. Jimmy had once told Hannah that he wasn't sure if he ever wanted to get married after seeing how his parents acted with one another; they had worn each other down over the years, and he never wanted that for himself.

Hannah looked away from Jimmy, staring into the yard as rain fell heavily, and considered what she would want her future family to look like. "You shouldn't let him have that much power over you to determine how your life turns out. It's fine if you don't want kids, but don't deny that for yourself just because he's an asshole."

Jimmy turned back to the sky, still watching the storm. "You're right, though. Fuck him."

Jimmy didn't get the job with the record label or any other job he had applied for back in March. He spent a couple of weeks walking dozens of city blocks, spending through the funds he had preloaded onto his subway pass, hunting for anything to pay the bills. Eventually, he found a job at a small music venue, saying it was only temporary until he found something more substantial. The pay wasn't bad, though, and he had a more consistent work schedule. Jimmy also had the best stories about concert-goers, never failing to make Hannah laugh. She figured he would love a job like that, being able to interact with all kinds of people and be surrounded by music.

Hannah and Jimmy saw more of each other since he started that job, which helped her to feel more secure in their relationship. Hannah found herself daydreaming more about a future with him, allowing herself to live in a fantasy world much like that weekend they spent together at Jimmy's childhood home. He seemed happy again, too, but something was eating at Hannah that things just weren't as good as he let on. There was always a heavy-heartedness in his voice, even in the happiest of times. Hannah's self-doubt told her that Jimmy was falling more in love with the city and a new group of friends he had made through work. It reminded her that it was only a matter of time before his life completely split off from hers.

One night, at their usual hangout spot on the park swing set in Stonebridge, Hannah broke down and asked him, "Jimmy—what do you even see in me?"

He frowned at her. "What do you mean? How could you even ask me that?"

"We've always been so different, and we've been living such separate lives for a while now. I'm worried you have so much going on in the city: a new job and new friends. I don't know how much longer I can fit into it," said Hannah as she choked back tears.

"You will always fit into my life as long as you want a place in it. No one has ever understood me like you do or loved me in the way that you do. I know that you've got me. Like, *really* got me, and I've never had that with anyone else before. Not friends, not family, not anyone." Jimmy paused. "I guess I need to know… do you?"

"Do I what?" she asked.

"Do you still want a place in my life?"

"Of course I do, Jimmy!" Hannah shouted. "So what is it then? Because I can feel something is off with you. What are you not telling me? Is it something about Kelly?"

He looked at her bewildered. "What? Kelly? Why would this have anything to do with her?"

Hannah raised her voice to him, the anxiety in her growing. "I don't know! She's living in the city now, too. I guess she's on the same subway line as you. I can't imagine you've only seen her the one time!"

"Banana, it *was* the only time I've seen her," Jimmy told her. "Don't tell me you've been worried about it? I would've never mentioned it if I thought you'd get all paranoid about it."

"I'm not paranoid!" Hannah shrieked.

Jimmy sighed but didn't say anything. He simply stamped his cigarette out on the underside of the swing, forcefully flicking it into the grass somewhere.

Hannah couldn't help but press Jimmy more, almost itching for an argument. "I bet your mom would just love it if you and Kelly got back together," she said sarcastically.

Jimmy narrowed his eyes at her. "What? Why would you even say that?"

"Because it's true!" she shouted, "Your mom hates me!"

"That's not true!" Jimmy yelled back defensively.

Hannah rolled her eyes at him. "It *is* true, Jimmy! I can't believe you don't see how she looks at me or talks to me. It's like she can't stand how close we are!"

"Don't be ridiculous, Hannah," Jimmy growled.

Hannah opened her mouth to say something more, but she remained quiet. She had meant to find out what was going on with Jimmy, not cause a fight, but she was getting lost in the weeds of her insecurities. "Anyway—what is it then, Jimmy? You've been kind of weird lately, and I don't know what to think."

Jimmy stared into the distance before admitting, "I've been struggling a lot lately. It's like this black cloud keeps following me, but it's like it's swallowed me whole this time and won't spit me back out. I've been trying to shake it on my own, and I just can't."

"Why didn't you tell me?" Hannah asked. "I thought we were past not being able to talk about this stuff?"

Jimmy shrugged. "You've just had so much going on with school and everything. I didn't want to worry you or add more to your plate."

"Well, I am worried!" she yelled. Hannah took a calming breath before continuing, knowing that getting overly emotional wouldn't be helpful to him; it would just prove him right that it was overwhelming to her. "Are you still taking your meds?" she asked.

There was a long pause as Jimmy turned against the breeze to light a fresh cigarette. He confirmed what Hannah had suspected, simply stating, "No. I haven't taken them for a while, actually."

"Jimmy!" she yelped, feeling deflated by his admission.

"Things were so crazy when I was at the magazine. I was so consumed with whatever was going on—I don't even remember anymore. I was running late one morning before I left for work, and I forgot to take them. Then it was the next day, and it happened all over again. Then, it turned into a few weeks and then a few months. I felt okay, honestly, up until a few weeks ago."

"That's what happens, Jimmy. You have to take them all the time, not just when you feel bad."

He only nodded his head in response, focusing on inhaling the nicotine he needed to steady himself. Hannah noticed a tremor in his hands.

"Can you get them refilled?"

He shrugged again. "I have no idea. Maybe? My mom had all the information for the doctors. I'd have to ask her."

"Then let's go ask her. She's still home, right?"

Jimmy looked at the time on his cell phone. "She should be."

Hannah hopped off the swing, holding a hand out to him. She led him back down the path and onto his parents' street. "I'm just worried about you," she told him.

"I know, but you don't need to be so worried. I'm really okay." Jimmy tried to sound convincingly upbeat, but Hannah didn't believe it.

"Jimmy, you don't need to hide from me. Lean on me. Please. Just don't run from me," she pleaded with him.

He squeezed her hand. "I won't."

Back at Jimmy's house, his mother was upset to hear that he had been without his medications for so long. She immediately called the neurologist and psychiatrist to schedule appointments to get him back on track. Hannah had sat at their kitchen table, witnessing the delicate dance of anger and love between a mother and her son. Hannah hoped it would earn her some points with his mom, finally.

I hope I'm doing the right thing here, she thought. *What happens if his depression gets worse? What if he runs again? What if—what if he left? For good?*

She couldn't let herself even think about it, not outwardly. Hannah had to admit that she had worried about Jimmy's own internal voice, which had a history of trying to convince him that everyone was better off without him. She and Jimmy were too deep into it, with three years separating them from that day in Chris' driveway when everything had come to a head between them. It had been two and a half years since Jimmy's last major depressive episode. Hannah had to trust him to be more on top of his appointments and medication, believing he would be more open with her about everything. If she didn't trust him, Hannah feared his black cloud would consume her, too.

W ith only a week left until graduation, Hannah picked up her three tickets for the commencement ceremony. Knowing Hannah would have an extra ticket, Jimmy had already promised to be there with her parents. She immediately texted him to let him know she picked up the tickets, providing the necessary information so he could take off work if needed. Jimmy didn't respond immediately, but Hannah knew he was at work and had probably gotten lost in arranging the venue's scheduling calendar again.

When Hannah didn't hear back from Jimmy for the rest of the day, she was left on high alert with a tingle of uncertainty running down her spine. Jimmy had spoken to her daily for the last three months, so it wasn't like him to suddenly go quiet.

It's fine, she thought. *His phone probably died again or something.*

Jimmy was like that, not allowing himself to be tied down by a cell phone; he was so unlike everyone else Hannah knew in that way. He had often left his phone in random places, completely forgotten about. Or he would forget to turn it on in the morning when he woke up. Another possibility still was that he let the battery die without any thought of charging it. Jimmy had joked with her once while they were still just friends that his real connections always knew how to find him. As if it were as simple as lighting the Bat-Signal, capable of reaching him when he was most unreachable.

When Hannah awoke the following day, she promptly checked her phone for any new messages from Jimmy, but there were none.

Weird, she thought to herself.

Hannah felt a pit grow in her stomach. She navigated to her email, sifting through spam messages that had come in overnight until she saw an email from Jimmy.

Why did he email me, of all things? she wondered, clicking into it.

To: Hannah O'Malley

From: James Taylor

Subject: I'm Okay

Date: May 14, 2009

Banana,

By the time you read this email, I'll be states away. Maybe. I'm not really sure where I'm going, but I just had to get out and get my head straight again. That cloud is still here. It didn't leave this time. It just got bigger and darker.

I've been living in this city, and I feel more alone than I ever have in my entire life. There is just always this noise and activity and people everywhere I go, and I keep finding myself sitting at the bar down the street drinking to just try to quiet it all. I used to always feel alone no matter how many people I surrounded myself with. I would've given anything for them, but I knew it was never mutual. Then there was you, Banana. You made me feel like someone had *me* for a change. I am so sorry for leaving like this. I just can't knock this voice in me that's telling me it's all a lie, that no one will ever really have me. To shut it up, I just have to leave. There's no other way. I need you to know that there is no other way.

I did try another way, though. I got into a fight last night to try to shut it up. I punched a guy. I don't know what I thought it would do. I knew it wasn't him talking, but I couldn't help myself. I know you're wondering it, and no, I haven't been taking my medications or anything. I barely even started them again. I probably should, but I don't want to. I don't feel anything when I'm on them, not even happy. I'm sorry I lied to you about that.

Everyone has been on my back, especially my dad. The only thing I could think to do was pack my stuff and go. I guess I'll just see how far my money will take me. I don't really have a plan.

I sent an email to my mom, too, so she knows. I'll call, but I don't know when. I just need time. Please don't worry about me. I'll be okay, I promise. I love you more than anything, and I am so sorry.

-Jimmy

Hannah felt her stomach lurch and searched the bedroom for the trash can, just in case. Her mind churned with so many thoughts that she couldn't even pick one out to run with. Hannah considered Jimmy's welfare and asked herself if he would be okay out in the world or with himself. She thought of where he would go but had no idea aside from the usual neighborhood haunts. She checked the timestamp on the email: 12:03 A.M. She looked at the alarm clock next to her bed. It was 6:42 A.M. He had almost a seven-hour head start.

Hannah immediately tried to call Jimmy. The phone rang twice but then went to his voicemail, and she knew he had declined the call.

"What the hell?" she whispered to herself, redialing him. The phone rang three times before going to voicemail again, making Hannah think that he had at least considered picking up her call that time.

Hannah left a message. "Jimmy, it's Hannah. What's going on? I saw your email. I'm worried." She took a long pause as all of the horrible scenarios popped into her mind. "I'm afraid you're going to hurt yourself or something. Please call me. Or text me—whatever! Just let me know you're okay." Hannah took another long pause before ending the message with, "I love you."

Hannah wasn't sure what to do with herself. She sat in bed, tapping her fingernails against the back of her cell phone, thinking about what she should do next.

Maybe if I text him, she thought.

She quickly typed and sent: *Are you okay? Please call me.*

Hannah scanned the room, deeply in thought about Jimmy's email, before noticing the open textbooks on her desk. She groaned loudly, remembering that it was her last day of finals. She leaped out of bed, throwing on a SHU sweatshirt and a pair of jeans she had left on the floor from the previous day. Hannah grabbed her things and ran out the door, heading for Jimmy's house first. Whenever she reached a red light, Hannah called him until it went straight to voicemail. Then she switched to texts, even though she knew he had finally turned his phone off by then.

As Jimmy's childhood home had come into view, Hannah spotted that rusty gray Oldsmobile parked outside at the curb. "He's still home!" she gasped.

Hannah was running up the front walkway before she could even question why he would've sent an email like that if he were just at home. She pushed the doorbell several times in a row, the agony overwhelming her as she waited for the door to open. She wrung her hands and looked from window to window to catch a glimpse of his silhouette moving toward the door. After a few more doorbell attempts, Hannah turned to leave.

I guess he just doesn't want to see me anymore, she thought, affirming the fears that tormented her over the last several months.

Her foot hit the last step when she heard the front door lock shift and the hinge squeak as the door swung open. Hannah spun around to find Jimmy's mom, Bonnie, in the doorway. Her eyes were red and puffy, while the worry lines around them seemed deeper than ever.

"Is Jimmy home?" she asked. "I saw his car on the street while I was just driving by—"

Bonnie shook her head. "He's not, Hannah. Jimmy—he, um— he left. He's gone," she said as her voice wavered.

Hannah's shoulders dropped at the news. "Oh, yeah, I got an email from him. I just thought—I saw the car," she said again as she pointed to it behind her.

"He left it here sometime last night and left on foot. At least, that's what we think. I called the police already, and they seem to agree. Not that I think they're going to do anything—they didn't seem concerned even with his history." Bonnie pulled a wrinkled-up tissue from the front pocket of her tailored khaki pants, wiping her nose with it. "I wish I had heard him pull up. I could have talked to him, maybe stopped him."

"Yeah, I wish he had called me or something instead of just leaving an email for me to find this morning," Hannah stated.

"What did the email say? Can I see it?" Bonnie asked.

Hannah nodded quickly. "Yeah, sure. Maybe it can help the police or something." Hannah reached for her cell phone in the back pocket of her jeans, opened the email application, and handed it over to her.

Bonnie scanned the message, her expression changing with every other sentence. "It doesn't say much more than the one he sent me," she disclosed.

"Is there anything I can do?" Hannah asked.

Bonnie exhaled sharply, but it seemed to Hannah she may have suppressed a laugh. "No, honey. There's nothing to do right now; we're handling it. You'll let me know, though, if he calls?"

Hannah suddenly felt like a little kid who thought they were much more grown-up than they were. "I will," she said simply.

Bonnie gave Hannah a tight smile before closing the door on her. Hannah knew she didn't have much time left to make it to SHU for her first exam of the day, so she hightailed it down the walkway back to her car.

While she drove, Hannah practiced a visualization exercise she had learned in one of her classes that semester. She packed her worries, fears, and broken heart into fictitious boxes in her mind, compartmentalizing everything that happened that morning. She imagined herself placing each box onto imaginary shelves to be taken down later. Hannah had already given up on getting perfect marks on her finals, praying she could pass them to graduate.

Hannah had planned to meet with Whitney and Katie for lunch in the Student Center before her last exam of the day, something they had planned earlier in the week. She thought about canceling but wasn't sure what else she would do with her time otherwise. Hannah was distracted as she sat there with them, checking her phone every few minutes, hoping to see an incoming message from Jimmy. Her disappointment only grew every time.

"Earth to Hannah!" Whitney shouted as she waved a hand in front of Hannah's face. "What's going on with you today?"

Hannah took a deep breath before telling them about Jimmy's email and the visit with his mom, which left her feeling a little disregarded. When she finished, Whitney and Katie just stared at her.

Katie spoke first, "Oh my god! What are you going to do? What should we do? I feel like we should be doing something!"

Hannah shrugged. "I'm not really sure what to do."

"Well, should we call the police or something? Did his mom call?" Katie asked.

"Bonnie called, but she said they weren't really worried about it since he hadn't been gone that long, even though he has a history of depression and stuff. I'm worried. He's not answering my calls or texts, and—" The heat of tears stung her eyes while she finally allowed herself to feel the overwhelm that had been lurking there all morning.

Katie grabbed one of Hannah's hands, letting her cry. She said, "I think someone needs to be missing for twenty-four hours or something before they'll take it seriously. Or maybe it's forty-eight hours? I don't know. I just remember you have to wait. That's what they say on TV, anyway."

"Yeah, I think I heard that once," Hannah agreed. "I just don't get it—he told me a little while ago that I was the only person he knew who had his back and would always be there. Why didn't he call or something? I just don't understand." Hannah sniffled back the rest of her tears and chuckled softly. "I'm sorry for ruining lunch, you guys."

"Don't be ridiculous!" Katie shrieked. "This is a big deal! We're here for you."

Whitney screwed up her face for a moment, then said almost bitterly, "I just can't believe he would do this to you again! He says he loves you but then vanishes without a trace? Knowing you've got finals and a week before your graduation, and the best he can do is send a freakin' email? Which says what exactly? Absolutely nothing!"

Hannah saw red in an instant. She wanted to say so many things to Whitney, but none were polite. Hannah took a moment to collect herself, even though Whitney didn't deserve that courtesy. "It's so much more than that," she sneered through gritted teeth.

Whitney stared at Hannah before clicking her tongue and rolling her eyes. "I don't know. I think it's pathetic how much time you poured into him, like some sad little project. You gave him three years of your life, Hannah. He's just an asshole. It's time you faced that—wake up!"

Hannah's breathing turned shallow and fast as she lost control. Slamming her hands onto the table, she began shouting at Whitney. "What's pretty shitty is your attitude, Whit. You called yourself his *friend!* He could be dead by now—did you even think about that? He could have jumped off a bridge somewhere or hung himself from a tree in the woods! Maybe he's been dead for hours! I bet you didn't consider that!"

Whitney was stunned by Hannah's reaction, having never seen her fight back like that before. "No, it didn't," she managed to stutter.

Hannah stood from her seat at the table abruptly, nearly knocking the chair over behind her. "Of course it didn't! This has nothing to do with you, so why would you care? I feel sorry for you, Whitney. Do you know that? I've watched you be consumed with jealousy every time someone around you is happy or in love because you know you'll never have that! You can't see anything past your own nose, and *that* is pathetic!"

Hannah's rage threatened to suffocate her as she stared down Whitney and Katie, her chest heaving to take in oxygen. She plucked her backpack from the floor and stormed out of the cafeteria as dozens of eyes followed her. Whitney and Katie sat silently, afraid to move until Hannah was out of sight.

She knew that not everyone could understand the extent of Jimmy's illness, but she had at least expected Whitney and Katie to have compassion for someone they had considered a friend for the last four years. At the very least, for the person their best friend was in love with. Hannah had expected Katie to speak up, to defend her from Whitney's jealous anger, not just sit there. Her silence spoke volumes that day.

She could feel her heart pounding through her entire body, her cheeks flushed with resentment. Hannah took several deep breaths, trying to regain control of herself. She found her way to the library, needing a quiet place to calm herself down. She managed to find an empty chair in the back corner of the expansive room, still checking her phone for any communication from Jimmy. She wanted to be home, hiding under the covers in bed, pretending the day had never happened. What she wanted most of all, though, was to talk to Jimmy. To see him. She wanted him in front of her, to feel his skin on hers, and to know that he was okay.

By the time graduation day had arrived, Hannah was still giving Whitney and Katie the silent treatment. Katie tried apologizing a couple of times, but Hannah couldn't accept it; she was still upset and too stubborn to change her mind. She was just so numb to it all. Her parents were so proud, so Hannah did her best to plaster on a fake smile and go through the motions of the day: walking across the stage, shaking hands, posing for pictures, moving her tassel from right to left. If Hannah had ever been good at anything, it would have been masking what was happening inside her heart so everyone would think she was okay.

As Hannah milled about backstage at the SHU arena with the other graduates, she talked with professors she'd had classes with and took pictures with students she had been friendly enough with. She had spotted Whitney and Katie across the gathering space, giving them a weak smile. They both returned it but didn't dare approach her. Hannah half-expected Katie to come up to her and make another attempt to beg for forgiveness, but when she didn't, Hannah figured she didn't have enough nerve to do it in front of Whitney.

Hannah hadn't spoken to Jimmy either, but he had emailed twice since that initial message. The police had closed their case since Jimmy was in contact with Bonnie and Hannah, saying they were limited with what they could do since he was an adult. As sad as she was, Hannah breathed a sigh of relief every time she saw his email address appear in her inbox. She would remind herself that he was alive one day ago, two days ago, three days ago….

In his last email, Jimmy wrote that he still didn't have a destination but had traversed many miles and crossed several state lines. He was hitchhiking, riding midnight Greyhound buses, and even hopping on and off commercial trains. Jimmy had played guitar on the streets in towns throughout Tennessee to make money. He had found bars and coffee shops hosting open mic nights to play in, often finding a night or two of work helping to wash dishes or scrub toilets. He headed as far west as Kentucky. Jimmy had painted her the most beautiful picture of the landscape, people, and the fine bourbon he had gotten drunk on one night. The one thing that Hannah held onto was the fact that at least he was playing music. She wholeheartedly believed it would be the thing that could keep him breathing.

In his most recent message, Jimmy was headed back east, hoping to land in North Carolina within the next day or two. He had planned to keep heading south from there. *Maybe somewhere on the coast so that I can feel close to home,* he had typed.

Hannah didn't understand why he didn't just return to Stonebridge if he wanted to feel close to home. She had half a mind to pack a bag and search the streets for him, but she didn't. North Carolina was a big state, and she wouldn't know where to start. She also knew that if she found him, it would only drive Jimmy further away. Whatever his reasons were, he needed this. She had to trust that.

Jimmy continued to sign off on every email by telling Hannah how much he loved and missed her. As the days passed and the distance grew larger, Hannah doubted it more. She didn't want

Whitney to win, but sometimes she couldn't help but think she had been right all along. Hannah would shake the thought from her mind, telling herself: *At least he has his music. At least he was alive one day ago, two days ago, three days ago….* It had become something like a mantra to her, one she repeated when brushing her teeth, shampooing her hair, and driving to work. She recited it every night before falling asleep, like a sad and desperate prayer.

On the nights she couldn't sleep, Hannah laid in bed reading each email habitually. She read the words in his voice as if it might reveal something more to her. When that didn't work, she read between the lines, searching for some hidden meaning or clue. Hannah never knew what she was expecting to find, though.

Going back over the messages, she echoed his sentiments about feeling more alone than ever. Her mind often returned to the first time Jimmy had disappeared from her life as if someone had flicked a light switch off. Poof! The way she felt so unwanted and unloved back then was nothing like how she felt in those moments, questioning if she could even continue breathing without him for another day.

Hannah wished Jimmy would call, begging her to meet him wherever he was. She knew she would follow him to the ends of the Earth if only he would ask. At the same time, though, Hannah also knew that she was watching the destruction of her dreams, and it only confirmed what she had feared a year ago: dreams were only ever meant to turn to dust. That they weren't meant to be lived. That there was no one out there in the universe who had been listening to her pleas.

Hannah spent most of the summer working at the same thrift store she had worked at since high school, signing up for as many overtime shifts as she was allowed. She had nothing else to keep her busy: no boyfriend, friends, or school. Her parents were nagging her about finding a job since she had a college degree, but Hannah quickly learned that she could only do so much with just a Bachelor's in Psychology. Her parents couldn't wrap their minds around the idea, like a college degree would allow her to skip the line into a great career. It's not like she was motivated to look for work or research graduate programs, anyway. Hannah spent the time she wasn't at work with her nose in a book or playing in the imaginary "Sims" world she built years ago.

Most days, Hannah haunted the record shop where Jimmy used to work, spending hours thumbing through the vinyl records and CDs. His old manager still worked there, letting her flit between the bins for as long as she wanted, even though she never bought anything. He would talk to Hannah sometimes, asking about Jimmy, but he eventually stopped when she could no longer hide the pain of his absence. When she was done there, Hannah would drive through all the towns they had aimlessly wandered. Hannah made it a point to always pass by his house to glimpse that dilapidated Oldsmobile still parked on the street. She spent hours sitting on the old swing set at the park near his home, staring into the void as little children played and giggled gleefully around her.

On her twenty-second birthday, Hannah went to the cafe where she and Jimmy had spent so many hours. She sat in a solitary armchair by the window and ordered a coffee and a cupcake. She thought she might as well have a little treat to celebrate, even if she was all by herself.

The server recognized Hannah, asking, "Is Jimmy joining you?"

Hannah's breath caught in her chest at the sudden mention of his name. "Just me," she squeaked out.

The server smiled and nodded, leaving to put her order together. Hannah pulled a $10 bill from her wallet, slapped it on the table, and ran out. She dashed around the corner, crumbling into a crying heap in the alleyway next to the building.

One hot and muggy evening in August, when the houses in the neighborhood had gone dark, Hannah found herself sitting on the back porch in the stillness of the night. She stared at the stars, wondering if Jimmy was staring at the same night sky. Hannah slid down the steps until she reached the cool pavement of the driveway and laid herself out like a starfish. She closed her eyes briefly, reminiscing about the nights she and Jimmy had spread a blanket out on the lawn to stargaze, still grasping at her memories of him just to feel close to him again. Hannah looked for the constellations he had taught her, then tried to identify other planets before giving up because she couldn't remember where they would appear.

Hannah's cell phone buzzed beside her from an incoming call. She ignored it, knowing she no longer had anyone left in her life who would call, especially at that hour. The phone buzzed again, but she ignored it; Hannah figured the caller was trying to drunk dial their ex and couldn't remember the number. When it buzzed a third time, she picked it up without looking at the Caller ID and yelled, "Look—you've got the wrong number! I don't know if you're dialing wrong or maybe someone purposefully gave you the wrong number, but please stop calling me!"

Before she could hang up, she heard a voice on the other end say her name. "Banana?" She put the phone back to her ear. "Banana? Did you hang up? Are you still there?" Her heart skipped a beat, recognizing the gravelly voice on the other end.

Hannah sat upright, her eyes searching the darkness in front of her as if the voice was emanating from it. "Hello?" she said to the void.

"It's me, Banana."

Hannah gasped and covered her mouth with her free hand. Through her fingers, she whispered, "Jimmy?"

"Hi," he breathed.

"Hi." There was a long pause as Hannah's mind raced to process the moment, unsure if she should cry or scream. "Where are you?" she finally asked.

Hannah heard Jimmy inhale from his cigarette and then exhale it deeply. "I'm in Riverside Springs. In South Carolina."

Hannah fiddled with a pebble she had found on the ground. "You haven't emailed me in a while," she said, her voice glum. "Does your mom know where you are?"

"Yeah, I've been calling her pretty regularly."

"Oh." Hannah felt jealous and hurt that Jimmy hadn't called her, or that Bonnie hadn't mentioned it.

"I miss you so much, Banana," Jimmy confessed.

"Don't call me that," she replied coldly.

Jimmy blew out a puff of smoke forcefully. His tone had changed to one of annoyance as he repeated, "I miss you."

Hannah sucked her teeth. It all felt like a lie, just something he was saying at the moment to quell whatever anger might bubble up inside her.

"It's true whether you believe it or not," Jimmy continued. "I needed to do this—for me, but it doesn't mean that I don't have regrets. The timing sucked, I know. I regret not waiting until after your graduation and not asking you to come with me. These last few months have been pretty great, but I've always been so aware of this hole in my heart. I was out here doing my thing, finding some peace, but I just couldn't fill in this one damn hole. I couldn't figure it out, and then I finally realized it was because the hole was you."

Hannah swallowed back her tears, reaching out for her anger instead. "But you promised, Jimmy. You promised me you would never do this to me again, and you did! You made me out to be a damn fool—everyone thinks it, and they're not wrong! I have no more friends because of this. Because I defended you."

"Wait, what? What about your friends?" Jimmy asked before taking another deep inhale from his cigarette.

She scoffed and tossed the pebble as hard as she could. "Exactly! What about them? They're all gone, gave up on me, the fucking idiot who stood by your side this entire time."

"Hannah, I—"

"Whatever, it is what it is," she said, cutting him off.

"Hannah, I'm sorry. I didn't know."

"Yeah, you wouldn't, would you?" Hannah asked sarcastically. "You don't know shit about what I've been through, Jimmy."

"But I want to—"

"Maybe it's too late for that," she scowled.

"Is it? Is it really too late?" he asked.

The weeks of anticipating that moment felt so far away. Hannah was too angry, too confused, to consider whether it was too late or not. A part of her said it was, while another part, a bigger part, told her it wasn't. That it would never be too late. Deep down, Hannah knew she would do it again for him. She knew he could break her, and she would just let herself drown in the pain.

"Banana—" he sighed. "I don't care if you don't want me to call you that. You'll always be my Banana, so you'll have to deal with it. Look—I know it probably doesn't mean much, but I love you just as much today as I did that day in Chris's driveway. More, even. I just miss you so damn much."

She could hear the sincerity in his voice. Even though she still did love him, she couldn't let herself give in so easily. "Right. I'm supposed to believe that after you abandoned me for all these months while you traveled around, you didn't meet anyone who caught your eye? That you didn't get too drunk one night and fall into someone else's bed?" Hannah's heart raced, and her breath quickened as her irritation grew.

Hannah could hear the scratch of the flint as Jimmy lit another cigarette, inhaling deeply. "I did meet people. I did crash on strangers' couches, but never a bed. I told all the women I met about my girlfriend back home, about how she always believed in me and stood by me when no one else did. Which I wasn't wrong about, apparently. But more importantly, I told them no one would ever compare to her."

Hannah laughed, brushing off his attempt to woo her. "I don't believe it for a second, and I think it's cute that you still think I'm your girlfriend."

"You have always had my heart, Banana, whether we're together or not. You always will. I know I can't really say anything to make you believe me, but I am asking you to try. I am sorry I put you through hell. I didn't think about the effect my leaving would have—"

Hannah slapped her hand down on the pavement. "Right! That's the whole thing, right? You didn't think! If I always stood by you and believed in you and blah, blah, blah—why on Earth would you think it wouldn't be hell for me? Why couldn't you just talk to me?"

Jimmy paused to take another pull from the cigarette. "That's a good point, and you're right. I didn't think about you. I was selfish. I felt like I wasn't worth anything to anyone and, with me gone, I figured you'd realize I wasn't worth anything to you, either. I knew you'd move on, graduate, and do cool things… you'd find someone who could give you the life you deserve. I didn't want to call and hear your voice because I knew I'd just ruin you. I'd ruin any chance you'd have for all of that."

Hannah quickly tapped the center of her chest with her fingertips. "There's nothing left of me to ruin, Jimmy! I am nothing, and I've got nothing left! Everyone is gone—you, my friends. I'm still working the same shitty retail job I've worked for the last five years."

There was a long pause in their conversation as Hannah held back sobs. Laying bear the emptiness of her life had exhausted her defenses, allowing every emotion she had tried to hold in to spill out from her.

Jimmy broke the silence first. "Come here then."

Hannah shook her head in bewilderment. "What are you talking about?"

"Come here. To Riverside Springs," he repeated.

"Jimmy, I can't just—"

"Why not?" he asked. "You just said you have nothing left there. Why stay?"

"My parents, though, I—"

"They'll be fine without you, Hannah. It's not like you'd never see them again," Jimmy interjected.

She closed her eyes and sighed, feeling more annoyed than anything. "Jimmy, I'm not like you. I can't just get up and leave.

Besides—you left me, remember? Why should I come there? Why should I be with you?"

"Because I love you. I'm telling you—this place has done something to me. It healed me, and I know it can heal you, too. It can heal us," he told her emphatically.

"That all sounds very romantic, but how can I possibly trust you again?"

Jimmy's voice wavered as he spoke, "I know, and I am sorry for it every day. I think you need this just as much as I do. I think you just need to take a leap and have some faith in me that I mean it."

"If only it were that easy. Jimmy, I am so hurt and so angry—" Hannah paused. "You really want me there? I mean, where would we even stay? What would I do?"

"Yes, I want you to come here. More than anything, I want you here with me. I have a place—an apartment. Well, it's half a house. A duplex. Whatever—it doesn't matter. I have a job waiting tables, but I make good money. Enough to get by. You'll figure out something to do; you're smarter and more resourceful than you give yourself credit for."

Hannah didn't respond for a long while, letting the scenarios of what might happen play out in her mind one by one. She couldn't believe she was giving the idea serious consideration.

I'd be crazy to go. It would never work out, she thought.

Jimmy continued, "When I got here, I was just sleeping on a couch for a couple of weeks but fell in love with this place. I know you would, too."

What do I even want from this? Hannah asked herself. *Is it right to get back together with him? To pick up my life and move states away to be with him?*

Part of her wanted to go and run away from everything that had left her behind. She knew her parents would be a giant hurdle to clear, especially after they watched her deteriorate all summer because of him.

"Banana? Are you still there?" Jimmy asked nervously.

Startled out of her thoughts, she replied, "I'm still here."

"You're thinking about it, aren't you?" he teased.

Hannah could hear that sly, crooked grin in his voice, and she couldn't stop herself from smiling as she pictured it. "I might be."

"Look—I know it's a big decision. I know it's scary. It's, honestly, crazy! But I'm asking you to leap, to find this courage inside yourself that I know is there. Come here to Riverside Springs. Be with me. Let's build a life here," he pleaded.

"What about us, though?" she asked.

"What about us? I love you. I want to be with you, and I know you want to be with me. I know you still love me—I can hear it in your voice. I know you, Banana, it's still there. You can't tell me that what we have could ever really die. Besides—you haven't hung up on me yet," he said with a chuckle.

Hannah found another small stone in the driveway and rolled it between her fingers. "It's not that simple."

"Of course it is. It's always been that simple," he told her.

She thought, *Maybe he's right. Maybe the only thing complicating this is me. Maybe love is that simple. Maybe it is enough.*

Hannah tossed the stone in the air and caught it. "Okay," she said in an instant.

"Okay? Okay, what?"

"Yeah, okay. I'll come," Hannah repeated, smiling genuinely for the first time in months.

W hen the sun rose, Hannah was already gathering her belongings in the middle of the bedroom floor. She had dug out the extra-large duffle bag she had received as a high school graduation gift. It would fit her entire wardrobe without issue. Hannah instantly froze when she heard her parents moving about the house downstairs but delayed talking to them for a little longer. Instead, she picked out her most beloved books to pack while she quietly practiced the speech she would deliver to them.

I guess I can't put it off anymore, she thought, walking down the stairs like a prisoner approaching her fate at the gallows. Hannah was confident that her parents would chain her up in the basement for the rest of her life if it meant she couldn't leave.

She stood on the bottom step, motionless, just staring at them. Her parents sat on the couch in the living room, drinking their coffees and watching the morning news.

Her dad looked over at her, surprised to see her. "What are you doing up so early?" he asked.

Hannah shuffled into the room, biting at her cuticles nervously. "Can I talk to you guys?"

"Sure," her mom said. Hannah noted that she hadn't turned off the television, let alone lower the volume; their attention was still focused on the weatherman rather than her.

"I talked to Jimmy last night," she started.

"What did that asshole want?" her dad asked with a grunt.

Hannah sighed. "He's not an asshole, Dad. He's got a lot going on, you know that." She thought about saying more, trying to explain his illness to them for, what seemed like, the millionth time. She decided that would only make things worse, though.

Her father grunted again and sipped his coffee.

"He's in South Carolina. He set himself up there with a job and an apartment." Hannah went back to chewing on her fingers, looking between them. Her parents remained expressionless, still gazing at the TV around her, so Hannah continued, "I'm going to meet him down there."

Hannah's father shot her a look, one she'd only seen once before: when their dog had run through wet cement on the front walkway years ago. His face turned bright red. "The hell you are!" he boomed.

Hannah's mom slammed her mug on the side table, causing some coffee to splash out of it. "Absolutely not!" she shrieked.

Hannah gulped in some air, searching for the bravery she had suddenly misplaced. "You can't really stop me," Hannah told them defiantly.

"Wanna bet?" her dad asked menacingly as he, too, put his coffee mug down hard on the table.

Hannah flailed her arms open, her palms to the sky, pleading for them to understand how much she needed this. "I'm well over eighteen now. You can't hold me here. Besides—what else am I doing? It might be a mistake, I admit that, but I need to find out if it is or not. I deserve a chance to make a life for myself, to be happy again!"

"You can do all of that here, Hannah!" her mom shouted as she jabbed her finger hard into the couch cushion. "You just have to get your ass up and do something! Stop being so goddamn lazy!"

Those words stung more than Hannah cared to admit. She hadn't been lazy, just depressed. Hannah shook it off, searching for the right words to say. "I know I can build a life here, but that's not what I want. I'm not happy here, as if you hadn't noticed! I just don't see any way that I can be, so I'm going regardless of what you think."

Hannah's parents raised their voices over one another, but Hannah couldn't make out what either one was saying. It was all just noise.

She struggled to raise her voice over theirs, shouting, "I'm leaving in the morning! Early! So maybe don't let this be the last conversation we have!"

Hannah turned her back on them, retreating up the stairs to her bedroom to finish packing.

In her room, Hannah continued organizing her belongings into the duffle bag, a backpack, and a large storage container. She knew her parents wouldn't be happy with her plans, but she didn't anticipate it would get as loud as it did. They had watched their daughter fall into a bottomless pit since graduation, standing still while everyone else moved on without her. The last thing they would have wanted was for Hannah to throw herself back onto the bomb that had destroyed her twice already, but she wouldn't let them keep her and Jimmy apart. She knew somewhere deep within her that the thing between them needed to play itself out, whatever the outcome was.

Once everything was secured into boxes and bags, Hannah called Jimmy. She was apprehensive about whether he would pick up, hoping their call last night hadn't been a fluke. Hannah walked back and forth across her bedroom, bracing for the voicemail to pick up.

After the phone rang several times, a breathless Jimmy answered, "Banana! Hey!" She could hear him transition from the noisy restaurant to the quiet alleyway outside the kitchen.

"Hey, you," she said. "Are you busy?"

"Kind of. I'm at work right now, and it's the lunch rush. I've got, like, maybe two minutes. What's up?" he panted.

"I'll be quick then. I have everything packed, and I'm leaving tomorrow morning. Early. Like, three o'clock. I just talked to my parents," Hannah said quickly.

Jimmy let out a long breath, his lips sputtering. "How did *that* go?"

"Well, they're not happy about it. Let's just leave it at that," Hannah shared.

"And you're sure about this?" Jimmy questioned.

Hannah stopped pacing. "More than sure. I need to do this," she said confidently. She heard Jimmy sigh. "Don't tell me *you've* changed your mind?"

"No!" he shouted. "No! This is great! So, wait—you'll be here tomorrow?"

"Is that okay? I know we just talked about it last night, so if it's too fast, let me know. My navigation says it should take me, like, twelve hours or so. I'd be there late afternoon," Hannah told him.

"That's perfect, actually! I am only working half the day tomorrow, so I'll be out by the time you get here." Jimmy sounded downright giddy. "I can't wait to see you!"

"Me too, but I am a little nervous. It's a long drive," she said, pursing her lips together.

Hannah could hear the heavy kitchen door screech open and a voice telling Jimmy that one of his tables was looking for him. "I have to go, but you'll text or call me along your travels all day tomorrow, right? Starting the second you pull out of your driveway, okay?"

"Sure," Hannah said.

"Cool. I love you, Banana. I have to go—love you," Jimmy said quickly before hanging up.

Hannah carried her things downstairs and out to her car parked on the street, loading everything into the trunk. Her parents didn't say a word to her, or lend a hand to help, as she worked. Hannah left abruptly to put gas in her car so she would be ready to start the journey early the following day.

When she returned, her dad quietly slipped out of the house. He went out to her car to check the air pressure in the tires and to ensure the necessary fluids were full and clean. Hannah smiled tearfully as she watched him work from her bedroom window. Her dad may not have given his blessing, but this was the next best thing; he'd always been a man of action more than words.

Hannah's cell phone alarm went off promptly at 2:50 A.M., but she had been awake for at least an hour by then. She felt too excited for the adventure ahead to get much sleep that night. She dressed in gym shorts and a T-shirt, wanting to be comfortable for the long drive. Hannah made her way downstairs to brew herself a thermos of coffee. Her parents stirred as the smell drifted into their bedroom, prompting them to get up and give her one last hug. They all pretended their fight the day before had never happened, but Hannah hadn't expected anything different.

At 3:02 A.M., Hannah texted Jimmy: *It's a little after 3, and I didn't want to call and wake you, but I'm heading out now.*

He responded to her message right away: *Don't worry. I couldn't sleep. I can't wait to see you, Banana. Get here safe.*

Hannah placed her book of CDs on the passenger seat next to her for easy access, set the address into her GPS mounted to the dashboard, and pulled away from the curb. Images of what she imagined Riverside Springs to be flashed through her mind as she got onto the highway heading south. She had researched the area between fits of sleep the night before, looking wide-eyed at cobbled streets, colorful buildings, palm trees, and roads lined with canopies of Weeping Willows. It seemed quaint and enchanting, almost unreal, like a Hollywood movie set.

Hannah called home every so often to let them know her location and that she was okay. She did the same with Jimmy, who had responded when he could; it had been a busy breakfast crowd of tourists that morning.

As the clock and the mileage gauge ticked on, Hannah wondered what their reunion would be like. Would Jimmy kiss her? Would he hug her? Did she want either of those things? The possibilities made her head ache.

Geez, this is so crazy, she thought as she fought the urge to turn around and drive back home. Her conversation with Jimmy replayed in her mind, and Hannah found the courage inside herself to leap. To keep traveling south. To follow her True North back home.

It was nearly 4:30 P.M. when Hannah pulled into the left-side driveway of a brightly painted light blue stucco duplex in Riverside Springs. She parked behind an older model, dark green Honda Accord with South Carolina plates, wondering whose it was. When she parked her car, Hannah spotted the front door opening, feeling the breath catch in her throat as Jimmy walked out of the house. He looked healthier than he had in a long time. He had put some weight back on and shaved his hair into a buzzcut. He looked happy, too. Genuinely happy. A big, crooked grin spread across his face, the same one that had mesmerized Hannah from that very first day.

Jimmy hopped down the front stairs, walking quickly to the driver's side door. He opened it as she stepped out, standing to meet him face-to-face. Hannah felt her knees buckle under the weight of her body, her heart racing. She had thought about that moment most of the way there, but standing there in front of him, she still felt unsure of how to approach him. Before she could move, Jimmy pulled her tightly into a hug that squeezed the air out of her lungs. She wrapped her arms around his mid-back, overcoming the initial shock of his affection, and squeezed him hard. She breathed deep into the crook of his neck, feeling at home in the unique smokey haze.

At least not everything has changed, she thought.

"I can't believe you're here, Banana," he whispered in her ear.

"You and me both!" she replied with a nervous laugh as those old familiar feelings stirred inside her. Hannah knew this was where she needed to be, feeling so confident in her love for him.

Jimmy pulled away from her, smiling still. They stared at each other for a moment, weirdly feeling like they were meeting again for the first time. Maybe they were. There was no doubt that the time apart had changed them both.

"Is that your car?" she asked, pointing to the green Honda.

Jimmy turned around to look at the car. "Oh, yeah. I just got it a couple of weeks ago. It's not much better than my gray Oldy, but it works." He gently rocked himself from the balls of his feet to his heels and back again. "Well, I guess I should show you inside. We can come back for your stuff later."

Hannah nodded. "Lead the way."

Jimmy gently took her hand, leading her up the small staircase and across the large front porch. She spied two rocking chairs facing the street with a small table and a full ashtray between them. The inside was so clean and modern, which took Hannah by surprise. The living room had an oversized, squishy couch and a television mounted to the top of a brick fireplace. Hannah scanned the walls covered in pictures of Jimmy and friends she had yet to meet, old and battered skateboards, and artwork he had collected on his travels. He showed her the small galley-style kitchen. A door to the left led out to a small patio with a table and chairs set up, which extended to a side yard with a cinderblock outbuilding at the back of the property. Jimmy explained that the washer and dryer were in there, which was only inconvenient when it was raining. "Which, unfortunately, it does often," he told her with a laugh.

Back inside, down the long hall to the left, was a bathroom with a small window of stained glass overlooking the side yard. A small bedroom sat opposite the bathroom door, while a second, larger one was positioned at the very end of the hallway. That was Jimmy's room.

"When I got home from work last night, I spent so much time straightening up. I was afraid to touch anything this morning before I had to head out again," Jimmy told her as he shoved his hands deep into the pockets of his jeans. Hannah felt comfort in knowing he was just as nervous as she was.

She whistled and nodded slowly. "I'm impressed, Jimmy. This place is really nice."

"Thanks. I, um—I do have the small guest room there. I don't know where you would be more comfortable. I didn't want to assume anything," he stammered.

"Oh," Hannah said, a little taken aback. She felt silly for assuming they would share a room and a bed, not even thinking he'd have an extra space for her. She felt the heat rise in her face. "Well, I don't mind. I guess I did assume, but if you would rather have me stay in there—"

"I don't," Jimmy said, looking down at the circle he traced on the floor with his toes. "I don't want you to stay in there." He looked back up at her expectantly, hoping it was okay to want her in his bed again.

She smiled. "Okay, then. I won't."

Jimmy let out the breath he'd been holding in. "I guess we should bring your stuff inside then?"

Hannah followed Jimmy back to the car, moving her bags and boxes inside. They placed everything in the corner of his bedroom, feeling too drained to unpack. Hannah asked if he would mind if she took a short nap to re-energize herself from the long drive. Jimmy pulled back the sheets on his bed as she lay down, then tucked her in, promising to wake her up before dark.

"If you're up for it, I'd like to take you out tonight for dinner. I can show you around a little, too," he suggested.

Hannah closed her eyes as Jimmy kissed the top of her head. "I'd like that," she said.

When she didn't hear the door close, Hannah opened her eyes to see Jimmy lingering in the doorway with a hand on the doorknob. A small smile spread across his lips before diverting his gaze to the floor again and gently closing the door.

Hannah had so much nervous energy pent up inside her that she wasn't sure she would fall asleep. She inhaled deeply, breathing in the scent that lingered on his bedsheets, thinking that none of it felt real just yet. Before she could form another thought, though, she drifted off into a happy dream.

When Hannah awoke about an hour and a half later, the house was eerily quiet. She had to remind herself where she was, feeling disoriented in the new space when she opened her eyes. She walked out of the bedroom and crept down the hall, peering into the open bathroom and then the guest room, but she didn't see Jimmy. Hannah kept moving forward, her bare feet leaving light footprints on the cool hardwood floors. She looked out the back door, then around the kitchen and living room. Jimmy wasn't anywhere in the house. Hannah looked around for a note, but there was none. Panic and fear crept in, the voice in her head telling her that he had abandoned her in this unfamiliar place.

Hannah heard the light strum of a guitar, which sounded like it was coming from outside somewhere. She opened the front door, leaning out onto the porch to look down the length of it. Jimmy sat in one of the chairs with his old, painted acoustic guitar, strumming lightly with a cigarette hanging from his mouth.

"Hey," Hannah said to get his attention.

Jimmy shook, startled. The strings on his guitar squealed as his hand quickly slid down the neck, and the cigarette fell from his mouth. "Geez, Hannah!" he shouted.

"Sorry! I'm sorry!" she apologized. Hannah felt terrible for scaring him but couldn't help giggle at his reaction.

Jimmy's face went tight with annoyance as he bent down to pick up the cigarette and smashed it into the ashtray.

Hannah stopped laughing. "I'm sorry," she whispered again.

Jimmy looked up at her, letting the tension in his face go when their eyes met. "No, it's okay. I'm sorry—you just really scared me. I'm just not used to someone else being here." He motioned to the chair in front of her. "Do you want to sit?"

"Sure," she said quietly. Hannah cautiously eased herself into the rocking chair, looking up and down the quiet side street. The early evening was beautiful—the air had cooled, and the sun was setting, casting a warm glow of oranges and pinks over the town.

"Did you sleep okay?" Jimmy asked, trying to make some neutral conversation after his outburst.

"I think so," Hannah replied with a shrug, her voice still hushed from the tension of the prior moment.

"Are you hungry?"

"Starving!" she gasped. Hannah hadn't realized it, but she was totally famished, having not eaten anything since stopping for lunch at a gas station just before the North Carolina border.

He stood up fast. "Good! Let's go get some food, then!"

"Can I just change first?" Hannah asked, looking down at the T-shirt and shorts she was still wearing.

Jimmy walked past her, and into the front door. "Yeah, of course! I guess I should probably put something else on, too."

Hannah followed him inside and shut the door. She dug through her clothes in the bedroom, trying to decide what to put on. "Where are we going exactly? Like, what should I wear?"

"I thought I'd take you to the restaurant where I work," Jimmy said, coming up behind her. He wrapped his arms around her waist, resting his chin on her shoulder. Hannah tensed as he pressed his body against hers. "I wanted you to see where I work, and I know my friends really wanted to meet you. I talk about you all the time. It's pretty annoying, actually," Jimmy told her, tilting his head to look at her, still resting on her shoulder.

Hannah rolled her eyes, playfully pushing him away. "That doesn't help," she said with a laugh. "Is it a casual place? Fancy?"

"Eh, it's just a little cafe. It's not fancy or anything," Jimmy explained, pulling off his T-shirt and tossing it onto the bed. He then did the same with his jeans.

Hannah watched Jimmy in his blue checkered boxers search for a shirt in the closet, noticing fresh scars and bruises on his body. She knew they were likely from some crazy new tricks he had been practicing on his skateboard.

Jimmy settled on a short-sleeved button-down shirt and a pair of brown Dickies pants. Hannah dug through her bag some more, finding the one nice pair of jeans she owned and a green and white floral camisole. Hannah undressed, noticing Jimmy watching her from the corner of his eye as he buttoned his shirt. Once she had some clean clothes on, she turned to the mirror on the wall and brushed her hair, deciding to wear it down.

From behind her, Jimmy cleared his throat. She met his eyes in the mirror. "You look beautiful," he said simply.

Hannah felt her cheeks flush and her eyes roll unintentionally. "Thanks," she said.

"I mean it, Banana. You really do." Jimmy grinned, but his expression changed quickly to one of regret. "I'm sorry it took me so long to call you."

Hannah opened her mouth to say something, but Jimmy raised a hand to stop her.

"No—let me say this. I need to say this to your face." Jimmy took a couple of steps toward her, grabbing Hannah's hands. "I'm sorry, Hannah. I'm sorry I am so broken that I couldn't do anything but run away. That all I can ever seem to do is run away. I know I hurt you, and I hate myself for that." Jimmy paused to clear his throat, trying to rid himself of the guilt building in it. "I just felt like there was no good choice to make—I was either going to hurt you by leaving or by staying and rotting away, or even coming back home before I was strong enough. I need you to know that I love you, Hannah O'Malley. Everything, and I mean *everything*, kept leading me back to you. I know I don't deserve you, but I am so incredibly grateful that we get to have this right now."

Without thinking, Hannah kissed Jimmy quickly, her hands still in his. She pulled away, embarrassed by her spontaneous affection, unsure if he had hungered for her in the same way. Hannah opened her mouth to apologize, but Jimmy suddenly dropped her hands and cupped her face. His lips surrounded hers as he gently pushed her up against the dresser. Hannah felt the comfortable warmth of his body leaning into hers, each of them moving their mouths with a sense of urgency, unable to deny that their love for each other was still very much alive.

Jimmy pulled away from her and looked down at the floor, worried that he had taken things too far. "I'm sorry—that was too much, too soon."

Hannah placed her hand on his chest. "No, it was fine. Besides—I started it," she said with a smile, trying to lighten the tension.

Jimmy nodded. "Maybe we should just go eat for now."

Hannah and Jimmy chose to walk several blocks to the downtown, where the restaurant was located since the afternoon heat had cooled throughout the early evening hours. To Hannah's surprise, the cafe had been converted from an old white house with a big front porch and classic Southern Colonial features. Outdoor lights were strung up along the walkway and around the covered patio, creating the most enchanting glow. A large Weeping

Willow drooped beautifully out front, both sad and elegant all at once. Hannah fell behind Jimmy and extended her hand to brush its branches as they walked up the front path, letting them dance from finger to finger.

"Jimmy! What's up? I didn't know you were working tonight!" A slim, twenty-something, blonde-haired guy approached them at the porch's top step, giving Jimmy an intricate handshake.

"Not tonight, man. I'm actually taking my lady out tonight," Jimmy replied as he gestured toward Hannah, who had peeked out from behind him.

The stranger's eyes went wide in disbelief. "Oh, shit! Is *this* Hannah?" he asked.

"That's me," she announced, flashing an awkward smile.

The stranger smiled so big that Hannah could count each of his teeth. "Wow! I'm Alan. It's so nice to meet you! Come here," he said, pulling Hannah into a hug when she had only been ready for a handshake. "Jimmy talks about you nonstop, but I wasn't convinced you were actually real! But here you are!"

Hannah laughed uncomfortably, looking from Jimmy to Alan. "I'm not sure if that's a good thing or not!"

"All good, I promise! Well, come on, I'll seat you guys!" Alan gestured them forward. "Did you want to sit out here or inside?"

"Outside would be nice," Hannah told him.

"All right, outside it is." Alan scanned the tables, spotting an open one. "There's a table over there. I'll grab some menus from inside."

Hannah and Jimmy made their way to the last table on the right side of the porch.

"He was nice," Hannah said as she sat at the table. "I didn't expect a hug, though!"

"Alan's a friendly dude. I should have warned you, but he's totally harmless. I know he was really hoping I would bring you by," Jimmy said.

"He's a good friend of yours?" Hannah asked.

Jimmy told her excitedly, "Oh, yeah. He's my best friend here. More like a brother, really. I met him on my second day, I think it was. He played at this open mic night in this coffee shop down the street from here." Jimmy pointed behind him with his thumb. "He's got, like, a country/folky vibe. Anyway—we started talking after his set, and I told him I had just got to town and didn't have a place to stay. Alan offered me his couch that night, and I wound up sleeping there for a while. He helped me get this job here, and he knows my landlord. So that's how I got into that place on a really good deal."

"Wow," Hannah said in surprise. She couldn't think of anyone so generous back home except Jimmy. Hannah had known him to give winter coats to the homeless huddled at the train station and run errands for his elderly neighbor back in Stonebridge.

"Yeah, he's cool people," Jimmy said. "I think you'll like him."

Alan reappeared with menus for them as if on cue. "You probably don't need these. This guy has the whole thing memorized from front to back," he joked, referring to Jimmy.

"That's alright. I like to see my options in writing so I can think on it," she told him.

"More like, so she can change her mind about twenty times before you come back to take our orders," Jimmy quipped.

Hannah looked at him with mock disbelief at the joke he made at her expense, unable to think of a comeback fast enough. Alan just laughed at them as he walked toward another table who had waved him down to pay their check.

Hannah soaked in her surroundings before looking at the menu, too distracted by the beauty around her that night. She turned to look through the window into the main dining room. The inside matched the casual, cozy vibe of the outside. She especially loved the old brick facade along one of the walls and the worn wooden floors. Scanning the dining room, she noticed a small cluster of employees huddled together, looking out the window at her.

"Oh my god," Hannah whispered, turning away from the window.

"What?" Jimmy asked.

Hannah leaned back in her chair. "I think your coworkers are watching us," she hissed, her voice still hushed as if they could hear her from inside the loud dining room.

Jimmy looked around. "What? Where?"

Hannah discreetly pointed toward the window. Jimmy scanned the room inside and laughed loudly when he finally spotted them. He waved at them as Hannah buried her face into her hands, trying to remain unseen. She peeked through her fingers to see them waving back at him.

"C'mon," said Jimmy as he stood up and reached a hand across the table to her.

"What? Where are we going?" Hannah asked nervously.

"I might as well introduce you to them. They'll either all come out here and make a big show of it, or they'll keep staring at us," he laughed. "C'mon, I know you want to just get it over with."

Hannah took Jimmy's hand as he led her inside, her stomach flipping from nerves. She flexed the fingers of her free hand, trying to shake off the anxiety. Hannah was worried about not making a good first impression, knowing it would be important to Jimmy that they all got along. It was important to her, too; these people would inevitably be her new friends.

Jimmy's voice boomed. "Real smooth, guys!"

The group laughed in unison, and then everyone began speaking all at once. Hannah was trying to grab onto one voice, but they all bled together, along with the noise of the crowded dining room.

Jimmy leaned over, his face so close to Hannah's that she could feel his body heat radiating onto her face. He pointed down the line of people, naming them off, "Hannah, this is Matt, Josh, Steph, Mandy, and you met Alan already." Jimmy turned to them all with a big grin. "And this is Hannah. I told you all she was real!"

Hannah raised her hand feebly in a wave. "Hi," she said with a shy smile.

"It's so nice to meet you, Hannah! You're going to love it here," Mandy said as she quickly walked toward a table that had flagged her over.

As she walked by, Hannah noticed how pretty she was, and the sweet smell of her perfume hanging in the air after her. Mandy's straight blonde hair barely brushed the tops of her shoulders, and not a single hair was out of place. Hannah instinctively put a hand on the side of her head, feeling all the strands curled up out of place by the day's humidity. She looked at Steph—she was beautiful, too, with eyes the color of wildflower honey. Hannah suddenly felt self-conscious about her appearance in comparison, questioning why Jimmy still wanted her around if these were his other options.

Jimmy put an arm around her shoulder, feeling Hannah slip away from him and into her mind again. "All right. Well, we're going to sit and eat. In peace, okay?"

"Bye, Hannah," Steph said with a sweet smile.

"Bye, nice to meet you," Hannah replied politely with another small wave.

Once they were seated back at their table, Hannah laughed, sucking in the cool night air to calm her down. "Well, that was a lot," she said.

"I knew it would be. They were all just so excited to meet you," Jimmy told her again.

"Yeah, what did you tell them about me, anyway?" Hannah inquired.

"Just how cool you are. That you're, like, the smartest person I know. Also, that you're the prettiest girl I've ever seen, and gentle, too, but that you've got a hell of a jab—I know, I've been on the receiving end of it," he teased.

"It was, like, one time, and you totally deserved it! You might have another one coming to you," she threatened facetiously. Jimmy laughed at her and took a sip of his water. Hannah's insecurities wormed their way back to the forefront of her mind in the silence. "Steph and Mandy are so pretty," she suggested.

"They're cool chicks. I think you could have another little girl gang with them like you did with Whitney and Katie," he said innocently.

The mention of their names felt like a punch to Hannah's gut. She still felt so angry and hurt over their fight, yet she missed them both fiercely; Hannah had wanted nothing more than a friend to be there with her that summer. By her expression, Jimmy knew he shouldn't have mentioned them. "Sorry," he said quickly. "I didn't even think—"

Hannah brushed it off. "No, it's okay," she replied. Changing the subject, she said, "Well, I guess I should look at this menu if we're ever going to eat."

Hannah opened the menu, skimming her options. Jimmy offered suggestions to help her choose, knowing she always had difficulty deciding. She ultimately settled for the crab cakes with rice and beans, while Jimmy ordered a fried pork chop with collard greens.

They talked over dinner somewhat uneasily at first, still feeling each other out after months of separation, hurt, and healing. They walked a fine line between strangers and lovers. Jimmy had asked Hannah what she had been up to since graduation, but she wasn't sure how honest she should be with him. After some hesitation, she told Jimmy about the well of depression she had fallen into, the sleepless nights and the lack of friends. Hannah watched him drum his fingers against the table and tighten his jaw repeatedly as she told him everything. She knew it was hard for him to hear, but she kept talking, wanting to let him know how his leaving affected every part of her life.

Clearing his throat, Jimmy asked, "What exactly did happen with Whitney and Katie? You guys were the best of friends. I just don't get it."

Hannah frowned as she detailed their fight that day in the cafeteria, from Whitney's meltdown to Katie's indifference. She told him about the uncomfortable moment at their graduation ceremony and how they all chose to go in separate directions. "Something just broke in us, I guess. I haven't been able to feel like they deserve forgiveness yet," she finished.

Jimmy fidgeted with the utensils on the table in front of him. "I am so sorry for that."

"Don't be. It's not your fault," Hannah told him.

After dinner, Hannah and Jimmy strolled deeper into the downtown neighborhood. Hannah felt thankful for the walk, which allowed the food in her belly to digest a little easier. Her eyes darted around the streets, taking in the French-inspired architecture and beautiful botanicals in bloom. As they walked down the cobblestone streets, Jimmy pointed out some of his favorite places: restaurants, bars, and a coffee shop. Most of the places were ones he had played music in, which wasn't surprising to Hannah.

Something shiny caught her eye in the window of a gift shop. She stopped walking suddenly, causing Jimmy to stumble backward at the tug of her hand. She moved closer to the glass and saw the most beautiful journal she thought she'd ever seen: a light turquoise cover with bits of seashells embroidered in an origami crane pattern. Every piece was handmade, from the paper to the binding in white thread and the shells sewn onto the cover. Hannah entered the shop without thinking, or even looking at anything else, and purchased the diary. She had packed two empty notebooks from home but decided she needed something different for the new chapter of her life.

Once they exited the shop, Jimmy pointed out a small mom-and-pop ice cream stand down the street. "You want some ice cream?"

Hannah let out a small groan. "I don't know. I'm so full."

"When have you ever turned down ice cream? Come on—a little mint chocolate chip?" Jimmy taunted.

"That's tempting, but—"

"Fine. We'll just split a cup, then!" he announced. Jimmy walked up to the window to order and introduced Hannah to the woman behind the counter, Rachel. He continued chatting with her as she scooped their ice cream.

She shook Hannah's hand, telling her how nice it was to finally put a face to the name that Jimmy was constantly mentioning.

Who didn't Jimmy tell that I was coming to town? Hannah wondered.

All of these strangers seemed to know so much about her, but she knew nothing about them. It was confusing to Hannah to hear so many good things about herself when she had spent the last few months feeling like nothing more than an afterthought.

It wasn't about you, she had reminded herself.

Once they had walked far enough away, Hannah asked Jimmy more about Rachel, having picked up on her distinct accent. He explained that Rachel and her husband had moved from New York to South Carolina about two years before, bringing their ice cream business with them. Jimmy had connected with them because they were northeast transplants, a familiar voice in a sea of southern drawls.

"That, and their ice cream is amazing," he told her.

They took their dessert to a nearby pocket park, finding an empty bench to sit on as they ate. Hannah turned the conversation to Jimmy, asking for more stories about his travels. Jimmy's voice filled with enthusiasm as he recounted his journey for Hannah, primarily focusing on the dozens of strangers he met along the way. Hannah listened to his stories, enthralled by the cast of characters. Their kindness rejuvenated her faith in humanity.

Once their ice cream cup was empty, Hannah and Jimmy walked lazily back to the house. Jimmy took out a cigarette to enjoy on the walk home, holding it in his left hand while holding tight to Hannah's hand in his right.

She watched him from the corner of her eye, taking in every detail of his face: the way his lips circled the cigarette filter, the sharp angles of his jaw, and the high arches of his eyebrows. Hannah felt the recognizable hollow ache in her chest, but something about it was different then. She felt a certain sadness for all the time they had missed out on that summer, and the depth of how much she had missed him seemed to hit her out of nowhere. She missed the simple moments the most, just walking hand-in-hand with him like they were.

Hannah gently laid her head on his shoulder as they slowly strolled down the sidewalk, feeling Jimmy kiss the top of her head. She looked up to see him looking at her with nothing but love in his eyes for her. Without another word, they continued to walk back to their home.

Continued

Hannah held the journal gently in her hands. Time had not been kind to its delicate cover and hand-sewn binding. She reminisced about seeing it in that shop on her first night in Riverside Springs, how she'd fallen in love with the way the streetlights bounced off the iridescent pieces of shell on its cover. Few of those shells remained, having slipped off the delicate thread over time.

Hannah ran her fingers over the napkin she had taped onto the page. "Magnolia Scoops" was printed in a funky font at the bottom. There were streaks of chocolate on the napkin from where the chocolate chips in their ice cream had melted on their lips. Above it was the receipt from their dinner at the Sweet Grass Grill, where they had eaten dinner that night. The paper had become worn, and the ink faded, but she could still make out their orders and Alan's name as their server in the top right corner. She wondered what had become of Alan, and if he and Jimmy had remained close friends in the years since then. She hoped they had, remembering just how tight their bond was.

Hannah climbed down from the attic and grabbed her car keys hanging next to the front door. She drove to the fish market in town, feeling a sudden hankering for crab cakes.

Continued

W hen they returned to the house, Hannah walked back to the bedroom to change out of her jeans, which were feeling way too tight around her midsection after all that food. She dug through her bags for a pair of sweatpants and a T-shirt, making a mental note to unpack in the morning; she felt frustrated not being able to locate her things quickly.

Once Hannah had found what she was looking for, she peeled off her clothes, bending down low to squeeze her feet from the tight pant legs. In the next moment, Jimmy shuffled into the room and delicately brushed the tops of her shoulders with his fingertips, tracing a line back down her arms. Jimmy tenderly kissed the curve of her neck as Hannah closed her eyes at the sensation. When he pulled away, she turned around to face him.

"You're so beautiful, Banana," he whispered, taking her in as she stood in her bra and underwear.

Hannah snorted a laugh. "Please," she said with a roll of her eyes. "Not as beautiful as all those girls you work with."

Jimmy shook his head. "What girls? I only saw you tonight. I only ever see you."

She laughed again. "Right. You've got game, Jimmy, I'll give you that." She turned away to start getting dressed in her comfortable clothes.

Jimmy looked at her confused, wondering where the forward and affectionate Hannah had gone. With a hint of annoyance in his voice, Jimmy crossed his arms. "Dammit, Hannah, it's the truth! When are you going to get over it? When are you just going to accept how I feel about you?"

She froze, caught off-guard by his attitude shift. Hannah had always struggled to feel good enough for anyone, not just Jimmy. Friends and family, too. She knew her insecurities had the power to ruin the moment, but she couldn't help herself, grasping for the affirmation she needed to quiet the spiteful voice in her mind. "So you really never hooked up with anyone all this time?"

"I really didn't," Jimmy assured her. "I'm not Manny. I wouldn't do something like that to you."

Hannah kept poking at the issue. "Yeah, but it's not like we were really still a thing."

Jimmy ran his hands over his short stubble of hair, sighing heavily. "We were still a thing to me, but I am sorry I made you feel otherwise. I have only wanted you, okay? I don't know why you can't see what I see."

Hannah only shrugged in response as a sense of shame came over her. Maybe Jimmy was right. Perhaps her relationship with Manny had scarred her more deeply than she realized. Or it was the loss of so many friendships in the last couple of years that had taken its toll. Maybe it was the sum of all the parts. Regardless, Hannah knew that Jimmy had always told her, always shown her, how special she was to him. She wished she could fix that broken part of her, fearing it would inevitably push him away.

Jimmy promptly stepped closer, running his fingers up and down her arms again as he stared intensely into her eyes. When he moved his hands upward again, he traced along her collarbone, both of his hands meeting at the notch in the middle. Jimmy brushed his fingers down her sternum, between her breasts, and then up and out over the tops of them , then back down her sides. Hannah shivered.

She reached for the top button of his shirt, undid it, and continued down the line. Once his shirt was open, Hannah placed her hands on his bare chest, moving them to his shoulders and down his arms so that his shirt fell freely to the floor. Hannah reached down to undo his belt, struggling to release it. They laughed nervously as Jimmy took over the task, then unbuttoned his pants and let them fall to the floor.

He took her hand, leading her to the bed. In the next minute, Hannah lay stiffly in the middle as Jimmy hovered over her, only letting some of his weight rest on her. Hannah lifted her face to his and kissed him deeply, just as she had earlier in the night, as the hunger for his love grew more intense. Jimmy released his mouth from hers and began kissing her neck, her chest, and her belly. He kissed her up and down, taking his time to remember every curve of her body, every dimple on her stomach. Hannah closed her eyes, taking small gasps of breath with each touch of his lips on her skin.

When Jimmy's face reappeared in front of Hannah's, their mouths met again with more urgency, while the rest of their clothes came off without much effort. Hannah and Jimmy lay entwined so tightly, afraid they might lose each other again if they let go even a little. They fought the intense hunger of their needs, taking their time as if meeting like that for the first time. Their hands explored one another, re-learning the spots that felt the best and the ones that tickled too much.

Midnight found Hannah and Jimmy lying bare together on top of the bed sheets, a light sheen of sweat covering their skin. Before she drifted off to sleep, Hannah remembered what she used to daydream about when they would house-sit for his parents. There it was, all around her, the realization that they were in their own place at the beginning of their new life together.

It doesn't get any sweeter than this, she thought in the bleary haze of exhaustion. *Maybe dreams really do come true.*

The two were soon fast asleep, holding firmly to one another still, afraid to let go even in their dreams.

Hannah awoke early the following day to the sounds of the neighborhood coming to life outside the open bedroom window. Jimmy was still asleep, with his arm wrapped around her waist. Hannah delicately moved under its weight, careful not to wake him. She found the T-shirt and sweatpants she had picked out the night before and put them on for the time being. She quietly went down the hallway and into the kitchen to make coffee.

"If only I knew where to find the coffee. Or coffee cups," Hannah whispered, thrumming her fingers against the counter.

She opened all the cabinets and drawers, eventually finding what she was looking for. Hannah brewed a whole pot so there would be plenty left for Jimmy when he eventually woke up, assuming he still drank about a gallon of coffee a day.

Hannah found her new journal on the kitchen counter in the shopping bag where she had left it the night before and then spotted a pen that had been left on the side table in the living room. With her mug of coffee, pen, and journal in hand, she walked out onto the front porch. Hannah stopped on the threshold, closing her eyes and taking a deep breath of the morning air. She had always loved the early morning quiet, being the first to greet the day.

She sat in the chair at the furthest end of the porch, with her legs tucked under her, leaning heavily on its arm. Hannah sat there momentarily, sipping her coffee and looking up and down the quiet street. She wondered about the neighbors, the kind of people they were, imagining them moving about in their own spaces. Many of the houses were brightly colored duplexes like Jimmy's. Her eyes were drawn to a pink one diagonally across the street as she made up some fictitious story about who lived there. She was sure Jimmy had already chatted with all of his neighbors for hours, privy to their deepest secrets.

Eventually, she opened the journal and detailed her journey from New Jersey to South Carolina. She wrote about seeing Jimmy for the first time in months, their dinner date that night, and all that followed. Hannah's hand ached as she finally finished, having filled several pages. She made a mental note to look for some tape later to add items she managed to sneak into her bag during their night out.

The front door suddenly opened, and Jimmy walked out onto the porch. He held an oversized coffee cup in one hand while the other clutched a pack of American Spirits with a lighter tucked into its wrapper. Jimmy hadn't bothered getting dressed, simply walking out in his boxers. Hannah could see his muscles visibly relax when he saw her sitting there.

She watched him stride toward the empty rocking chair and giggled. "'Morning," she said. "I think you're missing something."

Jimmy squinted his eyes at her. "Huh?" he asked, his voice still groggy from sleep.

"Pants, maybe?" Hannah plucked at the fabric of her sweatpants.

"Oh," Jimmy said, looking down at his half-naked body. "Nothing my neighbors haven't seen before." He lit a cigarette. "I'm not gonna lie, but I was a little nervous when I woke up and you weren't there. I thought maybe you had changed your mind after last night."

Hannah shook her head adamantly. "Nope! I'm still here. Why would that have changed my mind, anyway?"

Jimmy shrugged, the corners of his mouth turning up slightly. "I see you still sit like a pretzel," he added.

"And I see you upgraded to an even bigger coffee cup," she joked. "But I am sorry I scared you, though. I didn't want to wake you, so I figured I'd be safe out here."

Jimmy gestured toward the journal resting on the arm of her chair. "Did you have a chance to write? Do you need more time?"

"I did, yeah. I had plenty of time—got up a while ago."

"I hope you said all good things about me," he suggested.

Hannah winked. "Of course."

"Should probably put an X-rated label on that thing then," Jimmy joked.

Hannah laughed, choking on the coffee in her throat. She noticed Jimmy watching her, and she couldn't help but think how easy it all still felt with him despite the months apart and the what-ifs in between. The previous night had been proof that they could pick up right where they had left off, that they were choosing to leap together, and that they both wanted it equally.

Hannah's smile slowly faded. "Jimmy? Can I ask you something?"

"Anything," he replied.

"Why did you leave? I mean, I know you had a breakdown or whatever—I'm not sure what to call it. But—why did you leave?"

Jimmy contemplated her question. "Honestly? I've asked myself the same thing so many times, and the answer seems to always change. I'm not entirely sure," he confessed. "I felt... stuck, maybe? I just didn't feel right anymore—in the city or at home.

They both felt like clothes I had outgrown. It was like I was some monster that kept growing while my clothes got tighter and tighter. I was suffocating in this tightness! I had to leave just to breathe, or I was afraid I was going to die there. I just wasn't ready for that. Not yet." Hannah watched his jaw clench as he got lost in the past. "I was feeling more and more pressure from my dad to conform to what he wanted for me. He said so much fucked up shit to me, Banana. I can't even tell you. Then my mom was up my ass all the time, too. I just needed space from all the noise. From hearing how I was messing up not just my life, but yours, too."

Hannah blinked hard. "What?"

"Yeah, how I couldn't be the man you need me to be if I was just going to play around in these 'stupid, dead-end jobs' for the rest of my life."

"Your dad said that?"

He looked at her with a frown. "I woke up one day and knew I needed to escape or accept my fate. Just crawl up and die."

Hannah got up and padded over to where Jimmy sat, lowering herself into his lap. He leaned back in his chair, putting the mug of coffee down on the table next to them. He wrapped his arms around her waist as Hannah hugged him into her chest. They sat like that for a while, not saying anything. There was nothing either of them could say to fix it; they just had to find a way forward.

After some time, Jimmy asked, "What would you like to do today?"

"I don't know," replied Hannah.

"Well, I don't have work today. I could show you around some more, but I probably should hit the grocery store first. The fridge is looking a little bare."

"Sure, okay," Hannah said. "I do want to unpack this morning, and I *really* need a shower."

Jimmy lifted her arm and stuck his face in her armpit, inhaling deeply. He mockingly coughed in disgust, telling her, "You sure do!"

"Shut up, you jerk," she said playfully, standing up to return inside.

Jimmy stood up quickly, scooping Hannah off her feet and throwing her over his shoulder. Hannah screamed and laughed, kicking at him to put her down, but he refused.

"C'mon, smelly. Time for that shower!" he shouted, patting her bottom. Jimmy carried Hannah back into the house, her legs still kicking behind them.

At the checkout in the local Publix, Jimmy argued with Hannah about who would pay for the groceries. Hannah didn't want Jimmy to feel like he had to impress or take care of her, so she insisted on paying. She reminded him they were in it together, making their way forward as a team. Jimmy eventually relented, but Hannah felt the energy change with his short, serious responses to her attempts at conversation. When they returned to the house, Jimmy seemed more relaxed again.

He's so hot and cold, Hannah thought.

"You hungry?" he asked.

"Yeah, sure," she answered meekly, uncertain of his mood.

Jimmy glanced at her, seeing the strain on her face. "Everything okay?"

With a shrug, she admitted, "I don't know. I just felt like I made you mad back there. At the store."

"I'm sorry. I guess our conversation this morning just got in my head, remembering all that. I haven't thought about it all for a while, and then I was standing in the checkout line replaying how I would never be enough for you. It just got in my head, is all," Jimmy told her. "I guess I still feel like I don't deserve this…" His voice trailed off as he busied himself with making toast.

"If it's too much, I can take the other bedroom or something—"

"No. No, it's fine. I want you next to me," Jimmy insisted.

"Are you sure? It's not a big deal," Hannah said, trying to be reassuring.

"Hannah—I said it was fine," Jimmy told her with an edge back in his voice. He took a deep breath, steadying himself. "It's fine. I feel so much better waking up during the night, and you're lying there next to me."

"Okay," she replied quietly.

Hannah occupied herself by scrambling eggs and cutting open an avocado. Jimmy made another pot of coffee, which made Hannah smile; she found comfort in the fact that he was still as addicted to caffeine as ever. The two of them worked side-by-side in tense silence until the plates were complete.

"Do you want to eat outside?" Hannah asked. "It's such a pretty morning."

"Sure," Jimmy said flatly.

Hannah carried their plates out to the patio while Jimmy handled their coffees. Sitting across from one another, Hannah could feel Jimmy's eyes on her, but she fought the urge to meet them. This was nothing new for her, the variability of his moods on any given day. She was one of the few people who could handle him like this, who understood. Hannah knew she had to give him time to come back around again.

After she'd nearly eaten most of her plate, Jimmy finally spoke again, "I was thinking maybe we could go down to the park today. Just hang out for a little bit?"

"Sure," Hannah said.

"It's nice there—right on the water. We can walk around or set up a blanket in the grass or something," he suggested. "Maybe I'll bring my skateboard and ride around."

"Okay. That sounds nice. I'll bring a book or something."

Back inside, Hannah packed a small tote bag with a book and her journal while Jimmy grabbed an extra blanket and his skateboard. They walked a few blocks down to the park, talking about the neighborhood.

Jimmy led her down a path in the park lined with shrubs and an expansive umbrella of tree cover the whole way down. Hannah marveled at the marbled pattern of shadows along the concrete as they walked, feeling Jimmy's eyes on her again. He reached for Hannah's hand and squeezed it, giving her that usual half-smile. It was his unspoken apology. She smiled back, squeezing his hand, too, in unvoiced forgiveness.

"I love watching you out in the world," he said, carefully nudging her with his elbow.

Hannah chuckled. "What does that mean?"

"It's just fun to watch you take things in. You see the beauty in things I haven't noticed for a while."

Hannah still felt uncomfortable with his compliments after all the years together. "It's just things like this," she motioned toward the ground, "that makes me wish I were a better artist."

"You were always pretty good with a camera," Jimmy told her.

Hannah shrugged, never feeling very talented, not like some of her friends back home. "Eh, I don't know about that. I didn't bring it today, anyway," she said.

Jimmy gave a silly, exaggerated gasp. "What? You don't have your camera?"

"I just didn't think to bring it!"

Jimmy squeezed her hand again. "Well, we'll have to come back another day so you can do your thing. We'll have lots of time for that."

They found a patch of grass under some trees near the main promenade that ran alongside the bay. A few hundred feet away, a long pier jutted out over it. Casual fisherman stood along the rails with their lines in the water. Jimmy lay down on his back with his knees tented and threw his arms over his head before closing his eyes. Hannah pulled the book from her bag and lay on her stomach, her elbows propped up underneath her.

A few minutes later, she heard Jimmy's soft snores. She smiled, happy that a sense of peace had taken over him. She was always amazed at his ability to sleep with so much caffeine running through his veins, or how he could be in such a bad mood but still find a way to quiet his mind enough for rest.

"Jimmy? Hannah?" a man's voice called out.

Hannah looked down at Jimmy, who was still sleeping. She looked around to see where the voice was coming from and noticed a tall man waving at them. He was walking in the sun's path, causing her to squint to make out his face.

"Hey!" he called out again.

Hannah softly nudged Jimmy on the shoulder to wake him. His eyes shot open with a sharp inhale. "What happened?"

Hannah pointed toward their approaching visitor as Jimmy shielded his eyes for a better look. "Alan?"

"What's up, guys?" Alan asked as he sat at the edge of their blanket. He and Jimmy performed their usual handshake.

"Nothing really," Jimmy told him. "We just thought we'd hang out down here this morning."

"Cool, yeah, it's nice today. I see you brought your board," Alan nodded toward Jimmy's skateboard, lying in the grass beside him. "Matt, Josh, and Sven were going to meet me down here. You down?"

"Hell yeah, man!" Jimmy turned to Hannah and asked, "Do you mind if we ride a little?"

"No, go ahead," she told him, feeling a little relieved to have some quiet time to catch up on some reading.

"I think Sven was bringing his girlfriend down, too. And Josh said Mandy might come," Alan told Hannah.

So much for that, she thought.

"Okay, cool," she said to Alan with as much cheer as she could gather. Hannah worried about conversing with those girls while Jimmy was off with the guys. She wanted to make new friends, but being the girlfriend sitting alone with a book would be much easier.

Alan and Jimmy talked on the blanket about work. Hannah returned to reading, but Alan kept interrupting to include her in their conversation. She had maybe read two sentences by the time the others showed up. Mandy and Sven's girlfriend, Ali, joined Hannah on the blanket. Ali was a petite girl with short, pin-straight black hair and contrasting blue eyes. Hannah couldn't help but think the two girls looked nearly identical but with opposite coloring.

The conversation was initially uneasy, with Hannah feeling like the third wheel to their already established friendship. Hannah soon found herself loosening up as she imagined how Jimmy would behave if their roles were reversed. She learned that both Mandy and Ali were avid readers and loved the book Hannah was working through. She begged them not to spoil it for her, promising they could talk about it once she finished.

The three of them watched as the guys rode up and down the busy walkway, doing tricks off the stairs and railings of the water fountain in the main square area. Mandy told Hannah that she used to skate with them until she broke her ankle badly about a year ago; she had been too afraid to do anything more than just coast down the street since then.

Hannah thought about all the falls Jimmy had taken over the years and the many instances of road rash she had helped clean and bandage. She had lost count of how many times he'd smacked his head on the pavement, and the times she'd begged him to go to the emergency room. Hannah was thankful that Jimmy was playing it safe, opting for easier tricks and jumps, even if she knew it was only because she was there watching.

The group hung out until late afternoon, when everyone's stomachs started to growl with hunger. As everyone assembled around the blanket, the conversation turned to what they were all doing the rest of the day. Somehow, it morphed into a plan to meet at Jimmy and Hannah's for a barbecue to welcome her to town.

As they all split off in different directions, Jimmy turned to yell back to them, "Hey! Spread the word!"

A couple of them responded with a thumbs-up.

Hannah's voice rose anxiously, "I know we just went shopping, but we don't really have enough to make for them, especially if they're bringing more people!"

"It'll be fine," Jimmy said plainly.

"But—"

"Just trust me," he interrupted. "It'll be fine. Things are a lot different here."

Once they returned home, Jimmy moved swiftly through the kitchen, gathering paper supplies into a pile on the kitchen counter. When he went outside to check the gas levels in the grill, Hannah took some ground beef out of the freezer for burgers and some stuff for them to snack on. She asked Jimmy if he needed her to do anything else while he hopped in the shower to clean off the sweat and grime of the morning.

"Can you run to the corner store and pick up some beer?" he asked.

"Sure! What corner store, though? I don't think I've seen one around."

Jimmy yelled from the bathroom, "Make a right off the porch and go down a block. It's called Earl's. Just get whatever is cheap!"

Hannah walked down the street, taking her time to revel in her new surroundings. She passed a few yards with people outside enjoying their porches, hiding from the midday sun. Everyone she passed waved at her with a smile and commented on the weather. Hannah strangely felt more comfortable there than she ever had at home. It felt like her first semester at SHU, where no one knew her, and she could reinvent herself to be whoever she wanted.

Upon entering the store, she was greeted by an older gentleman with a thick drawl. "Hello there, young lady," he said with a tilt of the grungy ball cap he wore.

"Hi," replied Hannah, finding the refrigerators. She grabbed two cases of Coors Light, wondering if it was enough.

It's all I can carry, so it will have to do for now, she thought.

At the counter, she hoisted the two cases up to be scanned. "You new in town? I don't think I've seen ya 'round," the old man said. Hannah noticed his skin was deeply wrinkled, likely from all the sun he had taken in over the years.

"Oh, yeah. I just got into town yesterday—moved in just down the street."

"Is that so? Where 'bouts?" he asked.

Hannah felt slightly on edge with all the questions, but the older man's smile relaxed her. Besides, he looked too old, and seemed too nice, to break into their home during the night with murderous intentions.

Things are different here, she reminded herself.

"Campbell Street. It's my boyfriend's place, actually," she offered.

He thought for a moment. "You wouldn't happen to be Hannah, would ya?"

Of course, he knows me, too, she thought.

"That's me," she said with a polite smile.

"That boy, Jimmy, is always goin' on 'bout ya." He laughed and wiped some sweat from his brow. "He thinks you are something else, let me tell ya. He's a good boy, though. You take good care of him now."

"I will," she promised the old man, handing him cash for the beer.

Before she left, he reached out to shake her hand. "Well, it's been a pleasure to meet you, Miss Hannah. My name is Earl, by the way. Come down anytime you need anythin.'"

"Okay, I'll do that. Thank you," Hannah replied.

She walked back up the street with a case of beer in each hand. When she got within a couple of houses of theirs, she saw Jimmy jogging barefoot down the sidewalk in her direction. He had put on a pair of tan pants and a gray T-shirt with the name of a local band on the front. Jimmy grabbed the cases out of her hands to carry them the rest of the way.

"Is that okay?" she asked, pointing to the beer. "I didn't know what everyone would like."

Jimmy grinned. "It's beer, right? Trust me, it's not going to matter."

"Alright then," she said. "Oh, I got to meet Earl. I want to adopt him as my grandpa. He was so sweet!"

"Yeah, he reminds me of my Pop, my mom's dad," Jimmy told her. "Sometimes I walk down there just to talk to him."

Within the hour, people started to appear through the front gate leading to the yard. Sven and Ali arrived first with a barbecue grill in the bed of his pickup truck. Jimmy helped him move it into the yard while Ali wheeled in a large cooler packed with ribs. Hannah learned that Sven was a chef at the restaurant, which meant that he usually assumed cooking duties at every party.

"Not that he minds," Ali told her.

Alan arrived next with a large batch of coleslaw and a case of beer. Then Matt and Josh showed up with Mandy and their roommates, Tom and Ben. Hannah saw Mandy and Josh give each other a quick kiss, surprised to learn that they were an item. Steph came with a couple of her girlfriends. More people arrived that Hannah hadn't met; Jimmy knew most of them from the skate park, bars, and bands he had gotten to know since crash-landing into the town. Everyone who came brought something: beer, mixers, snacks, sides, meat to barbecue, and even chairs and tables. Both grills constantly rotated various meats and vegetables, churning out a random spread of food that covered the patio table outside and the kitchen counters inside. People, too, were spread everywhere throughout the house, the yard, and the front porch.

Hannah looked around at the strange faces surrounding her, feeling surprisingly calm. She scanned the crowd for Jimmy, realizing she hadn't seen him for a while. She spotted him with a group of guys by the grills with a beer in his hand. He had been watching her, ready to come to her rescue if needed.

Their eyes met as Jimmy raised his eyebrows in question. "You okay?" he mouthed to her.

Hannah nodded slightly.

The party continued well into the night. Some people left, while others came with even more food and drinks. At some point, a set of outdoor string lights woven into the fence turned on. Someone had brought tiki torches, which had been lit for the warm glow and to keep the mosquitoes at bay.

Jimmy grabbed his acoustic guitar while another unknown face with long dreadlocks appeared with a guitar he had retrieved from a car parked out front. Matt grabbed an empty bucket from the outbuilding behind the house. He flipped it upside down, testing the sound with a wooden spoon he had pilfered from the kitchen. The three of them started an impromptu jam session, causing the chatter to die down as people gathered around them to listen. Some swayed in time with the rhythm and sang along, while others simply stood there just listening.

Alan wandered over to Hannah, who had been sitting by herself in a rickety lawn chair. "Howdy," he said in greeting.

Hannah looked up to see him sitting down in the empty chair beside her. "Oh, hey," she said with a polite smile.

"Heck of a two days, huh?" he asked.

"Yeah, it's been pretty hectic," she laughed. "But it's been good. It's a good hectic."

"Glad to hear it. You'll learn to love it here. Everyone who comes here does, you'll see. It's already too late to get out, though, if you were thinking about it," Alan jokingly warned her.

Hannah laughed again. "You must be a local then."

Alan pursed his lips in disappointment. "Ooh, that is incorrect. I was born and raised in Louisiana. Guess I don't have much of an accent these days." He looked her in the eyes, pointed sternly at her, and said, "That's why I'm warning you—I got trapped here, too." He cracked up at his own joke, unable to maintain a serious front.

"So why'd you leave?" Hannah asked.

"Oh, ya know." He exhaled deeply and flipped his hands front of him. "It's the story you've heard a million times, I'm sure. I was just a small-town kid with big dreams, and I wanted out of Louisiana. I came here on a whim and, honestly, just fell in love with it. The people, the music culture, all of it. A lot of us here tonight came that way, you know, not just Jimmy and me. But—look at me! I wait tables and play in coffee shops for pennies. Some big dreams, huh?"

Hannah shook her head. "No, don't say that. I think it's great. As long as you're happy, right?"

Alan thought about it for a moment, eventually nodding his head. "Yeah, I guess so. Money is tight sometimes—hell, all of the time—but who here could say they live comfortably? Right? But, yeah, I am happy. I have a job that pays the bills, at least, and lets me do the other things I love to do."

"That's what should matter then," Hannah told him. A silence fell between them, but it felt comfortable instead of awkward for two people who didn't know one another. "Hey—" Hannah said, changing the subject. "I just wanted to say—Jimmy told me what you did for him when you guys met. Thanks for looking out for him and helping him out so much. He told me he considers you to be like a brother."

"Eh, it was nothing," Alan waved her off. "Someone did it for me when I came to town. I was just repaying the favor."

"Still," Hannah insisted. "It was really nice of you. I know he was kind of in rough shape when he got here, and I know it meant a lot to him."

"Well, anyone who is traveling around the country for shits and giggles on public transport is bound to be a little worn out." The look on Alan's face told her that he didn't understand what she was saying, that Jimmy hadn't told him about his breakdown or about all that had followed.

Hannah politely smiled at him. She didn't know what else to say, not wanting to be the one to tell Jimmy's secrets to someone he supposedly considered his best friend.

Alan exhaled deeply and said, "Well, I am going to go wander over to the food and see what else I can pack into my stomach." He stood up from the chair, but before leaving, he told Hannah, "I'm glad you're here, Hannah. The way Jimmy talks about you—there's just been a change in him since you decided to come down here. It's nice to see it. Anyway, I'll see you around."

Hannah watched him leave, letting what he had said sink in. She looked around at the scene from her seat, reminiscing about all the get-togethers *The Inkwell* staff used to have in Chris's basement. To Hannah, they felt more like a lifetime away rather than just a few months in the past. The new group of friends and acquaintances with her that night was an eclectic mix, just like their college friends had been. She took in the heavily tattooed and pierced bodies, the wildly dyed hair, and the prissy pretty girls.

She leaned back in her chair and looked at the clear night sky. She noticed how the stars seemed to shine so much brighter there than in New Jersey, remembering how Jimmy had told her once that he wished he could be in a place like that. A sense of peace spread in her heart, and she was happy that Jimmy had finally found that place for himself.

Hannah contemplated the changes that had happened in her life over just a few short days, still unable to believe she was sitting in that yard in Riverside Springs. A week ago, she could barely get out of bed, coasting through life with no idea what to do next. But, there she was, states away from that version of herself. Hannah felt that deep sense of belonging she hadn't felt since those newspaper days. The people before her had all acted like they'd known her forever. Probably because it felt like they did with how often Jimmy had talked about her. Things felt easy, like her heart could finally rest for a while.

Continued

A somberness overtook Hannah, who had not felt that warmth and connection for a while. She regretfully took those people and memories from SHU and South Carolina for granted back then, thinking they would always be a part of her life. Instead, Hannah found herself in the middle of her thirties with a splintered group of acquaintances. She thought how sad it made her that the only person she felt like she could be her real self around was Jake.

Growing into adulthood had been hard. People often diverged from the same path as Hannah, heading out on different journeys of travel, careers, marriage, and kids. Those who got to keep a core group of friends had something so rare and extraordinary. She yearned for that, wanting to go back and change how things had ended up.

She was still the same introverted person she had always been: afraid to trust and let herself be seen. Hannah had become even more of an expert in curating the best masks for any situation so she would fit into the moment simply. She could be who she needed to be more quickly than she could just be herself. Not that she even knew who that was anymore. Not like she once had, anyway, like on those nights in their yard on Campbell Street with an ever-growing and ever-changing group of friends. Some people fell off from them, their lives having branched off their path to seek a new adventure elsewhere. Others, though, stayed and became the chosen family that Hannah and Jimmy desperately needed at that time in their lives.

Hannah longed to be wrapped up in the warmth of belonging again, and the love only friends could give.

By late November, a cool Autumn air had moved into Riverside Springs, signaling the start of the holiday season. Hannah and Jimmy loved to walk the streets downtown, with wreaths already dressing the lampposts and white Christmas lights twinkling in the palm trees. They would stop at an empty bench overlooking the water on the pier, and Jimmy would wrap his arms around Hannah as she leaned back against him. She loved to close her eyes and imagine floating on the bay's calm water, its soft edges supporting all of her and leaving little spinning about in her mind. Moments like that with Jimmy were her greatest happiness, just being still in his arms without a worry about anything else.

Hannah had called her parents at the beginning of November to let them know she wouldn't be coming home for Thanksgiving or Christmas. The gift shop where she worked, the same one where she had bought her journal on that first night, was getting busy with holiday shoppers. She told them she couldn't take the time off, but the truth was that she also couldn't budget for the airfare or the gas to get home. To say her parents were angry was an understatement; Hannah's dad had always been deeply rooted in holiday tradition, and not having her home devastated him. If she had to guess, though, her dad was probably still more upset that

Hannah had left home to be with a boy that he didn't think was good enough for his daughter.

It's not like Hannah and Jimmy went entirely without, though. Every month, they scraped their pennies together, able to pay their bills and still have adventures with their friends. It was just that their life together was more prosperous than their pockets ever would be. To them, that was all that really mattered in the end, anyway.

Most of their friends were in the same situation, being far away from their families, low on funds, and nowhere to go for the holidays. Sven and Ali hosted the group at their house for a cookout with a mishmash of side dishes and desserts, which they had done the last couple of years. Sven had been up in the early morning hours to smoke a turkey, a skill he had mastered after moving to South Carolina from Sweden seven years prior.

They gathered around a couple folding tables in the yard under blinking rainbow-colored Christmas lights strung between the gutters and an old tree. Sitting down to dinner, they had toasted loudly: "To friends like these!"

Hannah watched Jimmy from across the table talking to Steph about something work-related, feeling something was off with him. He smiled, laughed, and responded at all the correct times, but his eyes seemed to be a million miles from that conversation. Jimmy eventually turned back, meeting Hannah's eyes before focusing on his food again. She saw that familiar emptiness in them—a warning sign.

On the walk home, Hannah held Jimmy's arm to help steady him. He had partied harder than he had in a long time, but she suspected he was trying to hide from something rather than celebrate.

"Are you okay?" Hannah asked. "You seemed a little distant tonight."

Jimmy didn't answer right away, too busy focusing on putting one foot in front of the other as he stumbled drunkenly next to her. "Sometimes I hate how well you know me, Banana."

That made her laugh. "Why is that?"

"Because I can never hide from you," he admitted. They walked in silence for a few more steps. "I'm sorry I fucked everything up for you."

"What?" Hannah stopped walking, holding his arm tight to prevent him from advancing further. "What are you talking about?"

Jimmy clasped his hands behind his head, his voice cracking as he spoke, "I feel like I've messed up your life. If I'm not abandoning you and running off, I'm just driving a wedge between you and everyone else."

Trying to decipher his drunken ramblings, Hannah asked again, "What are you talking about?"

"I heard you arguing with your dad the other day about not going home," he said.

"Oh, that. It's fine. He'll get over it," Hannah reassured him. "The holidays come around every year."

"Yeah, but I also ruined your friendship with Whitney and Katie," Jimmy continued. Tears flowed freely down his face as he released his hands back down to his sides.

Hannah wiped a tear from his cheek. "Jimmy, that wasn't your fault. Not even a little bit."

"If I weren't such a fucking wreck, it would've been fine. You would still be friends with them. You'd still be home where you wanted to be if I didn't drag you away from it all!" he shouted.

"Hey, please don't yell at me," Hannah said, putting a hand over Jimmy's heart to calm him. "I need you to hear me. None of that was your fault, and you didn't make me do anything. I did this all on my own. I am here because I want to be. I promise you that."

Jimmy stepped toward her, tears still streaming down his face, and laid his forehead on her shoulder. Hannah wrapped her arms around him. "Hey, it's okay," she said, rubbing his back. "Jimmy—hey—where is this all coming from?"

Jimmy lifted his head, collecting himself, and told her, "My dad called me this morning when you were in the shower, and he just—he laid into me about leaving home and how upset my mom was about the whole thing. He said she's been so worried about me, crying all the time and stuff. He called me a 'selfish asshole' for not coming home for the holidays, but I couldn't tell him I just didn't have the money. I didn't want to hear all about that—how I'm a loser, too." He paused to take a breath. "My mom must've told him you were here, I guess, and he went off about that, too. How I ruined your life, having you uproot everything for me."

Hannah stepped back from him, feeling disoriented by everything Jimmy revealed. From what he had told her, and what she had gathered from the couple of times she had met Mr. Taylor, Hannah could see how much he resented Jimmy's existence. She often wondered if he never wanted a second child or if he just saw Jimmy as some unruly thing that wouldn't obey. No matter the reason, Hannah could see that he would never meet his father's expectations.

"Jimmy, I—I'm so sorry. He had no right to speak for me or say anything like that to you. It's not true," she said.

Jimmy laughed half-heartedly, not fully believing her. Hannah took his hand in hers and continued walking.

"You did what you had to do, Jimmy, even if none of us understood it. It got you here to this place now, and you belong here. You've built a life that's all your own. Don't listen to him," urged Hannah.

Jimmy nodded slowly, his brow furrowed, thinking about what she had said. "You promise you're happy here?" he asked, searching her eyes for the truth. "That you want to be here?"

"Honestly, I wasn't sure I would be when I came. I wasn't sure I was doing the right thing, but I knew I needed to find out. I knew I'd regret it if I didn't come and at least see you again. When we met, my world became so much more vibrant and alive. Without you, though, it just wasn't the same. I had to come to see if there was still something worth fighting for," she told him.

"And? Was there?" Jimmy asked.

Hannah giggled. "Well, yeah! Of course, there was. There always was."

Jimmy held Hannah's hand so tightly that her fingers went numb after a while as they walked silently for a couple of blocks. She didn't tell him, though, wanting to be that steady something that kept him on his feet.

"Banana, I'm sorry," Jimmy told her, breaking the silence.

"For what?" she asked.

Jimmy chuckled, sniffling the last of his tears away. "For being such a wreck! I'm a fucking mess."

As they walked, Hannah laid her head on his shoulder, replying only to say, "Well, you're *my* wreck."

They strolled the rest of the way home like that, holding one another up in more than just a physical sense. Hannah had only gotten Jimmy as far as the couch once he had fumbled with the key in the front door lock for a few minutes, refusing to let Hannah help. She took his sneakers off, resting them on the floor by the front door. When she turned back to him, Jimmy had already fallen asleep. She laid a blanket over him and stood momentarily watching him. The worry and sadness had gone from his face, lost to the ease of his dreams. She left a glass of water and a couple of aspirin on the coffee table before kissing him gently on the forehead, and put herself to bed.

J immy's mood didn't improve much after Thanksgiving. Hannah did everything she could to help bring him around, even finding a local community center that offered free mental health services. That fight with his father weighed heavy on him, and the guilt of his mother's pain lingered. Jimmy spent much of his time on the front porch with his guitar, strumming the hours away. He went through a lot more cigarettes than usual and seemed to be drunk more often than not.

As Christmas approached, though, Hannah noticed a change in him. He had been able to talk with a counselor regularly at the community clinic, which seemed more helpful than medications had ever been. Hannah respected Jimmy's wishes about not wanting to rely on prescriptions anymore, so she let it go. It had also helped that Jimmy started a new band with some of his friends, returning to himself a little more with each practice and show they booked.

Jimmy woke up one morning a few days before Christmas, suddenly excited for the holiday. He asked Hannah if she wanted to find a small Christmas tree for the living room, to which she agreed; she wanted to decorate for the holidays but felt it was pointless if Jimmy wasn't into it. They walked through town and found a small lot with some scraggly little trees still left. Hannah picked out one that was light enough for Jimmy to carry home in one hand. They then drove out to the dollar store for a tree stand and string lights.

The winter chill had finally set it in that night, so Jimmy lit a fire and put on some obscure punk rock Christmas album. Hannah microwaved popcorn for tree decorations. She sat next to Jimmy on the couch with the bowl of popcorn, prepping two sewing needles and long strands of thread they had found at the store earlier.

Hannah worked diligently on her popcorn garland, slipping kernels down the needle to the end of the thread, one piece after the other. After a few minutes, Hannah felt she hadn't made much progress, though. She looked at Jimmy's strand, which was much further along than hers, and heard a loud crunch. Hannah turned to him just in time to see his jaw moving slowly as he tried to chew inconspicuously, stifling a laugh.

"You jerk!" she shrieked. "Are you eating my strand of popcorn?"

Jimmy nodded as he fell backward, laughing so hard that he nearly choked on the popcorn kernel in his mouth.

Hannah shoved him, grabbing at his popcorn strand, but Jimmy yanked it away quickly. She wrestled him for it, and he shouted at her through laughs, "No! Banana! You better stop! I'm warning you!"

She felt Jimmy's hands move to her waist, causing her to release the garland and instinctively find his hands at her midsection. "No, please don't tickle me!"

"What? You *want* me to tickle you?" Jimmy asked playfully.

"No! Please, Jimmy! Don't, please!" Hannah begged, trying to pry his fingers from her sides. Her body seized just then as Jimmy's fingers pulsed into her skin, causing shockwaves of laughter to overcome her. Hannah gasped for breath as she continued to beg, "Please, stop!"

Jimmy relented after just a few seconds as Hannah buried her head into his chest, trying to catch her breath. He wrapped his arms around her, leaning forward to kiss her forehead.

"Oh, *now* you want to be all sweet!" she said mockingly. "That was not very nice!"

Jimmy laughed. "It was a peace offering."

Hannah lifted her face, eyeing him suspiciously. "I'm not buying it," she teased.

He planted a quick peck on her lips. "I love you, Banana."

"I guess I still love you, too," Hannah replied with a smirk.

Jimmy moved an arm under his head, staring at the ceiling. "Seriously, though. I just wanted to say I'm sorry I've been off lately. Thanks for being there for me. For loving me."

Hannah laid her head back on his chest, telling him, "I know I can't save you from this, but I will always walk through the fire with you. I'll always be here."

Her head bobbed up and down in time with Jimmy's breath as they both eventually fell asleep. Hannah dreamed she was floating out on the open ocean, just letting the rhythm of the water carry her away.

On Christmas morning, Hannah and Jimmy both awoke earlier than usual. Neither of them had work to fill their time, so they moved slowly throughout the morning. They curled up on the couch together under a blanket, with a fire in the fireplace, slowly sipping their coffees from two chipped Santa mugs Hannah had taken out of the trash from work. Her manager deemed them too broken to be sold, but Hannah thought otherwise. As she stared into the flames, she reflected on the last few days, thinking about how much Jimmy had improved. It felt like he was back to his usual self, and she was thankful for that Christmas miracle.

Out of the blue, Jimmy pulled a Christmas gift for Hannah out from under the couch.

She accepted the gift with a look of surprise. "I thought we weren't doing gifts?" asked Hannah. "Money had been so tight—"

"I didn't spend anything. Don't worry. I made it," he said.

Hannah threw her head back and cackled loudly. "Well, I made you something, too!" She skidded down the hallway to the closet in the spare bedroom, carrying back a wrapped package.

Jimmy shouted excitedly when she presented it to him, "No way!"

They opened their gifts at the same time like excited little kids. Jimmy made her a mixed CD of songs that reminded him of her, while Hannah curated an album of photos from SHU to the present day, a pictorial timeline of their relationship.

"I love this, thank you," Jimmy told her.

"I can't wait to listen to this!" Hannah had replied, getting up to put the CD into the old stereo on the small bookcase beside the fireplace.

Hannah wrote in her journal later that day, sitting on the front porch wrapped in a blanket, while Jimmy made dinner for them. She mulled over the last months she'd spent with him. They'd had their struggles and dealt with some heavy things, but they could climb mountains together. Hannah looked out at the neighborhood and smiled, knowing they would outlast anything.

The warm spring days had finally returned to Riverside Springs, meaning outdoor living had become the norm again. Jimmy returned from working at the restaurant one afternoon and found Hannah lying on a blanket in the yard with a new book. He told her he had made plans for that night to skate at an abandoned pool several towns over.

"Do you wanna tag along?" he asked.

Hannah furrowed her brow, worried about getting into trouble. "Wouldn't we be trespassing?" she questioned.

Jimmy shrugged. "I don't know—maybe? We've done it before."

"Of course you have, but that doesn't mean it's okay," she sighed.

"It's not that serious, Banana," Jimmy snickered. "Are you coming or not?"

Hannah stood up, gathering up the blanket. "Obviously."

The drive to the forgotten pool took nearly an hour, but Hannah had lost track of the time as she stared out the window from the backseat of Alan's pickup truck. The bed was filled with skateboards and a cooler full of beer. There wasn't much to see on the drive except trees, tall grasses, and the occasional horse.

As they pulled into the parking lot, Hannah noted the cracks in the pavement and the prospering weeds growing up through them. The property was poorly maintained; Hannah guessed it had been at least a year since someone had been there to cut the grass. She started to think of all the ticks hiding in the brush, scratching at her legs, which had begun to itch at the thought. Alan parked the truck under a grove of overgrown trees to avoid being seen from the road.

They walked toward a wall of thick bushes, which Hannah realized was a chain-link fence. "This way," Jimmy said as he took her hand and led her down a worn path to the backside of the fenced area. He stuck a hand into the brush, feeling around for something. Jimmy grasped a piece of the fence at the furthest corner and pulled it back enough for everyone to crawl through.

Once inside, Hannah was met with vast graffiti murals, broken bottles of Old English, and crushed beer cans. The area had certainly seen better days, but Hannah could see the draw. There was something romantic about it, like a secret concrete garden to get lost in. The pool was large with rounded edges, like a giant mixing bowl, with a shallow and deep end marked to be twelve feet deep. There was also a basketball court, tetherball, and two diving boards at varying heights.

This must have been a fun place in its prime, Hannah thought.

Most of their usual group was scheduled to work at the restaurant that night, so Hannah was the only non-skater there. She grabbed a beer and wandered around the property with her camera for a while, taking in the graffiti art as if walking around the quiet halls of The Met in New York City. She snapped photos as the sun set, noting the beautiful cotton candy-colored skies above her. In the hazy dusk, large park lights began to illuminate the pool area and parking lot.

Hannah eventually found her way back to the empty pool, settling on the edge with another drink to capture some action shots. The guys took turns dropping in and swirling around the curved walls of the pool, showing off their best tricks.

After a while, Hannah started to curiously eye the diving boards, having gotten bored with being the group photographer; she felt oddly drawn to them. Hannah had always been fearful of heights, even feeling anxious when she walked too close to the railing on the second floor of the shopping mall back home. That night, though, something in her stirred with a fearlessness she had never felt before. She grabbed the iPod from her bag and popped the headphones into her ears. Walking toward the pool's deep end, where the diving boards were, she set her music to play randomly.

Hannah gripped the handrails of the tallest diving board and stepped onto the ladder's bottom rung, feeling the grip of its rough surface under her sneakers. She climbed one rung at a time until she reached the top. Holding tight to the railing on either side of her, Hannah stood there looking out at her friends below, the neglected parking lot, and the open fields beyond. She spotted a light in the distance—a house, maybe.

As the music shuffled and the beer made her woozy, Hannah closed her eyes and slowly bopped her head with the music loudly pumping into her ears. She relaxed her grip on the railings while also letting go of herself just a little more. She tapped her toes to the beat, letting her hands off the rails completely, as her whole body swayed with the rhythm. Hannah felt abnormally free. She reached her hands over her head, leaning back to stare at the night sky. She reached out, thinking maybe she could grab hold of a star or even a galaxy. Anything felt possible.

Nostalgia flooded her thoughts as memories of her time back home in New Jersey danced with her. She remembered those nights in the park with Jimmy when he would fly so high off the top of the swings. Hannah thought she could fly up into the clouds, too, if only she could jump high enough. She spun in place, the beat of the music pulsating through every fiber in her body, like she was again back in the Stonebridge VFW hall with Jimmy twirling her around a mosh pit. Those days seemed to cocoon around her, fueling her body to spin faster as the night air swirled around her.

When the song ended and silence filled her ears, Hannah could hear the whooping and clapping from the empty pool below. She opened her eyes and looked down to see her friends watching, wide-eyed and laughing. She covered her face in embarrassment. When she removed her hands, Hannah caught Jimmy's eye as his crooked smile beamed up at her. She grinned big back at him, biting her bottom lip. When her feet were back on solid ground, she curtsied for her fans, who had been waiting below.

Everyone but Hannah took their time returning to the cars in the parking lot. She leaned against Alan's truck, legs splayed, waiting for the doors to be unlocked. Jimmy appeared before her, the smooth skin of the scar on his lip oddly shining in the overhead lamplight. He grinned at her as he touched her hip and shuffled his feet between her legs.

Placing his cheek against hers, he whispered, "I could watch you dance like that all night long, Banana. Even if you weren't twirling around to my songs." He lingered there momentarily before pulling away, sending a shiver through her with a simple wink.

Continued

Hannah smiled while reading those words, remembering how she had felt so confident that she and Jimmy would go the distance. She wasn't sure if it was the pull of young love or naivety, but she had missed those days of feeling so sure about something. Jimmy's ability to cope emotionally had been a strain throughout their relationship, but they always found a way through it. She saw now that there was so much beauty in, not just the good, but the bad times, too. They fought hard and valiantly together to overcome every obstacle. She just wished it hadn't come down to choosing who to save—herself or Jimmy.

But Hannah knew where this story would go, having replayed those next few months over in her mind more times than she cared to admit. It had gotten easier with the passing of each year, but that first one nearly broke her. However, that video reel in her mind had new life breathed into it with the news of Jimmy's passing. Hannah couldn't help but question everything that happened, all that had been said and left unsaid. She regretted the years and the silence between them, wishing something, anything, had been different.

Hannah spent most of her days breaking down into tears at random times. She'd find herself melting to the floor of the shower into quiet, painful sobs. There were days she would be out working in the garden when she'd swear she heard Jimmy call out to her. Hannah started to avoid walking the pathway in town that was laid out against the shoreline. It made her think of that park in Riverside Springs, and she could almost see Jimmy skateboarding down the path toward her if she squinted her eyes hard enough against the sun.

Jimmy haunted her. She couldn't shake his face from behind her eyes or drown out his voice that played over in her mind. Hannah woke each day with the same empty pit in her chest, realizing that she had woken up to yet another day in a world without him. Even though they hadn't been in touch, Hannah now understood that there was a sort of peace and comfort in her soul just knowing that he was out there somewhere. That he was living life like only he could. Now that he was gone, though, her world felt a little more bleak.

Hannah climbed down from the attic, bringing the remaining box into her home office. Her body was sore from sitting on the old floor, and the dust was getting to her after so many hours of existing in it. She went to bed early that night while Jake streamed some cartoon show on the television. She tossed and turned for a while, unable to find a comfortable spot, until she realized it was her heart that couldn't relax.

She thought of Jimmy and all the adventures he had in his short lifetime. Hannah had always been envious of him. Sure, he struggled, but he had always lived on his terms and with an open heart. Jimmy didn't know how to be anyone but himself, always approaching a situation authentically. All of those things within him came together to create this beautiful gift in the way he could make people feel so special.

Hannah could feel her list of regrets growing longer and longer with each passing hour. She wished things between them had ended differently. There was just so much she would say if she could, but it was too late for that. That's the thing about time—it goes by so quickly. Years slide by in the blink of an eye, and once they're gone, they're forever gone.

Tears slid sideways down her face, wetting the pillow. More than anything, Hannah just wanted to see his face now on the pillow across from her. She reached a hand out as if he were there, like she could stroke his cheek or glide her fingers through his hair.

One more time, she pleaded with God or the Universe, whoever was out there. *Just one more time, and I won't ask for anything else as long as I live.*

Hannah awoke one morning to find that Jimmy wasn't sleeping soundly beside her. His band, Lowcountry Riot, had a big show at The Swamp Stage the night before. He'd been feeling down recently but was excited about the show, as it was their biggest one yet. Hannah hadn't been able to watch him play since she had to work late, but she was eager to hear all about it that morning.

She left their bedroom, thinking he might have just crashed on the couch to avoid waking her, but he wasn't there. She returned down the hallway to the spare room, but the bed was empty. Hannah walked back toward the front of the house and stepped onto the porch, thinking that maybe he'd already be sitting there with a cup of coffee and a cigarette. The street was quiet, with no soul in sight, and Jimmy's car was missing from their driveway.

There's a perfectly good explanation for this, she thought, trying not to panic.

Hannah walked back into the house, noting the time on the stove across the room. 8:24 A.M. She hesitated to call Jimmy, not wanting to wake him if he was asleep somewhere. She waited through twenty minutes of pretending to tidy up the house when all she did was just move some things around. She started to brew a pot of coffee before finally caving and calling him. It went straight to voicemail, which wasn't unusual. She left a message and then sent a text to ensure he didn't overlook calling her back.

Hannah continued pacing the kitchen, staring at the cell phone in her hands, thinking about who Jimmy had been with the night before. She ran through a mental list of band members and friends she knew had been in attendance, but Alan was the only one she could think to call. He was the most dependable, the one Jimmy trusted more than the rest; she knew if he had said anything to anyone, it would have been to Alan. She hesitated momentarily, considering if she was overreacting, but decided to call anyway.

Alan answered on the third ring, sounding dazed out of a sound sleep. "Hello?"

"Alan!" she thundered. "It's Hannah."

"Hey, what's going on?" he asked, trying to sound a little more alert.

"Well, I was just wondering where Jimmy was. Is he with you?"

"No," Alan answered.

"Are you sure? He didn't crash with you last night or something?"

"I'm sure. He followed me home last night, and we got back here at about one o'clock. My tire had gone flat, and Jimmy helped me put the spare on before we left the bar. We were a little tipsy, so we weren't sure we did it right," Alan told her with a laugh. "So he followed me home to make sure it didn't roll off or something, and then he said he was heading home."

"Well, he's not here," she told him as she peeked out the side door to see if he was in the yard, but there was still no sign of him.

Alan perked up more. "Are you sure? He's not, like, sleeping in his car in the driveway?"

Panic edged into Hannah's voice. "His car isn't even here, Alan."

"Maybe he went out for bagels or something?"

Hannah shook her head, looking around the house as if she had missed something. "No, he would've left a note. I don't see one."

"We were all so beat last night from the show and the beers—maybe he just pulled over to sleep it off in his car," he suggested.

"Yeah, maybe," Hannah said thoughtfully. "I'm going to take a walk to your house. I know the route he would've taken back home. Maybe I'll find him along the way."

"Okay," Alan said. "I can put some coffee on for you."

"Please," said Hannah, forgetting all about the fresh pot on the counter. "I'll be there in a little bit." She hung up the phone and rushed down the hallway to get changed. Her nerves were getting the best of her as she noticed her hands shaking while she tied the laces of her sneakers.

"He's fine. Jimmy is fine," she whispered to herself.

She knew she didn't fully believe it, conceding that Jimmy had been slipping back into a heavy depression in the last few days. Hannah tried to help him through it, but he had been withdrawing from her. Jimmy had missed a few shifts at the restaurant, jeopardizing his job. It seemed like the only thing that remotely lifted his spirits was his music, so Hannah was happy that his band had recently scheduled a few shows in the coming weeks. Her shoulders settled a little at the thought that he did have his guitar with him, which had been his lifeline in the past.

Hannah walked the winding sideroads to Alan's house, gazing at every car on the street and even those parked in driveways. She passed a municipal lot, weaving in and out of each aisle, but there was no green Honda Accord in sight. When she reached the door of Alan's apartment on the bottom floor of a two-story row house, Hannah was nearly in tears.

Alan was confused by the state of her and asked, "Is there something more going on, Hannah? Did y'all have a fight or something? I expected you to be worried, but I can see you're more than worried. Aren't you?"

Hannah took a deep breath. "Did Jimmy ever tell you about how he wound up here? In South Carolina, I mean."

Alan thought momentarily. "Well, he just told me that he was doing some soul-searching, I guess. He took a road trip, fell in love with it here, and decided to stay."

Hannah took a sip of the coffee that Alan had brewed for her. "I figured. Jimmy hides a lot from people."

Alan cocked his head to one side. "What do you mean?"

Hannah took another long sip of coffee and began to tell the real story of Jimmy's grand adventure. "Jimmy had a breakdown," she started. "It wasn't the first one; he had been diagnosed at a young age with Bipolar Disorder. He never really believed it, and I don't know how accurate it was, either, but—there's that. He's been in therapy recently, but now I'm not sure if he is even still going. That breakdown was his worst, and he just ran away. He dropped his car off in the middle of the night, sent me and his mom an email, and left on foot. He'd email every so often in the beginning, saying that he was taking Greyhound buses to one place or that he had train-hopped somewhere else. Jimmy was just basically living on the streets, playing guitar and pouring drinks to make some money to keep going. Anyway, he just came here by happenstance. I guess the money ran out, and it seemed like a good enough place to settle for a while. Obviously, you know that he just stayed."

Alan, who hadn't moved a muscle throughout the retelling of the story, slowly started to move his limbs and blink hard. "I don't even know what to say. I thought I knew him so well," he said, stunned.

"You do, Alan. You do know him so well. It's just Jimmy—he never wants to worry anyone. I'm sorry," Hannah apologized. "It wasn't my place to say anything, and I know Jimmy would be so mad if he knew I told you now."

"Well, I can keep a secret from everyone else," Alan assured her, "but Jimmy will just need to deal with me knowing. He's like my brother, and I'll be damned if I let him go through this without me."

Hannah smiled at him, knowing she made the right decision to call him. Together, they called through their friend group to see if anyone had been in touch with Jimmy after the show the night before. Everyone they were able to connect with told them that they hadn't seen Jimmy at all. Hannah contemplated calling Bonnie but didn't want to raise the alarm carelessly. Not yet.

"Maybe he went out to the pool last night to skate?" Alan thought out loud.

Hannah nodded. "Yeah, that's a good place to look."

He stood and walked over to the kitchen table where he'd thrown his car keys the night before. He grabbed them and then headed for the front door. "Come on, I'll drive."

They pulled into the abandoned parking lot within the hour, but Jimmy's car wasn't there either.

"Stay here. I'll check real quick. Just in case," Alan told her, afraid of what he might find. Even though he hadn't known about his friend's hardships, Alan had quickly grown worried for Jimmy, for what he might be capable of.

Hannah nodded as Alan exited the truck and jogged out of sight around the lush shrubs growing through the fence. About two minutes later, he emerged from the thick overgrowth. Alan shook his head and threw his hands in the air. "He's not here," he shouted.

Hannah's face sank, not knowing where else he could be. She rechecked her phone, but there were no missed calls or texts. She thought to check her email just then, wondering why she hadn't thought to look sooner. She felt hopeful that maybe he had left a message for her there as he had done before. Hannah's eyes scanned the list of new emails, but they were mostly all marketing messages and spam. She let out a long, exasperated breath.

"So what now?" Alan asked as he climbed into the truck and settled behind the cracked leather steering wheel.

"I don't know," Hannah admitted. "I might have to call his mom. What do you think?"

"Maybe you should," he replied before pulling back out onto the road.

The phone rang a few times before she answered. "Hello, this is Bonnie."

"Bonnie, it's Hannah. Have you heard from Jimmy this morning? Or last night?"

"No, I haven't. Why? What's going on, Hannah?" Bonnie asked.

Hannah's voice caught in her throat as she spoke. "He didn't come home last night, and I can't reach him. I've been looking for him all morning. I don't know what to do."

Bonnie sighed, "Oh, Jimmy. Okay—where have you looked so far?"

"He played a show last night and had gone to Alan's house, so I walked the route he would've taken back to our house from there. I'm with Alan now—"

"Hi, Mrs. Taylor!" Alan shouted from the driver's seat.

"We went to one of his favorite skateboarding places, and we were going to drive around to see what we could see," Hannah continued.

"You haven't covered much ground then," Bonnie chirped. "And that's not much of a plan."

"Well, we called through our list of friends already," Hannah stammered, trying to find a way to show Bonnie that she was capable. "No one else has seen or talked to him since last night's show."

"Did you call around to hospitals? Jails?" Bonnie asked.

"Not yet," Hannah said. "I hadn't gotten that far yet."

There was a long pause, and Hannah thought Bonnie had hung up on her. "Alright, do that, and let *me* try him. Maybe he'll pick up for me. I'll call some of our family down that way, too. Maybe he showed up at one of their houses last night."

"I don't think he would've gone to one of them—" Hannah started to say.

"I know my son," Bonnie interrupted.

"No, I know you do—"

"Then make your calls, and I will make mine. Drive around with Alan, I guess," Bonnie said. "Text me with any updates."

When Bonnie hung up, Hannah leaned her head back and sighed.

"Everything okay?" Alan asked.

Hannah looked out the passenger window, watching the landscape pass by in a blur. "Pfft. She just—she's so difficult sometimes. I don't think she's ever really liked me, honestly. It's like she always pushes me away when Jimmy is getting bad again, like it's my fault somehow."

Alan looked over at her briefly before focusing back on the road. "I'm sure that's not true, Hannah."

"It's been years of this, Alan," she told him. "It's always been like this. She has this weird jealousy or something that Jimmy and I are so close. She hates that he tells me more than he does her."

Alan drove Hannah around for the next few hours, looking for Jimmy in shopping plazas, parks, and along country backroads. They kept dialing his number, but it only ever went straight to voicemail. According to the messages she sent to Hannah, Bonnie hadn't had any luck either; Jimmy hadn't returned any of his mother's voicemails, texts, or emails, and none of their family had heard from him either.

With sunset nearing, Alan drove Hannah home. "I just don't get it," she said, shaking her head in disbelief. "The last time, he left me breadcrumbs to follow, but he hasn't done that this time. What if something really bad happened to him, Alan?" Hannah clapped a hand over her mouth to stop her sobs from escaping, but it was too late.

Alan pulled the truck over onto the side of the road and embraced Hannah across the center console. She cried into his shoulder as he promised her, "Jimmy is okay. We're going to find him."

As she continued to weep onto his shirt sleeve, Hannah thought about how grateful she was to have Alan with her. He always seemed to know just what to do in every situation, and Hannah had needed someone like that to help her through the worst of it. She felt comfort knowing she could continue to lean on him in the following days.

It had been about two weeks since Hannah had last laid eyes on Jimmy. She had gotten a call from Bonnie the day after he disappeared to let her know that Jimmy had returned home to Stonebridge. Hannah argued with Bonnie for information, pleading to talk to him. Bonnie only told her that Jimmy needed space and Hannah should wait for him to be ready to speak.

Hannah raised her voice to Bonnie, shouting at her, "I have a right to know! To hear it from him!"

She immediately regretted losing control like that, especially since all Bonnie did was promptly hang up on her. Hannah was angry, though, at having always been kept at arms-length from Jimmy. It felt like Bonnie didn't respect her position in his life, or that she was important to him. That she was someone who had planned to be next to him until the end of time. Hannah hated feeling like she couldn't help him through the darkness then. After all, she had been Jimmy's only emotional support in Riverside Springs for the last year and practically the only one before that back home. Aside from Brad, anyway. So much of Hannah's time and energy had gone to Jimmy, to make him feel whole time and time again. Yet, there she was, still on the outskirts.

Hannah tried to be understanding when Jimmy eventually called her, but she was hurt that they were in the same situation again. She reminded him of his promise never to disappear again.

"You know—the one you've broken three times now?" she asked sarcastically.

Jimmy sighed. "I just needed some space."

"You need space? Couldn't you have stayed at Alan's or something if you needed space from me? And isn't your dad there? The very person you needed space from last year?" she questioned. "I don't get it, Jimmy. Just help me understand this."

"It's not you that I needed space from. It's just—I needed space from my life. And my dad isn't here. He left. He flew out to see my brother. It's just Mom and me," he told her.

"When are you coming home?" Hannah asked.

"Hannah, I—I don't know."

J immy drove home after nearly a month away. The anger that had built up in Hannah spilled over the night of his return. She didn't mind the mood swings—she could handle them well enough, but the running away was too much. She wasn't sure how often she could deal with Jimmy's disappearing act, knowing that he would probably just continue to run.

"I've tried to be understanding and patient, but I can't tell you how hurt I am that you keep doing this to me. I feel like such a damn fool!" Hannah shouted through tears.

Jimmy couldn't meet her eyes, staring at the hardwood floor underfoot. "I'm just a fuck up, Hannah. I'm sorry."

"Don't talk like that, Jimmy. You're not a fuck up. You're sick." Hannah took a deep breath. "I just don't know if I can go through this again. I mean, we all go through times when we want to burn it all down and move somewhere completely new. Just start over fresh. Be a stranger in a strange land kind of thing. But here we are, in this life we created together—that *you* started—and it's still not enough? I don't know if I have it in me to trust you not to do this to me again."

"You're right. You shouldn't trust me. I've given you no reason to," Jimmy admitted.

Hannah shook her head and shrugged, asking, "Where do we even go from here? Promises just feel meaningless now."

Jimmy looked her in the eye briefly. "I don't know. I just know I'm sorry."

"'Sorry' isn't good enough anymore, Jimmy," Hannah stated bluntly.

He stared at his feet again before finally saying, "You deserve better. "

"What I deserve is your respect, to be more open about your feelings before you run. Let me help you!" Hannah pleaded.

Jimmy shook his head slightly, still unable to meet her eyes and show her how much it was killing him to say it. "No. You deserve better than me, I mean," he repeated.

Hannah's mouth fell open as tears fell down her face. "You don't mean that, Jimmy. No."

His voice cracked with emotion. "I don't want to, Hannah, but I do. You deserve someone stronger than me, someone who can love you how you deserve to be loved."

Hannah sniffled and shook her head vigorously. "No one has ever loved me like you, Jimmy. No one. I don't think anyone ever could."

"And no one has hurt you as much as I have," he admitted.

She took a deep breath and stared at the ceiling to collect herself. "I can't believe this. After everything we've been through, this is how it ends?"

Jimmy looked up at her, his eyes red and glassy. "You said it yourself, Hannah. You don't know how much more you can do this. You can't trust me, and I've done that to you. I've ruined us."

"You haven't—" Hannah started to say, but Jimmy raised a hand to stop her.

"Don't spare my feelings. It's the truth." With his voice cracking, Jimmy told her, "Go find someone who will make you happy and love you right. You deserve nothing less than the world."

Hannah reached out to him, but Jimmy pulled away from her touch. She stared at him, shocked, grasping for any logical reason for the words he was saying. "Did your dad say something to you again?" she asked.

Jimmy's lips trembled as they stared at one another through bleary eyes."My dad has nothing to do with this," he said coldly.

Hannah scoffed and folded her arms, protecting herself from the inevitable. "So what? That's it? You're not going to fight for me to stay? You're not even gonna try?"

Jimmy opened his mouth to say something but quickly closed it; he didn't dare say anything more. He didn't want to bait her into enduring any more hurt, no matter how much he wanted her to just stay.

Hannah knew then that they were done, and she would need to be forever done with him. Perhaps she knew somewhere in the deep recesses of her mind that they couldn't go the distance, but she hadn't been ready for it to end so soon. Her heart broke into a million pieces that sunk into her stomach, causing the acid to churn. She called home, telling her mom through tears that she would be coming back to stay.

Hannah haphazardly packed her things into the car and left Riverside Springs without looking back. Jimmy had stood on the front porch, his shoulders slumped, as he watched her back out of the driveway and disappear around the corner toward the interstate. He had no more fight left in him to keep her, but he also knew it wouldn't have been fair of him to try. He had damaged Hannah enough. The only thing he could do was to set her free.

Once she crossed the state line into North Carolina, Hannah pulled over and broke down into hysterical sobs. The friendships she had cultivated, the home she had made, and the love that had completed her were all gone in an instant. She drove through the night back home to New Jersey, thinking endlessly about how she would rebuild her life all over again.

Hannah spent the first couple of weeks back home in bed. She lay under the covers most of the time, with her face hiding from the bright summer sunshine. She barely found the strength to get herself up to meet her basic needs, not just the physical strength, but the emotional will to even want to. Sometimes, breathing felt like it was too much of an effort as the burning, gaping hole in her chest grew more prominent with each sunrise. Every morning only counted as another day without Jimmy. It had been one thing to feel the emotional ache of his absence, but she could also physically feel it in the center of her stomach, which was even more challenging to ignore.

Hannah's phone buzzed with notifications of texts and phone calls throughout the day and night—all from friends in Riverside Springs. She never answered or bothered to respond, thinking a clean break was better for everyone involved. She often wanted to contact one of them but would remind herself that there was no need to make things messier than they were.

At first, Hannah's parents were just happy to have her home. They had been surprisingly gentle with her, seeing how shattered her heart was. After the second week, they became less understanding. Her mom constantly intruded into the safety of her bedroom, going on about this thing or that, or something one of the neighbors had done. Hannah wasn't sure who or what her mom was talking about, and she barely heard the sound of her voice. Hannah only ever heard Jimmy's voice in her head, and the strum of his guitar became the soundtrack of her isolation in the all-encompassing darkness of each night.

Hannah's dad eventually lost his cool, screaming at her one afternoon about how she was wasting her life away over someone who was never worth her time in the first place. Hannah yelled right back at him, defending Jimmy yet again. Her father was right, though. She was being dumb. She was a fool. As much as she wanted to just lay in bed and rot for the rest of her life, she knew she couldn't. Life would still move on, and she had to choose whether to continue moving with it or not. Deep down, Hannah knew Jimmy wouldn't come back for her. She also knew she couldn't go back even if he did. She knew she had to choose herself.

Hannah called her old manager at the thrift store, practically begging for her job back. The tears she had shed probably earned her some pity points because she found herself back on the sales floor two days later. There was still something comforting to her about being there again, with the repetition of folding shirts and pants, the smell of rubber sneakers, the resistance of the cash register buttons under her fingers, and the beep of the scanner. It was enough to make her forget her loneliness, the aching in her heart, even just temporarily. Hannah took her breaks in her car, just like she always had. When she started seeing the ghosts of her and Jimmy lying on the trunk of his old car, though, Hannah would end her break early in favor of the soulless routine.

She worked alongside a group of college kids who always invited her out after their shifts. Hannah initially declined every invite, feeling too old to hang out with them. Sometimes, she just felt too sad. They wore her down until she agreed, having grown tired of the long nights at home. Then, it became part of her routine, yet the first of many bad habits. On those nights out, she struggled to find the line between enough and too much, letting the alcohol fill the well in her. It was the only way she could feel free from the weight of her decisions, even just for a night.

Pushing past her limits, Hannah found a place within her where she couldn't remember Jimmy's face or his gravelly voice. How he smelled like nicotine and patchouli. The taste of coffee on his mouth, or that stupid scar on his top lip that accentuated the chip in his front tooth. Sometimes, she barely remembered his name. It was always temporary. Everything was.

One late night in July, when she wasn't out trying to drown Jimmy in a river of vodka, Hannah was researching graduate school programs on her laptop. She wasn't sure what she wanted to do with her life, having spent the last year thinking her life was in South Carolina with Jimmy. She wanted nothing more than to be everything he needed, but she wasn't. She never would be, but maybe she could be the difference for someone else. Hannah found a counseling program at SHU, whose fall enrollment ended the next day. She worked through the night on her application and submitted it by the time the sun rose in the early morning.

Hannah continued to spiral as July dragged on. She found solace in chatting with strangers online. They were primarily men looking to take advantage of a sad, forlorn girl, but she found a boost in the compliments she received from them. Hannah would eventually meet them out in public for dates that usually ended in sloppy, meaningless sex.

She dated one guy from work, which ended faster than it began, and then moved on to someone she met on Facebook. Then another, and another. In between, she found comfort underneath the weight of another body. Hannah had convinced herself that it was all she was good for since that was all any of them wanted from her; those men didn't even pretend to want to actually date her.

More often than not, Hannah carried herself through the back door in the early morning, quiet enough not to wake her parents. She'd put herself to bed, tears in her eyes, for yet another piece of herself that she had left behind in someone else's sheets.

Hannah often felt an unpleasant feeling stirring in her, one she couldn't identify. Or maybe she didn't want to admit how ashamed she was about her behavior post-Jimmy. She had tried hard to bury him so deep inside her memories that she would never be able to find him again. Under it all, she desperately wanted to be loved again, like he had once loved her. To feel important to someone.

That she was worth something. So Hannah kept hunting for love in hollow people and places, even if it left her feeling numb and devoid of any human connection.

At the end of the month, Hannah found out she had been accepted into SHU's counseling program. She recognized a small glimmer of hope that maybe things could get better, a feeling she hadn't experienced since she parked her car for the first time in that driveway on Campbell Street.

The first weeks of her grad program at SHU were the most challenging days Hannah had experienced since she left South Carolina. The shadows of her former self and Jimmy still lingered on the sidewalks and in the halls. She had her first panic attack in over a year, feeling overwhelmed by all of the memories. Hannah broke down in that same second-floor hallway in the Student Center with Room 202 just around the corner; part of her had expected to hear Jimmy's heavy footsteps running toward her. She worked hard for weeks to fend off the feelings that enrolling at SHU had been a mistake and that she should figure out another direction to take. However, the days on campus got easier as she made acquaintances in her new program, filling her time with studying rather than partying.

She still felt empty without Jimmy. She felt so isolated even though she was building friendships with people in her classes. Hannah was sure her friends from Riverside Springs wouldn't want anything to do with her anymore. Besides, they weren't her friends to keep. They had been Jimmy's friends first.

Whenever Hannah saw one of them sign into Instant Messenger, she would hover her mouse over their usernames, wanting to start a conversation. Sometimes, she double-clicked on them but would leave the cursor blinking and the text box empty, figuring it was probably too late. She would see Jimmy's screen name flash on the chat box as he signed on and then always quickly signed right back off. Hannah felt the hole inside her grow bigger each time, thinking that he couldn't even bear to be online at the same time as her.

When Hannah signed in to Facebook, Jimmy's name would often appear on her newsfeed. Lowcountry Riot was making a name for themselves, playing gigs nearly every weekend. She watched grainy cell phone videos of their performances, feeling the hole grow bigger still. It felt like torture, yet she couldn't stop watching them. Hannah missed her life with him—the rundown bars, learning his new songs, dancing nights away in their kitchen, and the late-night barbecues. She missed her friends, sure, but she always missed Jimmy the most. She had to believe being apart was for the best, no matter how much it hurt.

Jimmy reached out to her on Instant Messenger in early November, but they both avoided ever talking about what had happened on her last night. They chatted like they had no history at all, pretending to be mere acquaintances making small talk. Jimmy told Hannah all about Lowcountry Riot and his new job at a bar managing their concert schedule. He was happier there than at the restaurant, and the money was pretty good. Jimmy was excited that Hannah was pursuing an advanced counseling degree and told her she would make a great therapist one day.

Hannah never said anything, but she didn't care about any of it. She hated having to act like they didn't know one another as well as they did, that they hadn't shared the last few years of their lives with one another. It was never more evident than in the midst of small talk that they were just two separate entities and that their love was just some crazy thing that neither could even acknowledge anymore. Jimmy didn't reach out again, and neither did Hannah, wanting to avoid another conversation that felt sadly scripted. Hannah and Jimmy, simply and slowly, disappeared from one another's lives.

Hannah met one of her coworkers at a small music venue, The Junction in Stonebridge, for a concert line-up of miscellaneous local bands. It was a wet and cold day, with rain and snow falling since the morning. It was the kind of day that made Hannah miss Riverside Springs with its warm, humid temperatures. As much as she had been looking forward to the show, her mood had shifted with the weather, and all she wanted was to stay in the warmth of her bed. Hannah also felt weird being back there again; the last time she had found herself inside those walls, she was with Jimmy at Cat Hair's final performance.

After the first band finished their set, Hannah walked back to the bar for another beer. The wait was long since the venue was crammed with concert-goers. With a bottle of Blue Moon in hand, Hannah turned around to exit the crowd but went face-first into someone's chest. Startled, she backed up a step and tripped over a foot in the crowd behind her. A hand reached out to steady her.

Hannah laughed at her own clumsiness. "Thanks," she said, looking at the hand on her arm. Its fingers were strong and felt warm through the thickness of the sweater she had worn that night. For just a moment, Hannah thought of Jimmy and how his hands used to feel on her. She closed her eyes, shaking the thought from her mind, before looking up at the face in front of her.

Hannah was taken aback by the tall stranger. His strong face, framed by black rectangular glasses, stared back at her with a big smile. "Are you okay?" his deep voice asked.

"Yeah," she replied. "Yeah, but I think I lost some of my beer." She held the bottle up to show the stranger.

"Well, that's a damn shame," he said with a laugh. He let go of her arm then, but his smile didn't fade. "My name is Jake," the stranger said, sticking a hand out to her.

Hannah smiled and shook his hand. "Hannah," she replied.

"It's nice to meet you, Hannah," Jake said without letting go of her hand.

An old feeling rumbled within her. She couldn't ignore the strange sense of Deja vu that Jake felt oddly familiar. Hannah suddenly let go of him and asked, "I'm sorry—have we met before?"

He tilted his head to one side in thought and shrugged. "I don't think so," he answered.

It hit Hannah like a punch to the gut that she had felt that way before, with Jimmy. It was the same warmth and intimate recognition that had left her flustered when Jimmy had walked in the door to Room 202 more than six years ago.

Jake saw a change in her expression. "You sure you're okay?"

Hannah struggled to find her words. "Oh, uh, yeah. No, I'm fine."

"Well, I'm over there with my friend," Jake told her as he pointed to the left side of the room. "Do you want to join us?"

"Uh, sure," Hannah replied with a nod. "My friend is over that way, too. I'll go grab her."

Hannah and Jake joined their two groups together, standing close to one another for the remainder of the show. He occasionally leaned down close to her ear to comment on whatever band was playing at the time. Hannah kept stealing glances at Jake all night, unable to shake the feeling she got from him in just the first minutes of meeting him. She also couldn't get Jimmy off her mind either. Hannah chugged the rest of her beer, hoping it would help scrub her memories like it always had.

At the end of the night, Jake asked for Hannah's phone number, which she willingly gave. He called her shortly after she had returned home that night. "I didn't want to wait to talk to you again," he confessed to her. The conversation felt natural and flowed like they had known each other for years. Over an hour had passed before they hung up, but not before setting a dinner date for later in the week.

A few days after Valentine's Day, Jake took Hannah to a diner in Cedar Cove, the next town over from Harborvale, where he lived with his family. Hannah ordered a burger and fries, and Jake got a turkey club sandwich. The conversation poured out of them easily, without any breaks or awkward pauses.

As they walked out of the diner that night, Jake astonishingly said, "Can I just say how impressed I am? You ate that entire plate of food!"

Hannah's cheeks reddened, feeling oddly embarrassed. "I was starving," she said. "I promise I'm not a pig or anything!"

Jake laughed. "No! I didn't say you were! You're just so tiny; I would've never thought you could house a meal like that!"

"Well, in that case—not to brag or anything," Hannah smirked, "but I *can* eat a whole pizza by myself in one sitting."

Jake smiled coyly, "Then I know where to take you to eat next!" He laughed deep from his belly, spontaneous and loud. It was so loud that Hannah thought the houses a few blocks away must have heard him.

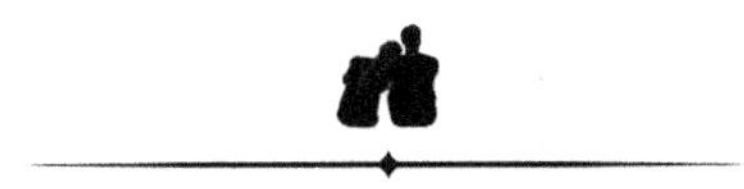

Hannah and Jake started dating each other exclusively within a week of their first date, and they exchanged "I love you's" after only two weeks. It seemed fast to their friends and family, but felt just right to them.

They saw each other every day, and Jake made it a point to take her to dinner at the only pizzeria in Harborvale; "I just had to see you in action," Jake had teased. He would pop into the thrift store for a quick "hello" when Hannah worked the evening shift, or they would meet at the Dunkin' Donuts after her shift for a coffee and a donut. On weekends, they drove around listening to music or walked hand-in-hand through the park in Stonebridge, sharing a hot pretzel. She made it a point to never stop at the old, familiar swing set. Sometimes, they would just aimlessly wander through bookstores, the record shop, or big box stores, browsing through merchandise but never buying anything.

Everywhere they went, though, Jimmy's ghost followed Hannah in remembrance of all the time she spent in his beater Oldsmobile driving around and loitering on the playground at the park. Jimmy's old manager, who remembered Hannah, still worked at the record shop. He stopped her once to chat for a few minutes but didn't bother asking about Jimmy after spotting Jake with her. Hannah was grateful for that, not wanting to relive that history more than she had to. It had been about a year since she had last heard from Jimmy, anyway— she wouldn't have known what to say.

"You know that guy?" Jake had asked once they left the store.

"Oh, yeah," Hannah said, "but that was a whole other lifetime ago."

Jake had come to Hannah one day after Thanksgiving, detailing a big fight with his family, and declared he would look for an apartment of his own. Hannah helped him in the search, but all the units in their area were outside of what he could afford. She sat back in her chair and thought about how she missed being out from under her parents. Hannah had a choice to make then, and she decided it was time to commit herself to Jake. He was thrilled by her suggestion that they move in together and start their own life.

They moved into an apartment in Branchtown just after the New Year. Their apartment was a quirky mix of furnishings and decor from nearly everyone they knew who was looking to get rid of their junk. It was small, and the neighbors were loud, but it was theirs. Hannah felt a sense of happiness that she hadn't felt in a long time, as if all the puzzle pieces were finally starting to fit together again.

One morning in early February, Hannah was home alone cleaning their apartment before going to work in the afternoon. She was jamming to music on her iPod when one of Jimmy's old songs came on. It had been a while since one slipped into the shuffle, and it caught her off-guard. Hannah felt the air catch in her lungs at the sound of his voice. She fumbled for the iPod in her pocket, quickly hitting pause and ripping the earbuds from her ears. Hannah sat on the edge of the sofa and grit her teeth in anger that, after all that time, Jimmy still had such a hold on her.

Hannah gathered herself and continued cleaning, picking a specific album to listen to rather than leaving it up to chance again. It was too little too late, though. Jimmy kept crossing her mind like he had set up a home right there in the folds of her brain. It had been nearly two years since they last spoke, but she still wondered what was happening in his life.

Hannah sat at her laptop, opened the Facebook website, and typed his name into the search bar to pull up his profile. She clicked on his picture, which had been updated two months before. Jimmy smiled at the camera with a guitar strapped across his chest. He looked more mature somehow. His face was full but more defined, and his eyes were upturned and full of life.

He looks good, she thought. *Healthy.*

She skimmed through his newsfeed, which was full of band announcements, his current thoughts on the upcoming presidential election, and skateboarding videos. Hannah couldn't help but click on a few of them, thinking she would remain anonymous, not knowing that he would be able to see who had watched his videos the next time he signed on. She kept scrolling and found a post from a year earlier about how he had quit smoking, which made her smile.

"Good for you," she whispered to his image on the screen in front of her.

She read that he bought a condo overlooking the water and scrolled through the photos he had posted, which had a noticeable lack of feminine touches. Hannah scrolled back to the top of the screen, glancing at the basic profile information to find that he still had his relationship status listed as "single." Hannah blinked hard, staring at the word, and felt a small part of her heart glimmer with the love that had once burned so brightly for him.

She hovered the mouse over the button to direct message him, feeling tempted to click it and talk to him again. Deep down, Hannah knew it wasn't a good idea to try to reconnect with Jimmy. To open that door to her past, to a love she knew she could never contain if it got loose again. She moved the mouse off the button, burying her feelings and memories of Jimmy, and turned off the computer.

That night, when Hannah got home from her late shift, Jake was still awake, waiting up for her. She had a difficult shift with customers who argued about every transaction, it seemed. She was tired and went immediately into their bedroom to change into her pajamas. On the bed was a greeting card with her name written on it. Jake crept into the room behind her as she opened it. Hannah was near tears when she finished reading his message of love and gratitude for their life together. When she turned to face him, Jake was down on one knee with a ring in his hand.

"Will you marry me?" he asked as his voice shook from nerves.

Hannah's emotions were so overwhelming she couldn't speak. She only nodded her head before collapsing into his arms. Jake slipped the small diamond ring onto her finger and kissed her sweetly.

One hot and humid afternoon in June, Jake and Hannah married on the beach by SHU with seventy-five friends and family members. Walking down the aisle toward Jake had been such a surreal moment for Hannah, who never thought she would have a wedding day quite like that. Years ago, she used to think she would one day marry Jimmy, but not in the usual, formal sense. No, she imagined their wedding would have been an impromptu shotgun ceremony at the Riverside Springs courthouse. They would have been dressed in whatever clothes they had thrown on that morning, asking anyone in the hallway to bear witness to their love. There wouldn't have been wedding rings, just the twisted foil wrappers from two sticks of peppermint gum that Hannah had in her bag. She was sure it would have been a rainy day, with their clothes soaked and water dripping from their hair, blurring the ink of their signatures. Afterward, they would have had one hell of a barbecue to celebrate.

Thinking about her old daydreams saddened Hannah because none of her old friends were there to celebrate her and Jake—none of them even knew him. Her heart was full, though, as Jake's large extended family welcomed her with open arms.

For their honeymoon, they took a road trip to Tennessee, enjoying the solitude of a small cabin in the woods. Hannah spent the week after their return making scrapbooks and photo albums from their wedding and trip. She had wanted to make sure their memories were perfectly preserved, despite not journaling very much at all. Hannah occasionally picked up her diary but could never commit to writing daily. She didn't want to admit it to herself, but she still felt broken by her past, and feared that her hand might be unable to stop writing once it started. That the agony of it all wouldn't waste another chance to bury her alive. Life was good, and there was no sense in resurrecting what she had already laid to rest.

As she sat by the pool in their apartment complex over the Fourth of July weekend, Hannah found herself scrolling through Facebook from her phone. She realized she hadn't seen Jimmy's name on her newsfeed in some time, so she searched for his name and clicked on his profile. Hannah found only limited information visible to her, like public posts about a promotion at work and various gigs he played with several different bands. Her eyes darted to the top portion of his profile to see the "Add Friend" button highlighted in blue; Jimmy had unfriended her.

Hannah's heart sank, feeling like she had been abandoned all over again. It felt weirdly permanent, and she wondered what had made him cut that last tie to her. As much as she didn't want to, Hannah knew she had to accept that Jimmy had made the decision for a reason. She felt sad that there was no longer any hope they might be able to rouse some kind of friendship in the future.

Hannah had always held onto this delusional thought that, maybe with enough time and distance, they could find a place for each other in their lives.

Hannah stared up at the clouds that passed lazily overhead. She knew she shouldn't even want a friendship with him, thinking they had never known how to be just friends anyway. She had a good life and a good man by her side, who she loved more than anything. Jimmy shouldn't be her concern anymore, and she had to face the fact that it was time to really let him go. Hannah closed the Facebook application and tossed her phone back into her pool bag, picking up the book she had brought. She found the spot where she had left off, the start of a new chapter.

Hannah called out from work for the second day in a row, which was so unlike her. Luckily, her boss didn't ask for a doctor's note to prove she was legitimately too ill to work. She didn't want to explain how she felt sick, but not in the obvious sniffling, coughing, or sneezing way. With Jake at the office, Hannah appreciated the quiet of the house, with the space she needed to consume herself with the past.

Jimmy's death brought his life back into full focus, plunging Hannah deep into the tidal wave for the first time in years. Nearly a decade had passed since she last spoke with him, but she had thought about him often. She never stopped caring in those years, frequently wondering where life had taken him. She would question if he had fallen in love again, and was curious about what kind of band he had been playing in. Hannah had sometimes searched for him on Facebook and Instagram, but both were private. She regularly thought about requesting to connect with him on either platform but never had enough nerve to click the button.

Now that Jimmy was gone, Hannah searched his name on Google to see what it might reveal to her, like a video compilation on YouTube of a skateboarding competition that he had entered back in 2019. She found all kinds of photos and videos that friends and family were sharing of him across social media platforms. The written tributes were short and sweet, some more emotional than others. She read the same theme in each one: a shallow promise to do better for the next friend in crisis. Hannah ached for these people whose names and faces she didn't recognize, feeling the same pain they did. She caught herself then, thinking that she didn't have a right to mourn him when so many people had known and loved him more recently than her.

Hannah examined each photo for hours and watched every video repeatedly, looking for some clue as to why Jimmy chose to end it all. She saw a posting for a memorial service at the waterfront park in Riverside Springs that some of Jimmy's friends had thrown to honor him. She recognized some of the names on the guest list, frowning at how much she still missed them and her old way of life. Hannah briefly felt sad that she had missed it but knew she wouldn't have gone anyway. She didn't feel like she belonged there anymore, that she wouldn't have had the right to be there. After all, Hannah had walked out on that chapter of her life a long time ago.

Hannah studied a video of another new band that Jimmy had joined, playing a concert in Riverside Springs only two months before his death. He looked good, having put on some weight again, his face vibrant. She watched as he swayed and tossed his head around while he played his guitar, but she couldn't help but notice his hesitance to take the mic. It was so unlike him to defer to another band member. For years, Hannah had watched him so easily take control of a crowd, never afraid to engage with them. Jimmy did loosen up after some time, telling corny jokes to the crowd between songs. She couldn't help but laugh at the punchlines every time she played that video, asking herself where it all went wrong.

That one video became a source of comfort to Hannah, one last thing that made her still feel connected to him. She could almost go back in time, watching him laugh so freely with his head thrown back and his eyes narrowed. She smiled, watching his fingers twitching at his side between songs, with chords always running through his mind. It made Hannah feel happy to see that Jimmy was still the same person he'd always been despite the downturn.

She kept scrolling through photos posted by strangers, stumbling on pictures of him looking too skinny again just two weeks before his death. His face looked sunken in and pale, his jaw clenched tight. Jimmy's hazel eyes looked blank and lifeless, a sign he was slipping away. Another photo, taken only three days before he died, showed Jimmy with friends goofing off in a parking lot behind a bar somewhere. He looked happy, with that crooked grin spread across his face. She didn't recognize the others in the photo and wondered if their core group of friends had still kept in touch.

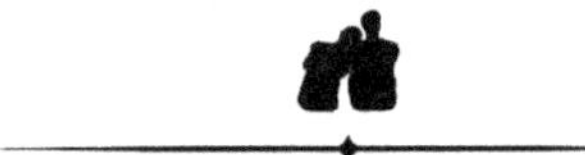

Hannah walked down to the beach in the afternoon, where she could do her best thinking. On the way there, she thought about all the kinds of love that existed in the world: romantic, friendship, and familial, just to name a few. Hannah had always considered Manny her first love since he was her first everything, but it just didn't feel true anymore. If she were asked now about her first love, Hannah's first thought would be about Jimmy. She loved Manny, but it had been nothing like what she had with Jimmy. Not even close. The love she and Jimmy shared had always been so much bigger than the both of them.

Hannah sat on an old post from a long-gone boardwalk that poked up from the sand. She put her feet into the gently lapping saltwater and looked toward the city. She contemplated all the lessons that Jimmy had taught her over the years. Perhaps the greatest one, though, was showing her what she wanted from love. Maybe Manny had been placed in her life to simply teach her what she didn't want, a lesson just as valuable. Each of them, though, had been a stepping stone to the next, ultimately preparing her the entire time for what was to come: Jake.

Tears flooded Hannah's eyes as she ruminated on her regrets with Jimmy. If only she had reached out to him any of those times she had thought about it over the years. She had let herself be so consumed with fear of what he might say or that she would feel so out of place in his life, so she kept herself separated from him. However, she had always known Jimmy better than anyone and could now see a change in him in those photos and videos. She let herself be swallowed whole every day by the guilt she felt, that maybe she could have done something to save him had she known, had she seen those images of him sooner. If only Jimmy had known how a part of Hannah's heart still beat for him, maybe he would've found some strength to keep his heart beating for her, too. If only.

Jake immediately launched into a knockdown, drag-out fight with Hannah over Jimmy when he came home from work that evening. His jealousy had gotten the best of him, telling Hannah he couldn't bear to hear her talk about Jimmy anymore.

"Do you even love me? Did you *ever* love me, or was I just your second choice?" asked Jake.

"You were never my second choice! *Of course,* I love you!" Hannah insisted.

Jake shouted at her, "Every time you talk about him, you just light up!"

"Because people light up when they talk about things that make them happy, Jake! I light up when I talk about you, my hobbies, or Diesel!" Hannah pointed to their dog, still asleep on the couch despite their argument. "Jimmy was a huge part of my life, and it's a part of my life that I admit I miss. Yes, we had our issues, but there were so many good things about him that I miss. There were so many good things about our life together that I miss. So I am choosing to remember those things because I miss him terribly, and he's fucking dead now! I will always have to just miss him."

Jake slept on the couch that night. Hannah felt like she was slowly losing her marriage, all because of a dead man. She spent the night alone, fidgeting and staring at their bedroom ceiling, trying to will herself to sleep. She felt a creeping unease that maybe Jake had been right, perhaps she was still in love with Jimmy after all these years.

No, she told herself. *I love Jake more now than the day we got married. He is who I am in love with.*

Hannah supposed a piece of her would always love Jimmy, though. He had greatly influenced her life, and that's just who Hannah was, anyway; she never fully let go of anyone she let peek into her heart. She would always love Manny, too, despite everything. Loving someone and being in love were two very different things that Jake didn't seem to comprehend, or maybe his anger had just gotten in the way of him seeing that.

Something else ate at Hannah, though. A looming sense of dread that she had been wasting some of the best years of her life just standing in one place. She had once been young and scared but so willing to leap for the things she believed in.

Hannah realized the last time she leaped was when she followed Jimmy to South Carolina. The very thought made her feel downright miserable. Hannah could feel it more than ever now, a desire and a need to get out of this place, to make a life somewhere new. Hannah knew she could leap into something completely foreign and be okay. She had done it before, after all. It was time for a fresh start. She just knew it.

Hannah finally found the motivation the following day to get back to work. She had also been dreading the number of sessions she would need to reschedule that week and the stack of documentation she still hadn't caught up on. When she got home that night, the air between her and Jake was still tense from their fight the night before.

Jake kept eyeing Hannah, trying to read if she would be open to a conversation. He cautiously asked, "How did things go at work today?"

"It was okay," she mumbled.

Jake nodded. "That's good."

"Yeah, I guess. How was yours?" she asked without looking up from her plate.

"Yeah, it was fine."

Hannah nodded. "That's good." She shoveled a forkful of food into her mouth, letting silence fall between them. She was still lost in her mind, rolling over her regrets and guilt some more.

"Is there something you want to talk about?" Jake asked hesitantly.

Hannah immediately felt the emotion lodge in her throat. She did want to talk about it but didn't think it would be well-received.

"I've just been thinking over all this stuff with… him," she choked out, afraid to even say his name.

Jake paused, taking a long time to chew his food, steadying himself for the conversation. "Anything in particular?" he asked.

Hannah recounted her regret for walking away from Jimmy and not trying to stay in his life. She admitted her guilt, feeling like she could have stopped him from going through with it. Jake assured her that wasn't the case, but it was hard for Hannah to accept that from someone who hadn't even known Jimmy.

Hannah poured out all her thoughts on love, the critical lessons she'd learned from it, and apologized for how much she had kept from Jake about her past. She acknowledged that she had shoved all the memories of her time with Jimmy so deep in her, only ever willing to have a surface-level conversation about it. Hannah knew she needed to dig it all out so it could finally breathe oxygen, to feel the pain all over again in the hopes of healing.

They sat for a long time at the kitchen table as Hannah opened up to Jake. She talked about her time in Riverside Springs for what seemed like hours. She painted pictures of her old friends, the love they all had for one another, and the home she shared with Jimmy. Explaining it in that way felt more like describing the plot for a sitcom or a movie, too beautiful to have been real. Hannah knew even then that she was still holding back some of it, unsure if she'd ever really be able to talk about it.

Hannah sighed deeply. "Jimmy meant so much to me. He taught me so many things about myself and life that I've never seen until now. That day at the comic book shop with him, when we were still at SHU, was the first time I really felt like I had been seen in my whole life. I was just always allowed to exist as I was with him, and he loved me anyway."

"Wow. It all makes so much sense now," Jake said with a big smile.

Hannah screwed up her face and stared at him, waiting for him to expand on his thought. When he didn't, she asked, "What does?"

"I've always seen how much it means to you when someone does something for you. Like, it's the only way you ever see the love that anyone else has for you," he told her. "It makes so much sense to me now why that would be. That day, Jimmy made such an imprint on you. He made you feel seen and cared for, which was something you were lacking. He did this one thing for you without expecting anything in return. He showed you the way gently so you wouldn't feel stupid. I mean, you said he wouldn't even take credit for helping. It was purely selfless."

Hannah stared back at Jake, eyes wide with understanding. "Huh. I think you're right."

"When I'm good, I'm good," Jake joked, which caused Hannah to finally smile again.

A few days later, Hannah's phone buzzed between sessions with clients. It was a notification from Facebook Messenger. She clicked it, and her eyes went wide with surprise. "Alan Reed wants to start a conversation with you!" That was a name she hadn't heard in a long time. Hannah accepted the conversation request and clicked on his profile picture to see her old friend's face again. Alan still looked youthful and happy, even if his hair had begun to recede. He posed with two children in his arms, which made Hannah smile; she had always thought he'd make a great dad one day.

Hannah returned to the message he had sent: *Hannah! It's your old friend Alan from Riverside Springs. Call me when you get this. I need to talk to you.*

Hannah read the number he had provided, one with a Louisiana area code.

Interesting, thought Hannah. *I wonder what he wants to talk to me about.*

Hannah had gotten lost staring at Alan's photo again when her computer chimed with a new email notification. It was her next client emailing to cancel their session. "Nothing like the last minute," Hannah quietly said to the walls of her empty office.

With her newfound time, Hannah decided to call Alan and clicked on the phone number in his message. Her stomach flipped with each ring, dropping out from under her when she heard the line connect.

"Hello?" said a familiar and friendly voice.

"Hi! Is this Alan? Alan Reed?" Hannah asked hesitantly.

"It is," the voice said wearily. "Who is this? Wait! Hannah?"

She laughed in response. "It's me!"

"Holy shit! Well, I guess you got my message. I wasn't sure you'd even bother to open it!"

"Give me more credit than that, Alan, geez," Hannah teased.

"Well, it wouldn't be the first time that you didn't return any of my messages," Alan said candidly. "I thought we were as good of friends as Jimmy and I were. I considered you my family, Hannah."

"Ouch," murmured Hannah. "I guess I deserve that, though." There was a moment of silence between them. "Alan, I just wanted to say I am sorry about how things went down. I shouldn't have ghosted you or anyone else. I was young and—I don't know—overwhelmed with the weight of everything. I was completely shattered at the end."

Alan let out a heavy sigh before responding, "It's okay. I understood why you did it more than anyone else. They all said things, but they didn't know about Jimmy's history—what it had done to the both of you."

It stung to hear that her old friends thought badly about her after she left, but she shouldn't have been surprised. Like Alan said, they were all in the dark because she and Jimmy had kept them there.

Hannah and Alan talked for several minutes, catching up on where life had taken them. Alan had moved back to Louisiana, to a small bayou town, with his wife and their two kids. They had only moved there within the last two years so Alan could work on his cousin's commercial fishing boat. The physical labor was already taking a toll on his body, though. His wife was a nurse at a hospital there. Hannah told him that she was working as a therapist in a community clinic, which hadn't surprised Alan. She talked about her wedding to Jake a few years before and that they had bought a home in New Jersey just down the street from the beach.

"You were always a child of the sea," said Alan, "I couldn't ever imagine you straying very far from it."

"I mean, it's been nice catching up with you, but it seemed like you had something specific you wanted to talk to me about," Hannah said as their conversation began to fade.

His voice was hesitant. "Yeah. Uh, Hannah—I need to tell you something."

"Okay…"

Alan exhaled deeply again, his lips sputtering. "I was never sure how I would say this to you, and now here I am having to say it, and I don't know if I can."

"Alan, what is it?"

He let out another long breath. "Well—Jimmy died. A couple of months back, actually. Suicide. I've been trying to track you down to tell you, but I could never find you."

"Oh. Well… I appreciate you telling me, but I already knew."

"You did? How?" Alan asked in surprise. "I didn't know you guys were talking."

"We weren't, but—I realize this is going to sound kind of stalkerish, I guess, but I sometimes looked him up to see what he was up to," she admitted as her voice started to shake. "He crossed my mind just a week ago—this one song came on that made me think of him on my drive to work. Anyway, I Googled him, and his obituary was the first thing that came up."

"Shit," Alan muttered. "That's a terrible way to find out."

"Tell me about it!" Hannah laughed as tears welled up in her eyes. Usually, she would have felt uncomfortable with the show of vulnerability, but the comfort she had always felt with Alan was still there. He was still her friend, and she knew he still had her back, no matter what she had done.

"I wish I had gotten to you first," he said. "I really tried. I did. I just didn't know your married name, and there was no record of it that I could find."

"It's okay. I appreciate you going through all that trouble to find me," Hannah replied.

Alan spoke to her sincerely, "Well, like I said, I considered you my family. I know it's been a while, but you still are, Hannah."

Hannah coughed, clearing her throat, wishing she could hug her old friend again. "I guess you and Jimmy were still friends then?"

"Oh, yeah. We were friends until the end. That guy was my brother from another mother, ya know? I should've known things had gotten bad again." Alan's voice broke with emotion. "That's what makes this hurt so much."

Hannah looked down at the keyboard on the desk in front of her, taking a moment to get her grief under control. "Don't do that to yourself," she told him. "I know it's easier said than done. I can't lie and say I haven't been thinking the same thing, though. That if we had stayed in touch, maybe I could've made some kind of difference. I don't know."

"Nah, I should've seen this coming. I knew him best by that point. I was thinking about it the other day, and I really think this was always in the cards for him. It was just a matter of when," Alan plainly stated.

"You might be right." Hannah frowned slightly, turning to look out the window of her office. "It just sucks—he had so much to offer the world. He had so much talent, and he was such a force!"

"Yeah, he was!" Alan exclaimed. "That dude walked into a room, and everyone knew he was there."

They both laughed, each at their own memories of Jimmy. Hannah recalled all the music clubs they had walked into and how it seemed like the attention of the room would turn immediately to Jimmy. She would often poke fun at him, saying he was some legendary local celebrity in the music scene. He hated that.

"I think some people are just never meant to grow up, ya know? That they're only meant to grow wilder. More free."

Hannah let out a long breath. "He never could be tamed," she said in agreement with Alan's sentiments. "It's weird. We hadn't spoken in years, but there is such a huge hole in me just knowing that he's not out there somewhere living his life and loving on everyone he meets."

"He never really dated anyone else after you left, you know," Alan blurted out.

"Wait—really?"

"Yeah, I mean, there were hookups. They were just girls he met online or at a show or something. Maybe a handful of them went past a night, but we all knew he wasn't invested in them. He was kind of seeing someone in the last year, but she was way more in it than he was—typical." Alan chuckled, then cleared his throat. "I think it was hard for all of those girls to live in your shadow."

"Oh," Hannah gasped as the ache in her heart grew stronger.

"I remember talking to him a few years ago after he had seen you lurking around on his Facebook page, I guess. He said something about his videos. I don't really remember, but he told me he wanted to reach out to you. He felt like maybe something was still there, because why else would you do that? I talked him out of it. I'm not sure if that was the right thing to do, but it seemed like things were going well for you, so I told him to leave you alone and to not fuck things up." Alan paused. "But—it was always you, Hannah. He told me he deleted you from his Facebook after you got married because it just hurt too much. It was weird for him to see you so happy. I mean—it was what he had wanted for you, but I think he always wished it could have been him. I know he regretted everything that happened the day you left, and I don't think he ever stopped regretting it. Or loving you."

Hannah clapped a hand over her mouth to muffle the sound of a sob trying to escape, but it was too late. She gasped as the tears flowed.

"Shit, I'm sorry, Hannah. I wasn't thinking. I was just running my mouth. I shouldn't have said any of that," Alan apologized. "That's not at all what you needed to hear."

"No, it's okay," Hannah squeaked out. "I deserve to know. I deserve to feel all of it. I know I hurt him. I mean, I did the very thing I had asked him not to do to me, right? I ran away when it got hard."

"You did what you had to do, Hannah. So did Jimmy. You guys were so right for each other but so wrong at the same time," he chuckled, trying to make light of it all.

Hannah knew he was right. Through tears, she told Alan about how she had regretted leaving, wondering what might have been different for both of them had she stayed. "I drove away still loving him, Alan. I just had to love him from afar to hold onto my sanity, even if it felt like it nearly killed me back then to do it. To be honest, I still do love him. I think I'm always going to, but I just wish he had known that before he died. That I still cared about him."

"If he didn't know it then, he does now. Trust in that, Hannah," said Alan pensively.

Hannah inhaled sharply and asked, "So—what happened? Like, what was going on in his life?"

"I've been trying to figure that out these last few months. I really didn't see this coming." Alan paused briefly before continuing, "There were things that weren't going right, but it was nothing he couldn't come back from."

"What do you mean?" Hannah asked.

"Well, they got hit with that hurricane this last season, which shut everything down. Jimmy lost his job because the bar was destroyed, and they couldn't start rebuilding until just a few weeks ago, actually. I know money was really tight. I lent him a few bucks to help out, but he had mentioned something about maybe needing to sell his condo because he couldn't afford it anymore. And that chick I mentioned before, she had walked out in the middle of all of that. I told him to give it a chance, to have her move in and help him with the bills, but he refused. I knew he didn't feel anything for her, but I thought if he just let her in, maybe he could learn to. I don't know—maybe the loneliness got to him? Then shit with his dad had boiled over again since he'd been out of work—you know how that goes—"

"Pfft, I shouldn't be surprised. Mr. Taylor was always such a bastard. It feels wrong that he outlived Jimmy," Hannah spat.

Alan chuckled. "You said it, not me." He took a breath before continuing, "Jimmy just always sounded so good, ya know? He was optimistic like he knew he would get through it. He'd even been playing guitar in a new band—had been with them maybe a year and a half? They were *really* good, too! They were working on recording an album and were playing a ton of shows. Hannah, you've got to hear their recordings; they were seriously going places. So, there were bad things, but nothing that should've sent him over the edge like this."

"He was always that way, though, Alan. You know that as well as I do. You never knew things were that bad until he—" she took a deep breath, choking back another sob. "Until he ran away."

"He really did run away this time, huh?"

"He really did." After a brief silence, she continued, "Jimmy had told me once before that he had always felt alone, even though he was surrounded by all kinds of friends. He never felt like anyone really had his back, and I was the first person who made him feel that way, that he was loved and supported. That I would be there to pick him up when he fell. I know he felt that way about you, too. I felt angry with him every time he ran because I felt like—he knew I'd be there for him, but then he never really let me. I wasn't sure if you guys still talked or not, but I figured you probably still did, and I felt angry with him all over again. I was angry that he had you and still did this."

Alan confessed, "I've had my fair share of anger, too. The hole in the wall of my garage would tell you the same."

Hannah swallowed hard. "I just think that some mean voice in his head, that depression voice, worked so hard to convince him that there weren't people who had him. I think it made him feel so isolated and alone. I think, over time, it just won."

"I can imagine after a lifetime of fighting it, it just wears you down enough," Alan agreed.

They chatted more about their memories of Jimmy, the good and the bad. Alan shared more recent stories about him, all the crazy things he'd done, and what a fun uncle he had been to Alan's kids. Hannah forgot to be sad then, only laughing as she imagined the scenes unfolding as Alan spoke.

Some people never change, she thought, finding relief from the pain in the stories about Jimmy's antics.

They recounted her last day in Riverside Springs and the camaraderie between them amid the turmoil of those days before it. Hannah had avoided talking about that day with anyone, not wanting to relive her pain, but it did feel good to dissect it all with Alan. He was the only one who could really understand. By the end of their conversation, Hannah and Alan had promised to keep in touch. She was grateful for that, not realizing just how badly she needed that connection to her old life, her old friend, and to Jimmy.

Jimmy appeared to Hannah that night in her sleep. He was solid and real. The two of them were young again like they had been in their days at SHU. Hannah and Jimmy walked down the sidewalk of Main Street in Stonebridge, approaching a group of people already sitting around a long dining table outside a restaurant. The street had been closed to traffic, allowing diners and pedestrians to enjoy the space on warm summer nights like this one they found themselves in; it felt almost like those summer nights in Riverside Springs. Hannah couldn't distinguish the words being spoken, but the tone of their chatter was so happy and carefree, with occasional laughter spilling over the conversation.

Hannah and Jimmy sat at the table next to one another. She looked around and recognized the faces before her—their old ragtag crew of friends from *The Inkwell*, the people they had cared for in another lifetime.

Jimmy turned to Hannah with that crooked smile of his. "Do you love him?" he asked sincerely.

Hannah knew he was talking about Jake. "Yes," she replied.

"What's he like?"

"Jake is so funny," she giggled. "He's got this laugh—it's so crazy and loud. You could hear it from a mile away. He's really smart. Carefree, like you. He's a good guy."

Jimmy smiled. "And he's good to you?"

"Yes," Hannah replied. "He's a good man."

"Then I'm happy," he said simply.

Jimmy wrapped his arm around Hannah's shoulders, pulling her in to gently kiss her hair. Hannah smiled and placed her head on his shoulder as Jimmy leaned his cheek to rest on top of her head. His arm stayed around her, protective and loving, as if to tell her he would always be there. Hannah let herself melt into him for the last time.

EPILOGUE
One Year Later

Hannah took a walk in the early morning hours down to the water. Being in the quiet of this place brought Jimmy to mind again as she remembered all the times they spent in that park in Riverside Springs. She stood there a while looking out over the still bay, her eyes focusing on the skyscrapers of Highgate City. She often thought about him during these in-between times of the day, as if he were still living and breathing. When the early morning sun glittered off the water with fresh possibility and adventure for the day ahead, and when the evening sky was painted in such vibrant oranges and pinks. They were colors as bright as Jimmy had been, unapologetic in how magically beautiful they were.

She could still faintly make out the shimmering stars overhead as the rising sun began to outshine them. Hannah's eyes scanned the sky, looking for Orion's Belt, remembering what Jimmy had told her to look for all those years ago when they used to lie back on the trunk of his car. Her face sank when she couldn't find it. She hoped that, wherever it was, Jimmy had finally found his place among the stars and gods. She was sure he had.

She leaned on the railing and watched fishing boats leave the harbor, inhaling sea air deeply into her lungs. Each new day still found Hannah struggling with the loss of Jimmy, but she hoped it would get easier to live with. She had put his old music back on her playlists to hear his voice again and keep his memory alive. She never failed to smile whenever one of those songs came on, remembering what it felt like to watch him sing them on a stage in a crowded room or when he played his acoustic guitar just for her on their front porch on Campbell Street. She'd often get lost in the memories, imagining him with a band of friends rocking out in a bar somewhere in South Carolina.

She ached for him, for the pain he must have felt at the end. Hannah often found herself tearful, knowing that so many people would never experience his magic, and those who had, now had to live without it. Sure, Jimmy's life was full, but it was still too short. She tried not to focus so much on that, as all it did was make that hollow ache in her core grow even stronger. It was there still, in the background most days now, but always present.

Hannah went to sleep that night, only to be looped into a cycle of one long, continuous dream that lasted the entire night. She was dropped into the same dream every time she woke and fell back asleep. Various scenes of her calling Jimmy danced behind her eyelids.

Sometimes, he picked up the call but never said a word. Other times, the call rang to a voicemail box where Hannah always left a message for him. She begged Jimmy to call her back in every single one, telling him how much she missed him. Sometimes, her phone would ring with his name on the Caller ID. She would answer, excited to hear his voice, but there was only ever dead air on the other end. In another scenario, Jimmy came to her and sat on the edge of her bed. He looked at her with sad eyes and that half-smile that was so uniquely his. Jimmy only stared at her, never moving closer, never speaking. He didn't even try.

Hannah finally awoke for the last time at 3:58 A.M. and decided to stay awake; she didn't wish to close her eyes and go through it all over again. She turned on her side to look out the open window, watching the sky become gradually lighter. Hannah considered the dream and Jimmy's silence. She knew, somewhere deep in her heart, that his silence answered every question she had asked over the last year. That it wouldn't have made a difference if they had kept in touch or had somehow made a friendship work between them. Jimmy was always going to hide it from her, how bad things had become again; he simply wouldn't want to worry her. Jimmy had always been that way, and he wasn't ever going to change, not even to save himself. So he ran again. He ran the furthest anyone could possibly run. Hannah just hoped that he had managed to outrun his pain this time.

The hollow ache in her faded just a little as Hannah put a hand over her heart and closed her eyes. She repeated that fact to herself over and over.

It wouldn't have made a difference.

She repeated it to herself until she started to believe it.

It wouldn't have made a difference. Our story was always going to end this way.

www.ingramcontent.com/pod-product-compliance
Lightning Source LLC
Chambersburg PA
CBHW070510310726
48976CB00002BA/400